This is Oliver's first novel, he started writing while his wife was working late during the lockdowns, surprising himself with his own dedication to the project. Oliver is a family man, daddy to two young daughters. Born and raised in West Yorkshire, he now lives in Kent with his family.

Dedicated to my wonderful wife, Emma, and our daughters, Anna and Hope, for all your love and support. Thank you to all my family for your help throughout this process.

Oliver Hurst

LOOSE ENDS

AUSTIN MACAULEY PUBLISHERS™

LONDON * CAMBRIDGE * NEW YORK * SHARJAH

A CIP catalogue record for this title is available from the British Library.

ISBN 9781398489677 (Paperback)
ISBN 9781398489684 (ePub e-book)

www.austinmacauley.co.uk

First Published 2024
Austin Macauley Publishers Ltd®
1 Canada Square
Canary Wharf
London
E14 5AA

Thank you to my parents, Beverly and Andrew, and my sisters, Lorna and Helena, for reading the first draft and giving their feedback. Thank you to my brilliant wife, Emma, for reading every draft I gave you.

Thank you to Austin Macauley for their belief in this story and for all their help bringing Matthew to life.

Chapter One

Leicester Square rocked as hundreds of late-night revellers and tourists weaved and ducked around each other. Each one looking for a certain bar, a certain theatre or attraction for a photo opportunity. The landmark was filled with the sound of laughter, taxi horns and the music of eager buskers hoping for another couple of coins before they went home.

Matthew Bartimaeus walked slowly and confidently through the crowds: up Irving Street, passing the many restaurants towards the last-minute ticket booth that stood on the edge of the famous Square; his white cane ahead of him, swaying gently left and right. Each step created a clear path through the large number of people eager to avoid knocking into a blind man.

He didn't need his cane, but it was useful for appearances sake. People don't usually suspect a blind man. Matthew could feel the path ahead of him, the vibrations in the ground from the hundreds of footsteps made him aware of the number of people around him. Their voices, aftershaves and perfumes helped him picture their faces and bodies in his mind's eye, letting him know who was innocent and who could be a potential threat. Over the years, Matthew had honed and perfected his other working senses so that even if, by some miracle, they worked again, he wouldn't need his eyes to see.

He walked the same familiar path towards the ticket stand and took his place at the back of the line—behind the eager tourists hoping for a last-minute deal on a West End show. As he waited patiently for the line to move forward, Matthew went through his plan again; reminding himself of his target's patterns, the strengths and weaknesses that he had picked up and memorised after weeks of stealthy observations. Standing tall with his back straight, Matthew removed his right hand from the cane held in front of his chest and ran it slowly over his short dark brown hair, scratching away an unwanted insect that had landed there. It was now Matthew's turn to be served. He took a few steps forward to the booth, resting his cane against the wall to his left.

"Good evening, sir. How can I help?" asked the young lady in the booth. For the sake of appearances to the people around him, Matthew smiled at her kindly while reaching inside his black suit jacket to pull out a folded piece of paper and sliding it across the table towards her, slowly and purposefully.

"I reserved a ticket for this evening," he replied simply. His voice was polite, but with a natural roughness. He took his hand off the paper as he felt her own soft, smooth hand slide over his own to take it from him. Matthew could smell her perfume as she leaned closer. It wasn't overpowering, in fact she had applied the perfect amount; a tempting concoction that complimented her smooth breathy voice and naturally curvaceous figure.

"I'll be right back, sir." She lowered herself off her chair and stepped away from him, moving across the small booth, holding the folded paper in her hand. Matthew could hear a soft clink of her heels on the floor as she moved to the back of the room, to a small black locked drawer. Heels, perfume, kind voice— Matthew couldn't stop himself creating a list about the woman in front of him. From the way her voice was raised up to him and the way both her feet tapped the floor together when she slipped off her stool, he guessed she must be short, around five foot two to five foot three. Her heels suggested she was dressed smartly, perhaps more than she should be for a ticket booth stand in Leicester Square. Most likely a simple blouse and black skirt combination. Although he had never seen the stand for himself, Matthew had associates describe landmarks and sites to him early in his career and suspected her blouse was the same colour as the sign above her, tight across her chest in an attempt to upsell tickets to the male tourists. Berkant expected all his employees to look the part, no matter where he had them working.

"Here you are, sir," came her voice as she returned, sliding a slightly thicker than normal white envelope towards him. Matthew registered the sound of her voice and the paper moving across the smooth surface between them and placed his hand gently on the envelope.

"Enjoy your evening, sir," she continued in the same silky, seductively smooth voice.

"Thank you," replied Matthew, his voice rich in natural gravely tones, slipping the envelope into his suit pocket. Picking up his cane, he nodded to the girl and walked away to his right, around the booth and up the Square past the Odeon Cinema.

Matthew turned right at the top of the Square, passing the casino and worked his way through the crowd slowly. His cane was slightly ahead of him, continually moving side to side. He made his way across the road, moving up the street and counting in his head every footstep as he walked.

As he reached his target number, he turned smoothly and confidently right into a side alley. Making his way to the end, he stopped next to a lone square bin. Matthew ducked out of sight behind the bin and slowly pulled out a pair of black leather gloves from his pocket. Once they were snugly onto his hands, he extracted the envelope, given to him at the ticket booth, from his pocket and began to open it. Running his index finger under the fold separating the glue from paper, he silently opened it. Holding out his left palm, Matthew tilted the envelope and felt a small flat knife land in his hand.

Tucking the now empty envelope back into his pocket, he ran his hand over the blade and handle, feeling every inch and familiarising himself with the small compact weapon. Built to order, the blade was no longer than his middle finger and the handle itself was just as thin as the blade, making it light and easy to conceal. He slowly and carefully slipped the knife blade first under his jacket sleeve and then tucked the dangerously sharp blade under his watch strap.

Listening carefully to the sounds coming from the main road, Matthew knew his target should be passing the mouth of his alley at any moment. Picking up his cane, he pressed a small button on the right side of his watch so that a robotic voice gently called out the current time. The target would be about to walk past the entrance to the alley any second now.

Matthew rose to his feet, buttoning up his jacket as he started forward. He made his way back to the noise of the passing crowds. As he approached the mouth leading out of the alley, he picked up that familiar scent of too much cheap cologne and the same annoying tune his target hummed everywhere he went. He stood waiting as the humming sound grew louder before passing right by Matthew. He waited, counting slowly to five before re-joining the throng of people following the man he had been sent to kill.

The man walking ahead of Matthew, unaware that his life would soon be coming to end, made the same familiar walk across the crowded Square, pushing aside tourists and drunks to keep himself moving at his brisk pace. Out of the Square, the crowd thinned as Robert Taylor made his way onto Charing Cross Road; walking up the street in the direction of Shaftesbury Avenue. Once there, he would head over to the same little bar that he always went to and would have his usual double rum and coke. If he timed it right, and he usually did, the drink would be on the bar waiting for him as he entered. Robert liked routine and would keep his to the second. To him, a solid routine kept life organised and made the world run smoother. Why couldn't anyone else see it his way?

Growing up, it was the same and many times Robert had to listen to lectures from his military Uncle about how people with routines were easier to kidnap. Kidnap, Robert scoffed at the thought, no one would dare even attempt to kidnap him. He was the one who did the kidnapping and ransom. He was confident in his ability to handle himself in a fight and with his connections to the criminal underworld of London, so he felt safe making his way for his evening drink.

Five paces behind Robert, Matthew was going through his plan step by step in his head and planning his next move. Soon the target would be passing a deserted side street, and this was when he planned to strike. While Robert continued on his straight path, Matthew took a sharp left and moved quickly up the side street overtaking Robert on the main road; all the time counting the seconds so that he could keep track of where the target was. Matthew soon reached the main road and turned back on himself, heading back in the opposite direction, towards his target. Matthew now slowed down his pace, tapping and swaying his cane ahead of him as he moved.

Robert looked around him as he walked, the street was beginning to thin out as it normally did at this time. People were heading to catch the last train home, looking for taxis or heading into the last bar or club to finish the night. He turned his attention forward, walking his familiar path. Soon he would be in his bar, on his stool with his drink. The pavement was almost deserted now. The only person coming towards him was a man in a suit. Robert almost froze and stumbled, but he caught himself and continued walking. He wasn't sure why, but something about this man made him nervous. He couldn't put his finger on it. Was it the expensive suit? The way the man held himself as he walked?

Robert breathed a sigh of relief when he spotted the white cane and the sunglasses at night. He's a blind man. Robert chuckled to himself, running a hand over his heart, telling himself to relax. Robert wasn't normally this jumpy, but recently he'd had reason to be. He'd agreed to a job for a rival of the Berkant family. It wasn't anything serious, just roughing up a few underground bookies and getting them to change their allegiance to a new family. He had worn a mask the whole time and had done his best to disguise his voice, but Robert had heard rumours about how Berkant handled those he considered enemies. After the beatings, he had gone underground for a few days, hiding out in different hotel rooms while the heat died down. That had been over a week ago and no one had come for him. He felt confident he was in the clear and he just needed to calm down and stop jumping at every shadow.

Matthew meanwhile, standing upwind of Robert, had picked up his scent again, the aftershave slowly assaulting his nostrils. They were getting closer; it was almost time. He listened carefully to his surroundings, making sure to keep his cane off the floor now so that the only sound came from passing cars, buses and the occasional shout of a party group passing on the other side of the road. As he moved closer to Robert, he could feel no vibrations in the floor except those of the man he was about to kill. Perfect. He had his chance. Matthew moved to his left as he walked, making sure he was closer to the road than his target. They were seconds apart now, it was time to strike; three, two, one.

Robert kept walking and looking at the approaching blind man, thinking to himself, *How easy would it be to pickpocket him? It's not as if this guy would know it was him. Fuck it why not?* Apart from his nightly drinks, he hadn't had any fun for a while now, since his last job and he needed to feel the thrill of stealing again. Even if it was just stealing a wallet or a phone. He ran through his method to himself in his mind, a reflex he had performed hundreds of times in his life. Preparing to 'accidentally' bump into his unfortunate new friend, he would catch him with one hand, 'apologising' for his mistake while his other would smoothly slip inside the jacket pocket and retract whatever he could find before his victim had registered his fake apology.

Robert flexed his fingers preparing them for the theft. A simple crime yes but, as they say, every little helps. The blind man came closer. *Here we go*, Robert thought to himself preparing his well-practiced stumble counting to himself 'one, two three'.

Matthew reacted first, the target directly to his right side. As a double decker bus rumbled by, he let go off his cane, leaving it balancing on its tip on the pavement. In one swift and precise movement, he extracted the flat knife from his wrist, striking the man in a quick 'one-two' movement. The blade pierced the man in the side of his body and then in his neck, puncturing an artery. Robert didn't see it coming. Matthew grabbed his cane with his left hand and pushed the dying man into a dark litter-strewn alleyway that they both stood in front of, just as he had planned.

Robert barely registered what had happened to him before it was too late. He had gone to reach inside the blind man's jacket, hoping for a wallet or a phone and the next thing he knew, he was being pushed against a large bin clutching his side and neck and feeling warm blood flow out of his fresh wounds. He couldn't speak. He opened his mouth but all that came out was his own coughed-up blood. He tried to look up at the man who had done this to him, but his vision was already becoming blurry. As he tried to remain conscious, he felt his attacker wipe something against his arm, cleaning the blade most likely. A trail of blood slipped out of the corner of his mouth as he tried to talk again. It followed the curve of his chin, dripping onto his shirt. With that, Robert let out his last breath and slowly dropped to the floor dead.

Matthew worked as quickly as he could, he needed to hide the body before he was discovered. He heard the last breath exhale from the lungs as Robert's life flowed out of him forever. The first part of the job was done. He stowed the now clean knife back up his sleeve carefully before throwing open the lid of the large industrial bin he and the dead man were next too. Careful to keep the open wounds away from his body, Matthew lifted the corpse and pushed up over the threshold into the bin dropping it onto a pile of overfilled bin bags and fast-food packets. Once he had dropped the corpse inside, Matthew closed the lid, picked up his cane and re-joined the main road walking slowly back towards Leicester Square. The kill and the hiding of the body had taken less than two minutes. The job wasn't over yet though. He had to dispose of the murder weapon. The body wouldn't be discovered for another two days when the bin men did their rounds and even though he had left no trace of himself on the blade (or the body for that matter), it would be a foolish mistake to leave or even keep the knife he had used on the victim.

Matthew walked down the high street, passing the closed shops and their dark windows. The sound of the crowds was growing louder as he approached the noisy Square in the heart of London. Counting his steps, he knew he was coming to his selected deposit point for the knife tucked up his sleeve. He moved closer to the side of the pavement, letting the tip of his cane glide along the concrete edge of the pavement. The storm drain he had chosen was getting closer. Matthew slowly slipped the knife out of his watch strap with his fingertips and held it up his sleeve as he went. His cane faltered as it hit the gap in the pavement. This was it. Never slowing his pace, he walked over the drain and released the knife. He felt it slide through his palm and drop perfectly into the sewer below.

The crowds in Leicester Square had started to thin now, people were arriving at their destinations and only a few were still milling around. Matthew walked past the large cinema used for the big movie premiers and back to the ticket stand he had been at only minutes earlier. He quickly slipped off his gloves and tucked them into his jacket pocket. The same girl was waiting for him at the stand, her perfume giving her away immediately. Her voice was calm, friendly and convincingly innocent as she looked up, watching him approach.

"Hello, sir, how was tonight?"

"A success as always," Matthew replied. He heard the sound of paper sliding across the smooth surface and reached out, his hands resting on a thick envelope. He ran his thumb gently along the edge of the large rectangular mass inside, his payment in full. Matthew said nothing as he slipped the money into his suit pocket and turned to leave.

"Excuse me, sir?" she called out. Matthew stopped in his tracks; this was unusual. As he turned back to her, he started to take in his surroundings, his senses now on full alert and searching for anything suspicious. He loosened his grip on his cane, preparing to reach under his jacket for his hidden firearm, when he heard that familiar sound of paper being pushed towards him. "Perhaps there's something you'd like to see tomorrow night?" she asked. Although it was a question, her tone was clearly telling him to take what she was giving him. Matthew slid his hand across the table and felt his fingers brush against what felt like a brochure. Picking it up quickly, he turned and walked away from the stand before anything else could be said and began walking down Irving Street at a brisk pace, past the restaurants and cafés and making his way to Charing Cross Station.

The train carriage was quiet and almost empty as Matthew sat in silence, his cane between his legs and held with both hands. He finally reached his home after a mile walk from the station. In his line of work, it was too risky for even a taxi driver to know where he lived. Only a select few knew where his home was located.

His home was a small bungalow built on the edge of a local forest and made out of several recycled shipping containers. Matthew's feet crunched over the gravel driveway as he approached his front door. Staying alert to all surrounding sounds, he pressed his thumb to the fingerprint scanner that operated the locks on his front door. There was a metallic click as the door unlocked and swung slightly inwards to let him in. The home's security alarm sounded, beeping incessantly until the correct code was entered. Matthew reached out with his right hand as he stepped in and felt for the pin box on the wall. Finding the marked centre button with his finger, he was able to work his way around the keypad and enter the correct code to silence the alarm. Once the alarm had stopped, he closed the door behind him hearing the locks turn and took a moment to enjoy the silence that enveloped him.

His home was his sanctuary and here, there was nothing but peace and quiet. He walked forward, dropping his cane into an umbrella stand, before stepping into the large open space that was his living room, kitchen and dining room. The layout of the furniture memorised in his mind, he moved confidently about his home, not hesitating in a step or reaching out ahead of himself with his hands. He passed a large leather sofa in his living room and moved into the kitchen area of the open-planned room. He tossed the brochure he had been given at the ticket stand onto the countertop, it could wait till morning. Taking a long deep breath, Matthew slowly took off his jacket, placing it carefully over the shoulders of a nearby chair and revealing his shoulder holster carrying the Sig Sauer P226 pistol, suppressor and spare ammunition that he kept on him at all times. He reached inside the jacket and pulled out the envelope that had been given to him earlier. Opening the flap with his finger, he pulled out the thick wad of notes. Twenty thousand pounds in a mixture of fifty and twenty-pound notes. All stacked Queen face up, the twenty-pound notes wrapped in one-thousand-pound bands and the fifties in two and half thousand. Matthew flicked the corners with his thumb. He didn't need to count it; it was there in full. It always was.

Exhaling slowly, relaxing his body and mind, he took off his glasses and rubbed his eyes with his hands. Leaving the money there on the counter, he turned away from the kitchen towards his bedroom. He walked through the doorway and into the room. Slipping his gun and cartridges out of his holster, he tucked them under his pillow should they be needed during the night. Matthew slowly sat down on his bed, undoing his tie and placing it next to him and replaying the night's events in his head. It was the new job that he had received that was sitting in the back of his mind. It was very rare, if at all, that he would be given two jobs back-to-back like this. Should he be worried? Matthew shook his head, attempting to remove the suspicious thoughts from his mind. The job and its details could wait till the morning, for now he needed to rest.

*

While Matthew was preparing for bed, deep in the heart of London's East End, Ruby Hardie was only halfway through her night. She walked slowly and confidently down the almost deserted street, sipping a coffee in a takeaway cup from an all-night café. In her pocket was just over five thousand pounds in cash. She wasn't worried about walking around with so much money in her pocket, no one would be stupid enough to try and rob her.

In her early thirties, Ruby was a beautiful woman, but there was a strong fire and toughness inside her. Her naturally dark red hair was tied back in a tight ponytail and her sparkling blue eyes kept a sharp look out as she walked. She was in excellent shape, slim but with the right curves to her figure. Her body and fitness built from a lifetime of martial arts, mixed with dancing at a young age and regular trips to the gym. Tonight, she was wearing her favourite brown leather jacket over a black t shirt with blue jeans tucked into her boots.

She turned left at a crossroads and walked the familiar route to her and her associate, Simon O'Neill's, base of operations. They both worked as part of the Berkant group but only as small-time drug runners and occasional muscle. Ruby had headed out solo tonight while Simon had stayed back at base, seemingly more distracted than usual. Something was up with him, and he'd barely let her out of his sight when they were together. He only let her do the collection alone because he claimed to be too busy. Ruby had gone to collect money from their customers who were behind on payments.

She finished her coffee and stopped to toss the empty cup into a nearby bin. She caught her reflection in the window of a parked car and paused to check her hair. Although tied back tightly, a few strands of her hair had fallen out during her confrontation with her clients. It was amazing in this modern day and age, that some men still thought they could push a woman around. Her clients had been reluctant to pay her when she had turned up alone and had instead suggested she put her mouth to a better use. This attitude had changed very quickly after experiencing Ruby's vice-like grip on their testicles and a couple of broken noses. Ruby smiled as she fixed her hair and then continued on her walk. She had left with her payment, plus interest for their disrespectful behaviour.

She had one more stop to make before she headed back to base; O'Neill told her to swing by a disused post box on a nearby corner. He had explained that she should be able to force open the door and inside there should be a bag that he needed. Ruby had asked what was in the bag but had got nothing more than a flurry of shouting and threats before she gave up and left. O'Neill really had been acting strangely. Something was up and Ruby herself was starting to feel a little paranoid. Recently she had felt like she was always being watched, that she was never truly alone and didn't feel completely comfortable doing her day-to-day tasks. Shrugging and trying to convince herself she was worrying about nothing, Ruby carried on at a slightly faster pace to find this oh-so-important post box.

*

Across the city, on the other side of London, there was another person who wasn't getting any rest, Chief Inspector William Blaine of the Met Police. He sat behind his desk, working late into the night again. Before him, mountains of folders and police reports of the various open cases within his department of The Undercover Crimes Unit. William sighed, leaning back in his chair and rubbing his eyes, before then pushing his hands through his swept back greying hair. 'Another late night', he thought to himself. How long could he keep this up? Looking back to his desk, he pushed aside a stack of notes to reveal the photo of his long-suffering wife, most likely tucked up in bed having attempted to stay awake as long as she could. William smiled down at her photo, reminding himself that retirement wasn't too far away. Soon he will be able to make up for all these late nights and finally spend some quality time with her.

William looked up at the sound of his office door being opened simultaneously with one sharp knock. Preparing to reprimand the idiot daft enough to walk into his office without permission, he rose from his desk with a heavy sigh. William's annoyance eased off and his face instead broke into a small smile as his old friend, Inspector Charles Thind, walked in. "Evening, Will," he said, kicking the door shut behind him, a steaming cup of coffee in a Styrofoam cup in each hand, "drink?" Charles placed a cup on the table in front of William before pulling a chair closer and taking a seat on the other side of the desk. He took a long sip of his own coffee as he did, letting the scalding liquid perk up his senses. William, thankful for the drink, picked up the cup before him, taking a quiet moment to enjoy the dark bitter flavours as he slowly drank, sitting back in his chair.

"Cheers, Charles," he said, looking across the desk. "To what do I owe the pleasure?" he asked, putting the cup down onto a badly written report from a new member of his department, something else to deal with tomorrow. William sighed, relaxing back into his chair more and smiling weakly at his friend, stretching his legs out under his desk.

William had known and worked with Charles for what felt like a lifetime. While William had been in the Met since he had left full-time education, Charles had transferred down to London from Manchester when he was in his late thirties. William had never found out why Charles had requested the transfer after establishing himself up north and his friend had always changed the subject when the issue was brought up, so William eventually gave up asking. Over the years, they had built a strong and competent partnership. Although now in different departments, they often crossed paths over ongoing cases and still made time for each other for a quick catch up and drink in the dark corners of even darker pubs. Charles relaxed back into his chair, his dark grey eyes taking in the mess of papers scattered over William's desk. His free hand scratched the growing bald patch on the top of his head as he chuckled at the amount of work his old friend was doing.

"Well, firstly, I was wondering why the head of the department was still here at this hour? So I said to myself, 'Charles, clearly your friend is in need of your help with something'." William chuckled as he leant forward to put his cup down on the table, using a stack of post it notes as a coaster. "So come on, old man, what's keeping you here so late? Why haven't you got those new recruits out there doing all your work?"

"Old man? I'll have you spending the night in the drunk tank if you keep that up," replied William, shaking his head at Charles. "One year between us and don't you forget it, just because I'm closer to retirement than you are doesn't mean I'm past it."

"I've never suggested such a thing," Charles added with a cheeky wink.

"Well anyway, between my own paperwork to file, a collection of badly written reports by the newbies—" William indicated the stack of papers, complete with a fresh coffee stain ring to his right—"I've now received word that one of my undercovers has gone silent. They haven't checked in for a couple of days now, which is longer than usual."

The cup Charles was lifting to his mouth stopped in mid-air. He looked away from his drink and up into William's experienced and tired eyes. "Is that so unusual? Who is it? Perhaps they're not in a position to check in?"

William ignored the question about which agent he was referring to. Undercover wasn't Charles' department and William felt that Scotland Yard had more leaks than the England back line. He shook his head. "No, this one always finds a way to let us know, even if it's just a text message. None of our officers have been able to find them either."

"So what's the plan?" asked Charles, downing his cup in one hot mouthful as if to prepare for action. William smiled at his friend's eagerness to help, "Don't worry, old timer. I'm just going to have to wait longer. Just because it's unusual doesn't mean something is seriously wrong just yet. Usually turns out the undercover was taking part in a job and forgot their charger. Couple more days and they'll turn up, you'll see."

"And if they don't?" asked Charles, a wary tone in his voice.

"We'll cross that line when we reach it," came William's simple response, letting his old friend know that it was time to get back to work. Charles rose to his feet slowly; groaning as he realised how worn out he really was. "All right, mate, take it easy and go home and see your wife at some point. I'm getting tired of having to fill in for you every night." Charles laughed, making for the door as William threw his now empty cup in his direction.

"Close the door on your way out please," shouted out William, laughing and enjoying the moment of normality Charles had brought him. Sighing heavily, William looked down at his disorganised desk and began to rifle through the paperwork to try and make sense of it all.

The door closed firmly behind him; Charles walked down the corridor towards the exit, nodding politely at a passing officer as he slipped into the stairway to leave the building. Charles overlooked the banister down the concrete passageway below him to see if anyone was coming up or down towards him. All clear. As he made his way quickly down the stairs, he pulled a small Pay as you go Nokia 3310 from his inside jacket pocket. There was only one number in the call history. Charles pressed the call button with his thumb, all the time double checking the stairway as he descended, making sure he was alone. After several rings, the phone was answered and a male voice greeted him, he sounded young and nervous.

"Hello?"

"There's been a development. I need information on all the agents in your department. Bring me everything you can about those who are active. Same place as before. Straight away."

Charles hung up the phone without waiting for a response. He tucked the phone away quickly as he went through the downstairs door and into the main hallway of Scotland Yard, taking a quick and direct route to the exit.

*

Half an hour later, Inspector Thind had driven over to the East side of London and was now waiting outside The Admiral's Arms pub. Standing alone, out back in the corner of the smoking area, keeping out of the light as best he could. He kept his eyes on the back door of the pub, waiting for his contact to arrive. He checked his watch for the umpteenth time again, shaking his head in frustration.

"Fucking late," he whispered to himself. He hated waiting, he hated standing outside of a run-down pub waiting for longer than he had to just for some paperwork. The door opened and out stepped that young upstart little prick, Detective Dickinson. Charles watched him as he stepped out into the back yard, a thick A4 envelope clutched obviously to his chest.

"Christ! Just waves it around so the whole world can see," Charles muttered under his breath, watching the young officer as he stood nervously, looking around the small square, concrete garden. Dickinson had been working in Blaine's department for little over a year now, still new to the role and still making the same mistakes. If it wasn't for Charles secretly moving him in the right direction now and again, he would have been back in a uniform, walking the streets of London with a traffic cone of a hat on his head. In exchange for his help, Dickinson had been only too eager to give Charles anything he asked for.

"Oi, lad. Over here," Charles called out, just loud enough for Dickinson to hear. The young man jumped and looked towards the corner.

"Sir, I didn't see you there," Dickinson replied, walking towards him. His eyes were darting left and right nervously as he moved, looking around the empty smoking area.

"You weren't meant to, boy. Did you bring what I asked for?"

"Yes, sir, I did. This is everything on the current undercovers operating in the city. All copied in full and the originals back in their place. No one saw me." Dickinson held out the envelope which Charles snatched out of his hand quickly, stuffing it under his coat. "Sir, can I ask why you keep asking me to take this information for you?"

"You may not," said Charles, pulling his coat around him to better hide the stolen information. Dickinson chewed his lip, fighting the urge that had been growing on his mind for months now. He couldn't take it anymore and the words he'd been wanting to say, since the first time the Inspector had asked him to deliver this confidential information, came tumbling out of his mouth.

"But sir, it's just that, well you don't work with the undercovers and, and I know you told me that you work closely with Chief Inspector Blaine," he added quickly, at the aggressive look Charles had suddenly given him for speaking up. "But if he knew that I've been taking these files and giving them to you, I'll lose my job or worse. Why do you need this information, sir? Why can't I tell the Chief Inspector?"

Charles looked down at the insolent pup before him. God, he could hit him. He clenched his fists tightly, resisting the urge to pummel the young lad's face. Instead, he took a deep breath, counting slowly to five in his head, he relaxed his fists and looked into Dickinson's worried eyes.

"Listen to me, boy. You've been giving me this information because I'm worried that an undercover police officer is in danger, maybe all of them. You're not telling the Chief Inspector because, like him, I'm worried that your department has been compromised. So the less people who know, the better. So keep your mouth shut, do your job and let me do mine."

The conversation over now, Charles walked away from Dickinson, quickly heading through the back door into the pub and leaving the underling standing alone and picking his nails as he mulled over what he'd been told.

Charles had headed straight home after that short meeting. A small one-bedroom flat that he kept Spartan with minimal furniture and decoration. After his messy divorce, a result of his troubles in Manchester, he had no desire for creature comforts. He flopped onto his sofa and opened the envelope. He pulled out the papers and flicked through them; some he had seen before while others were new to him. They all contained information on several undercover officers that he shouldn't know about. He was looking for one in particular. He found the file he was looking for halfway through the stack of papers, Sergeant Zoe Garland. Charles had never met her, but had heard good things from other senior officers in Scotland Yard before she had joined the Undercover Department. The papers in his hand contained information regarding the groups she had infiltrated and who she had been seen with, as well as small pockets of notes and text messages she had sent back with information on the underworld she had become a part of. Charles held up a new page in front of his tired eyes, it contained a photograph taken from a smart phone in a passing car of Zoe and a man Charles did not know. They appeared to be walking side by side, closely but not speaking. The notes below the picture said:

'Sergeant Garland and Simon O'Neill. Known associate of the Berkant family group'.

Charles ran his hand through his thinning hair and rested his head back against his sofa. Sighing, he reached into his jacket pocket and pulled out his Samsung smart phone. Opening the text app, he typed a message to a number with no name.

I have everything on Garland. Confirm she and O'Neil will be in the meeting place tomorrow.

He hit send and waited looking at the screen. Within seconds, a reply appeared on the screen below his sent message bubble.

Bring all information you've collected to the regular deposit point then head to targets. Confirmed, they will be there along with a third target.

Simple and to the point. Charles tossed his phone aside along with the papers. He sighed again; this was not the way he had seen his career going when he had first joined the police. Not long into his career and after achieving a number of quick promotions, he had been suspended and investigated on accusations of corruption. Eventually the charges had been dropped and Charles had been allowed to return to work, but the whole experience had put such a strain on his marriage and the trust of his co-workers that he needed to get away.

He hadn't been a criminal then, but, if people thought he was a criminal, well, if you can't beat them, join them. Once he had established himself in London, it hadn't taken him long to build a trustworthy reputation and eventually join and work alongside the underworld of the city. Pulling himself off the sofa slowly, he made his way into his bedroom to finally get some sleep.

Chapter Two

Matthew woke at six to the sound of his alarm. With one hand under his pillow, clutching his loaded pistol, he reached over to the bedside table to press the button on his digital clock and silence the incessant beeping. Once the shrill noise had stopped, Matthew sat up slowly in bed, pulling his gun out from under his pillow. He kept it in his hand as he rubbed it eyes with the other, listening to his surroundings. Apart from the occasional bird call, there was complete silence. After savouring the moment of peace and tranquillity, he tossed his covers aside and climbed out of bed naked. He walked across the bedroom in quick strides to the treadmill that looked out of a large window into the surrounding forest. He carefully placed his gun on a nearby table as he climbed onto the rubber track. Reaching forward for the controls, his hand glided over the familiar buttons, turning the machine's pace to a hard uphill run. As the treadmill began to pick up speed, Matthew forced his body to wake up as he pushed it harder and faster with every step.

His naked body was awash in scars from the knives of the enemies and opponents that had cut and pierced his skin, along with the many bullet wounds from the guns he wasn't quick enough to avoid. A hundred stories of violent confrontations and personal wars covered every part of his body like a tapestry of war.

He ran as hard as he could until the muscles in his legs and chest begged him to stop. Gasping for breath, he slammed his hand onto the stop button, making the machine slow down. Matthew's legs slowed with the treadmill before they gave way, causing him to fall to his knees and flow backwards, landing on the floor with a thud. He lay on the floor for a moment catching his breath, gulping at the air as he recovered from his self-imposed punishment. Matthew slapped himself in the face, forcing his body to carry on. He slowly got himself back on his feet and staggered across the room to the door of his bedroom where a chin-up bar waited for him. He slowly reached up one hand at a time, his fingertips brushing the cold metal bar.

"Get on with it," he ordered himself with a grimace. He leapt up, wrapping his hands around the bars and began to pull himself up, counting in his head each successful lift, his knees bent behind him as he pulled his scarred muscular body up and down.

When he had had enough, Matthew fell to the floor and laid there on his side gasping for air. When his breath had returned and his raging heartbeat had relaxed, he got back to his feet and made his way into his ensuite bathroom where, at the far end, was a walk-in shower.

After a scalding hot shower, Matthew walked back into his bedroom. Slowly, he slid open his wardrobe door, reaching inside, his hand wrapped around a black three-piece tailored suit that hung neatly for him next to a crisp black shirt. He took his time getting dressed, feeling that his tie and collar were indeed straight. Before leaving his bedroom, he wrapped his watch around his wrist and picked up his faithful handgun and spare ammunition before making his way into the kitchen.

Running his hand along the marble countertop, he reached the coffee machine sitting alone, waiting for him. Opening the cabinet above him, reaching instinctively for a mug, he placed it under the spout of the expensive machine in front of him. A small pod was already waiting inside, and he flicked the switch and stood there listening to the small machine fire up, heating the water before pouring out the smooth black liquid. Sipping the hot drink, Matthew turned towards the brochure that he had left on the side before going to bed. Laying it flat, he slowly flicked through each page, running his fingertips across the pages in turn until on the seventh, he felt the small braille bumps embedded into the page. Hiding in plain sight. Matthew smiled to himself as he placed both hands on the pages, finding the starting point and admiring the ingenuity of his employer and his people. He fingertips felt their way to the top of the page and found the first word of his next assignment;

'Targets: two. One male, one female. Male target – Simon O'Neill – drug dealer and known assassin considered armed and very dangerous. Female target – Ruby Hardie – has been seen with O'Neil on various operations and is assumed to be an associate or partner. Work out of the Motorbike shop and mechanics on

Rushey Green Street. Will be at location Thursday night. Eliminate and dispose of bodies. Payment upon confirmation'.

Matthew re-read the transcript again, taking in all the details it provided him. The job was tonight. He sighed and took a sip off his coffee. He preferred a minimum of seven days for a multiple target job, but, he supposed, needs must. He knew the location and two targets shouldn't be a problem. It would be getting rid of the bodies once he'd killed them. That would be the tricky part. He took the brochure and placed it into the recycling bin. He didn't need to destroy the document, no one would see the message on the page so there was no need for an over-the-top burning or shredding. He finished his coffee in one hot, mouth burning gulp and sighed to himself. He had the day to himself before he had to work. His hand slid out across the counter slowly, his fingertips brushing the corners of the bank notes he had left there last night. Time to go to the bank.

*

Matthew stepped out of London Bridge Station into the early morning sunshine. The warmth of the sun on his face balanced the coolness of the air around him. Pushing his glasses up his nose slightly, he moved with the crowd of commuters who had left the station with him and were making their way to work in the hundreds of offices throughout the city. Keeping his cane slightly ahead of him, Matthew walked at a slow pace. He felt men and women gently brush past as they moved quickly around him, muttering to themselves about being late for early morning meetings or talking too loudly and openly on their phones, like suit-wearing salmon swimming against the current.

He walked past the Shangri-La Hotel sitting at the bottom of The Shard. He carefully made his way along St Thomas Street, keeping close to the edge of the pavement. Under his suit jacket, his gun sat nestled against his body, comfortably in its holster, loaded and ready to be used at a moment's notice. On the other side of his jacket, tucked tightly into his pocket, was the twenty thousand pounds he had earnt the night before, five thousand of which was in a separate envelope.

He made his way up the long street, his cane swinging gently from side to side as he moved, occasionally tapping the edge of the pavement, streetlamps or post boxes. Matthew passed The Old Operating Theatre Museum. Stopping at the next crossing, he waited patiently for the lights to change, holding his cane in both hands. When the lights changed and the signal beeping began, he tapped his way across the street in front of the waiting cars, bikes and buses to the other side where the Barclays Bank stood, the doors of which were being opened as he approached by the Branch Manager. Matthew made his way inside the bank with the other early morning customers. Elderly pensioners, office workers nipping in before work and business owners coming to make necessary deposits and withdrawals.

Matthew was in no rush, he took his time, letting the other customers make their way to the counter before him. He used this branch regularly and knew the layout well enough. Counting his steps, he kept his cane ahead until it gently tapped the back of another customer's leg, signalling he had joined the queue.

"Sorry," he said innocently.

No reply from the other customer, either they hadn't felt his cane, or they didn't care to respond. He waited patiently, the line slowly moving forward. The branch slowly came to life as more customers came in. Polite conversations between customers and staff mixed with the growing sounds of the increasing traffic outside, flowing in through the opening and closing automatic doors.

"Can I help you, sir?" the voice called out from behind the glass screen, signalling for Matthew to approach. He stepped forward slowly, not wishing to appear as confident as he was with his surroundings. His hand reached out, feeling along the counter, following the guiding voice of the cashier. "Nearly there, sir, that's it. Yes, you're with me now. How are you, Mr Scrivinor?" she asked, leaning forward out of her chair, feeling that the closer she got, the better he would hear. This cashier, like most of the staff who had served Matthew in this branch, knew him as Gavin Scrivinor, a nice man who came in once a month to make deposits into his business account.

"Good morning, is that Carol?" Matthew asked, a kind and innocently-lost smile on his lips.

"It is, yes. Having a nice morning?" Carol asked, returning to her seat. A kindly middle-aged woman who had been with the bank for over twenty years. As she sat down, she smoothed out the blue dress of her uniform. Unlocking her computer, she prepared herself for the transaction. "Another deposit?"

"Yes, same as usual please." Matthew reached into his jacket and pulled out a white envelope with the five thousand pounds cash. He carefully placed it onto the counter, sliding it under the glass parting until he felt Carol's hands placed gently over his to take the envelope from him.

Matthew had opened this business account himself, in secret, without Berkant knowing. Using false identity documents and business plans, he had opened the account under the false name and with the impression that he was a teacher helping people who had recently become sight impaired learn how to read braille. He only deposited a fraction of his payment into the account as he knew too much cash would arouse suspicion with the bank and he wanted to keep a low profile.

The remaining fifteen thousand pounds, that he had been paid for the murder he had committed last night, was to be dealt with after he had finished in the bank. Although he had always been paid well by Berkant for his work and had been looked after by the organisation, Matthew always felt it was best to plan for the worst. Criminals had a nasty habit of turning on each other and organisations such as Berkant's didn't last forever, so Matthew believed it was good to have his own insurance plan in case of emergencies.

Carol finished his deposit, sliding a small square receipt towards him, smiling warmly at him even though he couldn't see it.

"Anything else for you, Mr Scrivinor?"

"No thank you, Carol. That will be all. Have a nice day," Matthew replied, taking the receipt from her and wondering to himself why she was giving him this? It wasn't printed in brail and she didn't tell him his balance, the paper was useless.

"You too, sir."

Matthew walked out of the branch and back into the busy London Street. The sound of traffic and pedestrians had increased to sound like a war zone of car horns and angry cyclists. He made his way back the way he came, towards London Bridge. The number of pedestrians around him felt like it had tripled while he was in the bank. Although they tried to avoid him as they rushed around him, he felt them buffeting past him followed by an occasional grunt and non-committal apology. He kept a straight and steady pace, never weakening or giving up his ground as he walked slowly back to the station. If only these people knew what he could do to them, they'd think twice about bumping into him.

Once he had arrived at the station, he found the line of waiting black cabs and climbed into the first one. The cabbie who had been deeply involved in his book, jumped slightly at the sound of his door being opened. He was even more surprised when he noticed Matthew's cane and glasses.

"Er, where to mate?" he asked, tossing his book aside onto the seat next to him and flicking the meter with a smirk to himself.

"Humber Road. Get yourself onto the A501, then join the A5 past London Zoo. It's a straight road there and I'd knock off a couple of quid from the fare seeing as you started the meter early." Matthew sat back, resting his cane between his legs and waiting for the motion of the car to begin. The cabbie fired up the engine, surprised and disappointed at his savvy passenger.

The journey was smooth and straightforward. Neither man said anything to the other. Matthew was lost in his thoughts and the driver was longing to get back to his crime thriller. Just over thirty minutes later, the cab turned onto Humber Road as requested.

"Where abouts do you want dropping off then?" the cabbie asked, turning off the meter and admitting defeat in his conning of another customer.

"On the corner of Tankridge Road please."

The driver saw the road Matthew indicated and pulled over without signalling. As the car came to a halt, Matthew reached into his pocket and pulled out his wallet. Without waiting to hear the cost of the fare, he extracted a handful of notes and passed them through the partition as he climbed out the cab.

"Thanks."

The taxi pulled away as soon as the door closed behind Matthew. He followed the same route on Humber Road he usually took, around the corner until he came to the storage facility. A large, grey industrial looking building covered in sheet metal. Inside were dozens of large storage lockers and rooms for hire with few questions asked.

After checking in, Matthew declined the offer for assistance to his unit. He walked down the corridor, metal shutter doors on either side of him, he ran his hand along them, feeling each door, its padlocks and the walls separating them. Eventually, he came to his own. He stopped outside the large metal door, pausing for a moment to listen carefully to make sure that he was alone. There was no sound, no one was spying on him. He was alone. From his trouser pocket, he pulled out two keys, one for each of the two heavy padlocks that locked his unit. He unlocked the one on his right first then moved over to the left. Tucking both padlocks into his jacket pocket, he knelt down and swiftly pulled up the large metal door. The unit was large enough to stock an entire living room plus a dozen large boxes, instead, it held a single lone wheely suitcase. The black case lay on its side, alone in the centre of the room. Matthew walked into the room then closed the metal shutter door behind him.

He knelt down in front of the bag. Reaching for it, he found the zip and pulled it round to open it. He flipped open the lid of the bag away from him, revealing neatly stacked piles of money. Inside was just over two million pounds, collected over the many years Matthew had been in service to Berkant. The notes had been carefully placed into the bag and then left alone in this cold metal storage unit until such time that Matthew felt the need to disappear. He reached inside his jacket and pulled out the remaining fifteen thousand pounds of his payment. As one hand held the notes, his other slid over the stacks of money, laid on their sides in the suitcase until he found the gap from his last payment. He carefully placed the notes next to the existing ones, making sure they were packed in tightly. Satisfied that it was all neat and correct, he closed the lid of the suitcase and pulled the zip back round, closing it up.

*

William had been the first one to arrive in the morning, as always, and by the time the office was up and running, he was already on his third cup of coffee. Although he had worked late into the night, the stacks of papers and files on his desk still covered it like a vast paper mountain range and looked even bigger than it had when he had left. Worse still for William, there had still been no contact with his undercover officer, Zoe Garland.

He had tried the number of her private phone, but she had not answered and none of the detectives he had sent to look for her, in her last known whereabouts, had seen her. William had reached out to other undercovers to check if they had heard anything as well, but so far no-one had any information. It was as if she had just disappeared. William didn't want to worry just yet, but the longer her silence lasted, the more likely that something bad may have happened to her. Sighing, he finished the cold dregs in his coffee cup and tossed the empty polystyrene cup into the overflowing bin next to his desk. Things were getting desperate. Zoe had been sending messages that there was a lot of suspicious movement coming from Berkant and his top people, but she had been unable to give him more information and now she wasn't checking in at all.

William had known her since she had first joined the London MET. She hadn't had the easiest of lives: her parents abandoned her when she was young and she was then raised by her grandfather until he too had passed away, just after she had joined the police service. Her reputation as a PC had caught the attention of many high-ranking officials during her short but awarded career. William had taken her under his wing when she was promoted to detective and made sure she became a part of his department when he was made the head of it. He had become a mentor and a father figure to her as they worked together, guiding her in her career and helping her through life in the ways a father should protect a daughter.

William looked out of his office window onto the busy, sunny streets of London below him. Desperate times call for desperate measures. Being on the force as long as he had, William had made plenty of connections to the less than reputable members of society who usually had an ear to the criminal underworld. He didn't want to, but under the circumstances, William needed to be sure that she wasn't dead. Turning back to his cluttered desk, he snapped up his smartphone and from his contact list he selected a number registered simply as 'unknown' and pressed the call button. Putting the phone to his ear, he listened to the electronic ring of the dial tone until the familiar gruff Scottish voice answered, "What do you want?"

*

Aaron Wilson had been the Landlord of the Admiral's Arms for the last two years. Having spent fifteen years locked at Her Majesty's pleasure for many crimes including; armed robbery, grievous bodily harm and being caught at the scene of a crime involving drug and gun smuggling. He was the type of publican that many of the cliental knew better than to get on the wrong side of. A tall but slightly overweight man, Aaron still had a presence about him that gave him an auror of strength and speed. His thick curly brown hair fell naturally down his back, blending into the matching beard that covered his face.

It was a quiet night in his bar tonight. Only a few regulars had come out, sat in the same corners, talking quietly amongst themselves and nursing the same pints in dirty glasses since they had arrived. Aaron grunted to himself as he wiped another glass, placing it on the shelf above the bar. He looked towards the door sharply as he heard it open and swing shut as a new patron stepped inside. Aaron's sharp eyes looked out from the mass of hair surrounding his face from his head and beard and saw the familiar, tired face of William Blaine. William had left his office earlier that evening, telling his team that he wouldn't be long and was going to take a walk to clear his head. Once out of sight of his office, he stuck the back streets of London as he made the long walk through the city to the familiar dark pub.

"Good evening, Aaron," William said, smiling a little in an attempt to show peace between them. Aaron merely grunted at him. Picking up another pint glass from the small washer behind the bar, he ignored William for a moment as he began to dry it. "Mind if we talk a bit more privately?" William asked, nodding to the only empty corner of the bar. Aaron looked around his small pub, a sarcastic look on his face as he counted the number of drinkers in his bar.

"Quietly?" he asked, the sarcasm ringing on his tongue. "Oh, aye let me get someone to cover me to deal with the crowd and I'll be right with you. Privately? Daft tosser." He slammed the cloth he was drying the glass with so hard on the bar, that several of the drinkers around the dingy pub jumped at the loud crack of the wet rag, nearly spilling their half empty pints. As William made his way over to the empty table in the corner, lowering himself onto a stool, Aaron poured them both a half pint of lager and brought them over, sliding one over to William as he sat down.

"Cheers, Aaron," William said gratefully with a nod to the gruff landlord, lifting the cold beer to lips and savouring the taste.

"Never mind that, you want to tell me why I've got more and more of your lot coming into my pub?"

William looked over his glass at Aaron as he spoke but said nothing. Slowly putting his beer down, he rested his hands on the small round table that separated them.

"If my people choose to drink here, that's their business. Like I said on the phone, I just have some questions, that's all."

"Well ask y'questions then and be on y'way," Aaron replied, sipping his drink, his own eyes locked on William's as they spoke.

"Have you heard anything recently? I've heard people associated with Berkant come and go in this pub. I just want to know if you've seen or heard anything while they've been drinking here?"

Aaron downed the rest of his beer in one and placed the empty glass on the table so hard the other customers jumped once again. William however did not flinch, his eyes still locked on Aaron's.

"Right, first of all. I'm no snitch," said Aaron, pointing a large thick finger at William. "And even if I was, I haven't allowed anyone associated with that Turkish cunt inside my bar since I took over."

"Why's that then?"

"After what he did to me? D'you really think I'd sit down with him for a friendly drink? Too much trouble, aren't they? Bring the police down here more often than I'd like. Better to keep that scum out and keep me head down."

"You've got a point there. Although you weren't exactly innocent." William took another long sip of his beer and sighed, feeling a little defeated that this trip had been a waste of time. "Sorry to bother you, Aaron. I'll leave you be. Have a good evening." He nudged a crumpled bank note across the table for the drinks.

"Aye, no bother—" shrugged Aaron, waving a fat hand at him—"you're all right, better than the last one of your lot, I had in here anyway." William stopped rising to his feet and sat back down.

"Who was here?" he asked, more curious to find out which members of the police might actually think to come and drink in this shit hole.

"That big lad you used to bring with you back in the day. The shady one you liked, when you'd come bother me like this for information."

"Charles?" asked William, surprised to hear he would be here by himself. "Was he working on a case?"

"Fucked if I know," replied Aaron shrugging and checking the bar for any waiting customers. "Didn't say nae word to me just went out into the back and was out there for thirty, forty minutes I'd say, mostly by himself. Some young lad, tiny wee thing, a breeze could knock him over, he eventually walked in and went straight out there. He wasn't out there for long. Your mate left a few minutes after the wee one arrived. Neither of them bought so much as a packet of peanuts. Cheeky buggers."

William looked into the cold eyes of Aaron, eyes that had seen so much over the years that he knew if he would be lying, "Thanks for your help, Aaron." William got to his feet and made for the door. "Take care of yourself." With that, he turned his back on Aaron, heading straight out of the bar to process this information.

Chapter Three

Matthew made his way up Rushey Green Street slowly, his cane held out in front of him. But he used it only for show, for the few cars passing by this late at night. He made no sounds as he walked along the pavement, his cane hovering just above the dirty concrete surface, counting his steps, as always, as he moved. He slowly lifted his left hand, waiting for the signpost that held the sign for the mechanics where his targets resided, unaware of their approaching deaths. The leather gloves on his hands brushed the cool metal pole, causing him to stop in his tracks. Matthew stood still, slowing his breathing and calming his mind. His senses were on full alert as he listened to everything around him. There was barely a sound: a car engine revved loudly in the distance; a slight breeze in the air; otherwise, he was alone on this dark street.

He folded his cane up quickly and tucked it into the specially designed inside-pocket of his suit jacket. He knew the layout of the business, having spent his afternoon here to get a lay out of the land. He had changed into a more casual look of jeans and t-shirt and had told the sales team of the bike shop that he simply wanted to feel the bikes, pretending to be a former rider who missed the thrill of a bike. They had been more than happy to leave him alone with the bikes inside and outside of the shop. These reconnaissance visits were vital to his job and prepared him for what was about to happen.

He stepped quickly towards the main gate, both hands reached out and rested against the wire fencing, testing it as he pushed against it. There was no resistance; it was open. Matthew pushed the gate slowly, making sure there were no squeaks or screeching of metal against metal. Once there was a big enough gap, he slipped inside, closing the gate quietly behind him. Straight ahead of him was the main entrance to the show room of the shop. Inside, motorbikes and scooters stood untouched from the wind and rain, gleaming under the streetlamps around the building. To the left of the main showroom was the garage where many vehicles lay in different stages of repair. During the day, the workshop was on show to the passing public, as the large metal shutter door was lifted open to show potential customers the hard, dedicated work of the mechanics.

Matthew suspected his targets were inside the repair shop, he stepped up close to the metal shutter, pressing his ears against the curved grooves of the door. He could hear a voice inside, a male voice, talking quickly. It was impossible to make out the words he was saying but Matthew got the impression that this man was either angry or upset. He stepped away from the door and unbuttoned his suit jacket, reaching inside he pulled out his trusty weapon from its holster, along with its suppressor from another pocket. As he attached the suppressor to his weapon, he moved silently away from the shutter, walking behind the building and away from the front entrance. The suppressor on, he kept a free hand to the wall, letting his fingertips glide over the old bricks of the building. When he reached the corner that led to the back, he turned, following the wall of the building. He kept his hand against it until he reached the door that the staff used to come outside, out of sight of the customers, for cigarette breaks or to place old or unusable motor parts.

His gun held in one hand, Matthew reached out with his other and placed it gently on the door handle. Slowly pushing down on the handle, he pushed forward against the door slowly and he felt no resistance. He paused for a moment, taking a deep breath to calm his heart rate and his thoughts, it was time to go to work. As he opened the door silently, the voice inside became louder and clearer.

Matthew stepped inside with the silence and quick grace of a ballet dancer, making sure to close the door completely behind him. His targets were close; Matthew could hear the voice bouncing off the many surfaces in the large workshop. His gun held up at shoulder level, but held back close to his body facing forward, Matthew held out his other hand slightly up ahead of him to feel for anything he might miss. He walked by several motorbikes, all currently in different stages of repair. His fingers could feel the spaces where the headlights used to be, feel the dents of damaged body work and the tears of ripped leather. He was getting closer to the two targets.

Matthew could hear the angry voice of Simon echoing around the room. He must have been pacing back and forth because the volume of his voice kept increasing and decreasing as Matthew reached the corner wall that separated him from them. Matthew stopped and waited behind the corner taking long, slow deep breaths as he listened, using the echoes of their voices on the walls to roughly position where they were for when he finally made his move.

He stopped his breathing ritual and concentrated, turning his head slightly to listen better. Something was wrong. He frowned as he leaned closer, trying to make out what he was hearing. There was the clear male voice of Simon O'Niell shouting, as he moved around the room. Matthew had assumed that the other target, his female partner, Ruby, had just been quietly listening, sitting in a chair or leaning against a workbench. But he could hear another sound, a sound he wasn't expecting. A sound in between the ranting and raving of O'Neill, a muffled sound as if someone was struggling to talk.

Matthew leaned closer; his head almost exposed around the corner as he tried to make out this mysterious sound. It was a higher tone; it must be the woman Ruby. Was she gagged? He leaned back around the corner out of sight, resting his head against the wall and thinking quickly as he processed this new information. *'Why has O'Neill gagged his partner?'* he asked himself. If she's been gagged, then she's most likely tied up to a chair. Matthew thought this over. If he was right, and he usually was about such things, then this Ruby was currently bound and gagged. Which would also mean that she would be unable to fight back when Matthew stepped out and revealed himself to them. He gripped his gun with both hands, clearing his head of all thoughts except those needed to end a life. He had to be careful though and quick.

Matthew stepped around the corner raising his gun in both hands aiming towards the sound of Simon's voice. Simon had his back to Matthew as he moved round. He heard Ruby's gagged voice became louder behind the duct tape that had been placed across her lips. Her muffled voice was suddenly full of panic and her eyes widened, as if screaming.

"Will you shut the fuck up?" Simon shouted at her, turning to snatch out and grab the gun he had left on the table next to him, amongst a stack of photos and printed emails he had tossed there when he had arrived. As his hand shot out to pick up the weapon to hit the girl again with the butt of the gun, he saw movement out of the corner of his eye. He turned quickly and froze; his whole body began to shake.

Moving slowly towards him, as silently as a ghost, was a man he had heard of only as a rumour, a legend, but had never seen himself: The Blind Man. Simon instinctively raised his hands as if to surrender then realised that this man, as dangerous as he might be, couldn't actually see him and instead made to grab his own gun. Matthew was quicker, sensing a rush of movement he pointed his gun towards the left of Simon's leg and fired a warning shot, missing Simon but striking the table with the bullet sending papers fluttering across the floor.

"I wouldn't if I were you," he said simply taking another step closer.

"Berkant sent you, didn't he?" Simon asked, unable to hide the panic in his voice.

"That's not really important now, is it?" Matthew replied, taking a moment to listen for Ruby's voice. She was to his right, behind Simon and still trying to speak behind her gag. "Let's make this quick, shall we? We've already spent too much time talking."

"Wait, don't kill me!" Simon pleaded. "You're making a big mistake!"

"Scary, isn't it, when you're on the other side of a gun? Sorry, as you know, this is just a job, nothing personal."

"No, you moron, listen to me! This is a set up! She's with the police!" Simon shouted, stabbing a finger in the direction of Ruby tied to her chair. "She's an undercover detective. I found out when I caught her trying to make calls to her boss. She's got info on all of us. Berkant knows, that's why he sent you!" Simon was really panicking now. Matthew just stood there and listened. If what he said was true, it made no difference to him. It just meant that he was wasting more time. He raised his gun to chest height as if to make his point.

"You can't kill me! You shouldn't kill me!"

"And why not?" Matthew asked, struggling to hide the boredom in his voice.

"Berkant hired me as well, to kill you."

Matthew froze, his gun still held straight ahead of him pointed at Simon's chest. "What did you just say?"

"Berkant hired me to kill you. I told you this is a set up. He knows that the police have managed to infiltrate his group and now he's tying up loose ends."

"What do I have to do with the police?" Matthew asked. He couldn't believe any of this, it was nonsense. It was clearly a last-ditch attempt by Simon to try and save his own skin.

"He's moving on, out of the country. Don't you get it? He's done here. With London, with England. He's been suspicious for ages, thinking the police were getting closer to him. He must have a man on the inside or something? He's going back to Turkey, to his brother, I think. They've been using us to kill people who know too much – think about it!"

Matthew didn't reply; he just stood there, his mind working fast. It's true, there had been more jobs than usual but that didn't mean anything. His face must have given something away because Simon had relaxed a little and even let out a small chuckle, "I knew it. See, it's just you and me. He set us up. We were supposed to kill each other and then that's another loose end tied up."

"And the girl?" Matthew asked, his anger rising inside him, coursing through his veins like a deadly poison. He nodded towards the now silent Ruby who had been watching the two men argue.

"Like I said, she's with the police. She's probably the reason why he's acting so fast to try and get out."

This job was falling apart and becoming a mess very quickly and Matthew was starting to lose his patience. He took a long deep breath and tightened his grip on the gun still pointed at Simon's chest.

"So, according to you, Berkant has put a hit on the both of us, in the hope that we would kill each other?" He asked taking his time with each word as if saying them out loud would make them untrue.

"Yeah," replied Simon simply, relaxing slightly, satisfied that he had convinced the man in front of him.

"Very well." Matthew pulled the trigger. The bullet left the gun with a soft 'fwump' hitting Simon in his chest. As Ruby let out a scream behind her duct tape gag, Simon simply fell to the floor, silent in shock with his hands across his chest where the bullet had hit him. Blood started to flow out over his fingers as he dropped to his knees. Matthew heard the gentle thud as his body dropped. Lowering his gun, he fired again; this time catching Simon in the head. His body jerked backwards as brain and skull fragments ejected out of the back of his head and onto the floor behind him. His now lifeless body crumpled to the floor as blood flowed, creating a crimson puddle underneath it.

Matthew quickly removed the suppressor, then tucked his gun back into its holster. Ruby was struggling against the ropes tied behind her back. The chair rocking side to side as she tugged and pulled as hard as she could, fighting with all her might against her bonds, the coarse rope burning her skin.

Matthew walked towards her, stepping carefully over the body on the floor. His leg brushed against Ruby's. He placed his hands firmly on her legs to stop her kicking out at him as he crouched down in front of her, his face level with hers. He slowly lifted his hand towards her face, his fingertips finding the edge of the tape across her mouth.

"I'm going to remove this. You're not going to scream. You're not going to shout. You're going to answer my questions. Understand?"

She was still trying to talk. Muffled sounds of panic and anger tried to escape from behind the tape as she struggled to speak. He could feel her body tense as he began to peel the silver tape off her lips, her skin red around her mouth from the adhesive.

"Now, my questions."

"Get down!" she shouted. What happened next was a blur and an assault on Matthew's senses. As her voice echoed off the surfaces across the workshop, she freed her leg from his grip and struck out hard and fast kicking him in his chest. He fell back into the body of O'Neill, one hand grabbing at his chest where her heavy boot had connected, the other reaching for his gun. As he hit the crumpled body of the dead man, he heard the sound of glass cracking, felt the rush of wind as something shot past him, only just missing him by millimetres. Matthew froze as he heard the sound of a bullet hitting the floor and felt the small pieces of glass rain down on him from a window above them.

As her foot hit his chest, Ruby had pushed herself away from him, crashing to the floor onto her back, only just getting herself out of the shooter's line of fire. She hit the floor hard, still tugging against the ropes behind her back. Her hair spilled across her face, as she looked across at the supposed blind man now lying there across the man he just killed. "Get me out of this chair!" she called across the room at him. Matthew shook his head, scattering broken glass from his hair over the floor where it tinkled and splashed into the growing pool of blood. Ignoring the pain in his chest, he rolled forwards across the floor towards the sound of Ruby's voice.

As he threw his body towards her, another shot was fired, followed by the sound of glass breaking as a bullet passed through it. The bullet landed where Matthew's body had been laying seconds before, hitting instead the corpse of Simon O'Neill. He reached Ruby and quickly extracted a small knife that was hidden up his sleeve. His hands roamed over her body quickly. Finding her arms, he slid his hands down past her elbows to her wrists, finding the ropes that held her in place.

"Hurry up!" she shouted again, tugging as hard as she could against the ropes causing her skin to burn and bleed.

"Stop moving or I'll cut your wrists open," Matthew replied, doing his best to keep calm. Knowing another bullet could come any second, he brushed the hand holding the knife against his other hand, searching for where to cut. Clutching the ropes, he began to slide the blade against the rough fabric to free her hands. As the blade slid back and forth quickly, he could feel the ropes, start to slacken as the bindings broke against the sharp steel. The ropes finally gave.

Her hands free, Ruby rolled over, grabbing Matthew by the shoulders and pulling him down on top over her. Matthew acted instinctively and tried to push her off. As he did there was an explosion of pain in his left shoulder as a bullet finally caught him. The window above them was now completely gone, broken glass had rained down, joining the ever-growing pool of blood on the floor. Matthew let out a shout of pain and fell to the floor clutching the upper part of his arm, his warm blood flowing out over his leather gloves and down his suit. Bent over on his knees, Matthew pressed his hand tightly against the wound, gritting his teeth against the pain.

Ruby was on her feet in an instant. While the man in front of her fell over shouting with pain, she jumped over him, rushing over to the table across the room and grabbing as many of the files and papers she could. She forced them roughly into a canvas rucksack that sat on the floor – from which they had be emptied earlier. Another bullet was fired, hitting the table and just missing her hand as she reached for more notes and photos. She snatched her hand back, jumping in shock. Leaving them on the table, she turned, rushing over to Matthew who was now on his feet, his free hand gripping his bloody shoulder hard, he had become pale, swaying slightly on his feet.

"Move, you moron," Ruby ordered grabbing his good arm, she pushed him forwards and through the door that led into the shop away from the line of fire. "Come on. My car's out on the street." She kept a tight grip on his arm as she pulled him quickly through the shop around the gleaming motorbikes and various accessories. "Give me your gun," she demanded, never breaking her pace as they got closer to the glass front door. Letting go of his arm, Matthew reached inside his jacket and pulled out his gun, the metal handle slipping against his bloody hand. Ruby reached across him with her free hand, yanking the bloody gun away from his grip and firing two shots straight into the door ahead. The glass cracked but didn't completely break. She fired a third shot as she reached the door, closing her eyes as she slammed her shoulder into the glass and threw them both through it. The glass exploded around them as they collapsed onto the cold concrete outside.

Matthew shouted out in pain again as he landed on his wounded shoulder. The shop's alarm activated, a high-pitched scream shouting out across the quiet street. Ruby was already on her feet looking around, checking for the shooter. She grabbed the rucksack and threw it over her shoulder. She then grabbed Matthew with her free hand, pulling him to his feet. All the while her other hand was still pointing the gun ahead, her eyes darting around for their attacker.

"Let's go," she said, dragging Matthew along beside her. He forced himself to move. *Ignore the pain and get away,* he told himself, groaning loudly. He met her pace, keeping close to her as they ran together. The shop's alarm was so loud he could hear nothing else. He was useless to her until they could get away. Blood was dripping from his body as they moved away from the shop, leaving a red dotted trail behind them.

Ruby led him back onto the main road tugging at him, encouraging him to move faster. Ruby dragged him to the right along the road, moving as fast as she could as she supported him towards a parked black BMW. As she reached the car, she pushed Matthew against the door, letting him support himself. Now gripping the gun with both hands, she crouched slightly looking around, the gun ahead of her as she looked up at the surrounding buildings, checking windows, fire escapes and rooftops looking for their shooter. As her eyes darted from roof top to window, she reached into the pocket of her red leather jacket and pulled out her keys, pressing the button to unlock the car.

"Get in," she ordered, opening her own door as she jumped into the car. Matthew slid his hands along the cool metal of the car searching for the door handle, he found it quickly and climbed into the car which lurched away before he'd even shut the door.

"Jesus!" he exclaimed as the car door slammed against him. The tyres screeched on the tarmac as Ruby's foot slammed into the accelerator, speeding them away.

"We need to get out of here and get somewhere safe," she said, constantly looking over her shoulder to make sure they weren't being followed. The burglar alarm now in the distance, the only sound was the roaring of the car engine. Matthew was able to clear his head and start to think straight.

"Well, I'll assume your place is out of the question? Most likely, there'll be people headed there now waiting for you just in case you escaped and were stupid enough to run home."

"Where do you suggest then?" she retorted angrily, brushing her hair back out of her face. "I assume they know where you live, seeing as you work with them? Do they know where you live?"

Matthew ignored her, the question jolted him into action like a shot of adrenaline. He pulled his phone out of his pocket, ran his finger over the unlock button and slid his thumb across the icons, feeling the vibrations that told him he'd found the dial pad.

"Hey, are you listening?" she demanded of him, finally slowing the car down to the speed limit. "You can't call anyone. For all you know, they're tracking you with that."

"I doubt that," Matthew replied as he slowly typed in an eleven-digit number. As he slid his thumb over the green call button feeling the vibration as the phone sent a signal out.

"What are you doing?" Ruby asked, her tone becoming angrier with each question. "Can we go to your place? Is it safe there?"

"It doesn't exist anymore," Matthew replied simply. He ripped the back off his phone, extracting the battery first, he then pulled out and bent the sim card, tossing all the separate pieces out the window. "Where's your phone?" he asked, Ruby shook her head as she drove on.

"O'Neill smashed it up when he first caught me and realised there was nothing useful on it." She sighed and looked ahead as she drove with no clear destination in mind. "So where do we go then? We can't just keep driving all night."

"I have a place. A safe house. No one but me knows about it," he explained, wincing a little as he pressed his hand against his open wound, trying to stem the bleeding. "Just keep driving, head into the city, I'll tell you more as we get there."

"How can you do that? You can't see shit," she replied gesturing towards his eyes with her hand.

"Just shut up and drive," Matthew groaned, resting his head against the car window.

*

On the roof over the top of the Mechanics garage, Charles was cursing himself as he packed away the stolen L115A3 Long Range Sniper rifle. He'd have finished the job and killed them both if the weapon in his hands hadn't kept jamming on him. It wasn't a gun he was too familiar with but he had needed something. The alarm was still on, deafening him as he moved as fast as he could. He needed to get away before the police arrived and if he was spotted anywhere near here before them, then he would be in real deep shit. The rifle locked away in its case, he looked around for somewhere to conceal it. He couldn't just leave it out and about, this was a weapon that had been stolen from the evidence locker. Even with the serial numbers filed off, it could be traced back to him.

Charles spotted an old rusty air vent towards the corner of the rooftop. Over the screech of the building's alarm, he could just make out the familiar sound of approaching sirens. Charles pulled off the grate to the vent and pushed the rifle inside, making sure to wedge it against the metal walls so it didn't drop away. He would need to return and retrieve the weapon when it was safe to do so. Replacing the cover quickly, Charles looked down over the edge of the roof. He'd have to time his descent perfectly. If he was on sight before the patrol cars arrived, questions would be asked. He'd have to wait for them to begin their investigation and simply blend into the eventual chaos. The wailing of the sirens was growing louder, mixing with the building's relentless alarm. Grinding his teeth against the noise, he pulled out his phone and began typing a text a fast as he could.

There has been a problem. O'Neill is dead but the girl and the other man have escaped. Simon told her everything. They've taken the evidence with them.

He hit send and looked over the edge of the building. The police had arrived and several officers were already rushing inside. Charles took his chance and quickly climbed down the exterior ladder to the ground, keeping himself as close to the ladder as he could. With the alarm still going and the flashing lights of the police cars, none of the dozens of police officers noticed him slipping into the crowd amongst their growing number. Charles took a moment before barking out orders, demanding someone turn off that bloody alarm and someone explain to him what the hell was going on here.

While he waited for his answers, confident in his performance and that he had not warranted any suspicion, he felt the phone is his pocket vibrate with the reply from the unknown number.

We'll take it from here. Stay out of the way.

Charles read and reread the message several times keeping the phone cupped in his hands. *Stay out of the way?* he thought to himself. He swore under his breath. He had already left the files he had been given at the drop off point they had instructed him to and from the looks of it, O'Neill had stolen the bag of evidence and now it was in the wrong hands. He had nothing left now. If this all goes south, he could be facing a lifetime behind bars. But he wasn't going to be pushed aside because of one small mistake, he would find a way. A Constable was rushing towards him calling his name over the screeching alarm. Charles tucked the phone into his pocket, deciding to plan his next move as soon as he could get away from here.

*

Berkant sat behind his desk in his dark office, his only sources of light coming from his laptop, a gold desk lamp and a cigarette sitting in a square black ashtray. He was a large man, tall with a strong chest and large arms. His muscles had been built through a lifetime of hard work and growing up fighting on a daily basis. His grey hair was cut short and straight, his dark eyes, always sharp and focused, were glowing by the light of his phone.

He had grown up in a small village in Turkey, with his older brother and father. Starting out picking pockets, Berkant and his brother started to move into bigger crimes as they grew older until they eventually became the heads of the largest organised criminal family in Eastern Europe. Their influence and power spread slowly west across the continent. Berkant left his brother to control the Empire alone when he moved to England, seeing it as a starting point to eventually move across the Atlantic, into North and South America. Berkant tossed the mobile phone he was holding onto the large oak table in front of him and leaned back in his chair, running his hands over his eyes, rubbing them before dragging his hands down his face in frustration against his grey stubble. This was getting out of hand. Everything had been going to plan, it was almost complete and now this had happened. It had been hard for him to give the order to have Matthew killed, he was his favourite after all, almost like a second son. But the police were getting too close, members of his team were starting to get sloppy, it was time to pack up operations and head home.

The last remnants of ash from his cigarette fell to the tray, catching his attention for a second. He considered lighting up another one but decided against it. The way he had been going through them lately, they would kill him before Old Lady Time did. Instead, he drummed his thick fingers against the armrest of his chair, checking his watch and wondering where his son Arif was? As if on cue, there was a knock on the door and without waiting for a reply, Arif walked into the office. He was very much like his father in appearance, slightly shorter and slimmer but with the same strong, muscular body type. Arif had chosen to shave his head bald and to keep his face free of facial hair; one less thing for his opponents to grab during a fight.

"You wanted to see me, sir?" he asked. His voice had a strong East London accent, having been moved here to be with his father after his mother had died when he was a year old. Now, thirty-five years later, he knew London better than most black cab drivers. He stood with his back straight and hands behind his back, looking his father straight in the eyes. Arif was more a soldier than a son, displaying nothing but respect and loyalty to his father and boss. Wearing a tailored grey suit with a black shirt but no tie, his shoes polished to a mirror shine, he gave an aura of style, confidence and fear.

"We have a problem," Berkant said simply, leaning forward and resting his elbows on the table, resting his clasped hands against his chin.

"Something went wrong between Matthew and O'Neill?"

"Not just that, turns out O'Neill had recently acquired a new partner."

"The girl Ruby?" Arif asked. He allowed a small smirk at the thought of the attractive red head he had met on a couple of occasions. Berkant caught the smirk and gave his son a look so stern that Arif instantly removed it from his lips.

"That girl," Berkant said slowly, doing his best to keep his temper. "Who I now ask, how have you come to know her? Is in fact an undercover detective and in turn has been collecting information on all of us and our entire operations. You, me, everyone we work with, our contacts here, our contacts abroad, she has everything!" Berkant's voice grew louder with each word and his face grew redder as his clenched his fists tightly, slamming them onto the table with the last word. "And not only that," he continued, sucking air in through his clenched teeth as he spoke, "it looks like the information that our man, inside the police, had left at the drop off site has been intercepted, most likely by this girl. So now, she has information on us and now probably knows that we have compromised the police as well."

45

"Fuck," replied Arif, looking away at the floor. Despite his strength and skill as a fighter, his father was the only man he was truly afraid of, not that anyone except the two of them knew that.

"Oh, fuck indeed, boy," said Berkant, rising slowly from his chair taking a long deep breath to calm himself.

"How do you know she has all this info on us?" Arif dared to ask his father, his eyes darting back to his father's own for a split second before looking away.

"That idiot O'Neill told me himself. He called me and had the nerve to accuse me of double crossing him. I tried to convince him he was in no danger, but I wasn't a hundred percent sure he believed me. So I sent our inside man as an insurance policy to make sure everything went to plan. Turns out none of it did."

"How has she got so much info if she's been hanging around with that idiot, he wasn't anywhere near the inner circle?" Arif asked, daring to make eye contact with his father once again.

"I was hoping you could tell me. Clearly you know this girl. Have you been fucking her like every other whore in this city?" Berkant stayed behind his desk, resting his closed fists on the hard wooden surface and looking like a dangerous gorilla.

"No," replied Arif, looking back into his father's eyes and holding his gaze with him, "Perhaps some of the others but she didn't like me, believe me, sir, I tried."

"Oh, I believe you. Well however she did it, she's got dirt on us all and now we need to fix it before we have the entire London Police Force banging on our door." Arif straightened his back again and raised his head ready to take his orders.

"What do you need from me, sir?"

"From what I know, she escaped with Matthew. We already know where she lives. I have some information on her." Berkant nodded across the room to a small safe on the floor in a lockable cabinet. "We had already collected that from the deposit point from other informants so it's unlikely she will head home now."

"Think she will go with Matthew to his home?" Arif asked, already itching to move into action.

"Possibly," said Berkant, stroking his chin as he considered his options, his rough fingers stroking his hard stubble, "go there. I don't think he'd be foolish enough to go there and hide, but it's possible he may go back to get supplies.

Take your best men; you know as well as I do, despite his disadvantage, he's still fucking dangerous."

"I can handle him." Arif's face had gone hard, clenching his jaw. Like an angry dog tugging at its leash, he wanted nothing more than to be told to go do his job. Berkant could see this and raised his hand.

"Calm down, boy, rushing is what got us into this mess."

"I will, sir, but don't worry I won't let you down."

"I know how you feel about Matt, don't let your emotions take over and steal your focus. Get the job done first." Arif had always made his feelings about Matthew known to his father. A mixture of jealousy and hatred towards the man who was basically his brother. Arif felt that Matthew shouldn't even be cleaning his toilet, let alone be so highly regarded by his father. "It's a shame you two could never get along," said Berkant, walking around his desk slowly, "but perhaps that was a sign from God that led us to this moment." He walked over to his son, gripping his arms in his strong hands. "You are my son, my flesh and blood. I'm sorry if you ever thought I favoured him more than you. I know you won't let me down." He released his son and nodded towards the door. Arif nodded, a glint of excitement in his eyes as he looked to his father before turning and walking swiftly out of the room, closing the door firmly behind him as he went to assemble his team. Berkant sat back against his desk, pulling his silver cigarette case and lighter towards him.

Chapter Four

Ruby and Matthew had been driving for over twenty minutes. He had managed to slow the bleeding in his arm, but he was going to need to get the bullet out and stitch up the wound before he lost too much blood. His clothes were soaked with his blood and the car seat wasn't faring much better. As they had progressed into the city, he had told her to call out the street names and the direction they were heading. He quickly figured out their location and guided Ruby with each turn.

"How do you know where we are?" She asked, unable to hide her suspicion. She looked sideways at him, trying to see his eyes behind his glasses, wondering whether this was all an act.

"I passed The Knowledge six years ago," he replied, shrugging slightly and wincing at the pain in his arm as he did.

"Why?" is all Ruby could ask him. This man was surprising her with each passing minute.

"It makes it easier for me to do my job," replied Matthew, in a tone that suggested she should stop asking questions. "We're nearly there, left here." Ruby did as she was told, turning the car into an unassuming dead-end street.

"Where are we?" she asked, slowing the vehicle down to a steady crawl. Except for one other car parked to the right and several bins, the street was completely empty. Either side of them, boarded up or darkened windows covered the buildings that surrounded them.

"Head to the end," Matthew instructed, "you can leave the car parked up by the door."

"What door?" Ruby began to ask, but the car's headlights answered her question. They highlighted, at the end of the street, a black, graffiti covered door. She stopped the car directly in front of it, cutting the engine. As she did, Matthew climbed out of the car as fast as he could. He ran his hand over the car, leaving bloody streaks from his fingers as he moved towards the front of the vehicle, right now he didn't have time to be careful. When he reached the tip of the bonnet, he extended his hand, reaching out for the door.

"Need a hand?" Ruby asked, she headed to the back of the car with a knife in her hand from her rucksack. She bent down and used the knife to pull the registration plates off the car roughly. She tossed the plates onto the driver's seat, grabbing her bag before kicking the door closed. She walked to the front of the car, standing next to him as he found the surface of the door.

He moved his hand slowly across the dirty door as if searching for something. He said nothing and kept moving his free hand. He stopped at a point towards the top right where the door appeared to be chipped. His fingertips picked at the damaged wood, pulling away a large chunk and then tossing it over his shoulder. Ruby watched him with a confused expression on her face. She looked over her shoulder, checking up the street in case they were being followed. When she looked back, he was holding a brass key that he had removed from the door. Matthew slid his hand down the door, holding the key. Finding the rusted lock, he turned the key and opened the door.

He stepped inside quickly, heading straight up the stairs ahead of them without a word or waiting for Ruby. Rolling her eyes, Ruby followed, closing the door behind her and hearing the lock turn automatically. She headed up the creaking wooden stairs. Matthew had already vanished from view; a door at the top of the stairs hung open and a light was turned on, penetrating the darkness. The door at the top of the stairs led into a small flat. She walked, in closing the door while looking around. She was standing in a living room, barely furnished; the only light source was a single bulb hanging from the ceiling. There was a dusty sofa and armchair facing a TV stand with no TV in the corner. The coffee table in between them had a thin layer of dust across it. To her left, she could make out a small kitchen that appeared just as unused as the living room. Matthew appeared from the room to her right which she guessed was the bedroom. In his hands, he was carrying a first aid kit.

Ruby was amazed at how well he moved around the room, almost as if he could see. He didn't hold out his arms as he walked, nor did he keep bumping into things. He had clearly spent time here. Matthew didn't have time to talk, he needed to sort his arm out and figure out what was going on.

"There's a bottle of Vodka in the freezer, get it for me," he demanded, slowly peeling off his bloody jacket to reveal a white shirt now soaked in red blood. Ruby knew what he was planning to do and headed into the tiny square kitchen.

In the small freezer above the fridge, there was an unopened, ice-cold bottle of vodka. By the time she had returned to the living room, Matthew had taken his shirt and glasses off. Ruby stood there for a moment looking down at this man. There was no scarring or damage around his eyes as she had originally suspected. Apart from being almost completely white, his eyes looked perfectly normal.

His body on the other hand was a different story; scars, bullet wounds and other marks covered his strong muscular frame. He had already pulled out a set of surgical tweezers from the first aid kid and was now sliding the edges across his skin towards the wound.

"What the hell are you doing?" she demanded, moving towards him and quickly grabbing the tweezers out of his hand as she sat on the sofa next to him.

"I'm getting the bullet out," he retorted his head turning towards her voice with an annoyed look.

"No, you're not, now just stop moving." Ruby pushed him back against the sofa and rested the tweezers on her lap. Quickly opening the vodka, she poured the liquid over her hands rubbing them together before pouring more over the metal tweezers spilling the clear liquid over the floor.

"Do you know what you're doing?" Matthew enquired, listening to the sounds of the spirit being spilt over her hands and the floor.

"Let's see," Ruby grumbled, focusing on the task at hand. She gave no warning as she poured Vodka over the bullet wound causing Matthew to inhale swiftly through his teeth as the cool liquid stung his flesh. "You know for someone who has clearly been in plenty of fights you're a bit of a baby aren't you?" she remarked, a slight playful teasing tone to her voice. Matthew said nothing, resting his head against the back of the sofa, he dug his nails into the dusty cushions as the smooth metal tools began to explore the wound in his flesh. Ruby worked silently and efficiently, she pushed into his flesh carefully exploring with a sense of purpose that told Matthew she had done this before. He said nothing as she worked; he wanted her to concentrate on his arm. He sat back, his jaw locked, he was doing his best to ignore the pain in his arm as she attempted to grab the bullet.

"Well, you're lucky it hasn't hit the bone and I don't think it's broken. It looks like it's all in one piece." She felt the tweezers grasp the small metal bullet and carefully began to remove the tool, holding tightly onto the bullet as she extracted it out of the bloody flesh. With her free hand, she reached over for the first aid box and grabbed a large white dressing, ready to wrap up his arm. The bullet was finally out. She pressed the dressing to the open wound, placing the bloody tweezers and bullet onto the coffee table. She picked up more dressings and medical tape and began to tidy up the wound.

"Thanks," he mumbled begrudgingly, sitting up slightly as Ruby finished covering his arm. He reached out over the table and finally found the bottle of vodka and pulled it to his lips. He took a long gulp and groaned as the liquid burnt his throat.

"Planning on getting pissed?" she asked standing up heading into the kitchen to wash her blood-soaked hands.

"It's for the pain," he said nodding to his wounded arm. "Thank you though." He looked towards the kitchen, his eyes staring blankly in her general direction, "Not just for the arm but for getting me out of there. I don't really know what happened to me back there." She came back and sat in the armchair opposite him watching as he took another long sip of vodka.

"Don't worry about it. Hard as it is for me to admit, you did save me back there as well. I don't think me kicking you helped you with your…magic powers," she said struggling for words as she waved her hand at him, acknowledging his skills despite his blindness.

"Nothing magic about me," Matthew grunted. His arm was feeling stiff, but the pain was lessening as they spoke. "How did you know there was a shooter on the roof?" he asked her, offering the now half empty bottle of vodka.

"They were using the laser sight. It caught my eye through the window they were aiming through. Whoever they were, they can't have been the best shot in the world if they couldn't kill a blind man or someone tied to a chair." She gave a light laugh and knocked back a shot of vodka, the strong alcohol relaxing her slightly. "So what's your story then?" she asked, brushing the bottle against Matthew's hand to offer him more. He declined, waving his hand at the bottle.

"You first," he said, his tone becoming more serious as he sat up, groaning against the pain in his arm. Ruby leant forward and pressed her hand against his bare chest, pushing him back into the sofa. She could feel the scars across his muscles on her fingertips.

"In the morning," she replied, in an equally serious tone, "right now we need rest and time to clear our heads after what just went down. You're no good to me in this condition." She removed her hand, looking at him again before standing and stretching her arms above her head with a small yawn.

"You might be right," Matthew agreed, feeling fatigue finally crash down on him. "How can I be sure you're not going to cut my throat while I sleep?" Matthew kept a straight face remembering he had given her his gun.

"How do I know you're not going to do the same?" Ruby answered, her fingertips twitching as she thought of the gun still tucked into the back of her jeans.

"I guess we're on the same page," Matthew answered after a pause considering his predicament, "take the bedroom, I'll sleep on the sofa. The sheets are clean and there's an en suite where you can wash up."

"Effective killer and a gentleman? And women say all the good men are taken." Ruby smirked as she headed over to the small bedroom. Matthew shrugged, smiling to himself, thinking how long it had been since he had spoken to someone in such a way, like a friend. It felt almost alien to him, as if he was in a foreign land and trying to speak a new language.

He leaned down, reaching under the sofa, his hand feeling around the dusty floor and pulling out an old blanket to sleep under. Ruby came back to the doorway of the bedroom, leaning forward with both hands resting on the frame. "Now listen. I just want to make something clear between us, regardless of what's happened tonight. I won't hesitate to beat up a blind man if I find you in here trying to kill me or trying to sleep with me. Either way, I'll snap your cock off, are we clear?"

Matthew froze midway through beating the cushions into a better shape to sleep on, he slowly turned his face towards the sound of her voice doing his best not to laugh in her face.

"I wouldn't worry about that, you're not exactly my type."

"Do you prefer your girls blonde to red heads?" she asked standing straight and watching him with a mild curiosity.

"I don't prefer girls," he replied simply turning away from her as he lay back on the sofa. Ruby stood there, surprise rushing through her.

"Oh," is all she could say. "Well sorry then, that was rude of me, goodnight then," she said simply, heading back to the room and preparing to close the door.

"Good night, Ruby," Matthew called over as he placed his hands over his bare chest.

"Oh well, if we're being honest with each other now. I'm not Ruby. My name is Zoe."

"Matthew," he replied, tapping his bare chest once, "good night, Zoe." He closed his eyes, signalling the conversation was over. Zoe gave him a nod and closed the door, relieved to be getting some rest at last.

*

Berkant was pacing back and forth across his office in front of his desk, roughly stubbing out a cigarette in the overflowing ashtray as he passed and instantly lighting up another. He checked his Rolex watch again, it had been nearly an hour since his son had left to go and search Matthew's home and still no word. He was about to give up waiting and go check himself, when the Android smartphone on his desk lit up and started vibrating loudly against the polished dark wood. He snatched it up, pressing it to his ear as he answered, "Yes?"

"We're here, sir," came Arif's voice. He sounded frustrated.

"Well? Any sign of him?" Berkant's temper was already rising, having to ask for more details.

"There's nothing here except fire engines and police cars. The house is a burning wreck. Looks like there was an explosion. There's debris everywhere." Berkant did his best to keep calm, squeezing the phone so tightly in his hand that he caused the screen to crack.

"Curses! Did anyone see you?" he asked. The last thing he needed now was his team being questioned by the police.

"No, sir, no one saw us," Arif replied. Berkant could make out the sounds of car doors closing over the phone. "We'll head back to the mechanics and see if we can pick up a trail there."

"Good boy. Keep me updated." Berkant ended the call, catching the sound of a car engine firing up as he did. He dropped the phone carelessly onto his desk and stood still, running his hands through his hair, pulling on it slightly as he did. He needed rest, the sofa against the far wall of his office looked more and more inviting. Trudging over, he sat back and closed his eyes, trying to relax his brain and figure out how he was going to clear up this mess.

Chapter Five

Zoe woke early the next morning, checking the watch on her wrist. She saw that it was nearly seven and slowly pulled herself up, sitting in bed yawning and rubbing her eyes. Looking around the unfamiliar room, it took her a moment to remember where she was and what had happened. She ran a hand through her tousled and tangled hair before tossing the covers aside and climbing out of bed. She had found a shirt hanging in the wardrobe and had helped herself to it to wear in bed, it was too large for her and hung down her body covering her underwear but revealing her strong thighs and legs. Her clothes had been left folded over a small wooden chair in the corner. As she reached the bedroom door, she paused, her hand on the door handle. On the other side, she could hear movement and deep long breaths. She slowly opened the door and stood in the doorway, looking across the small living room. Matthew was on the floor performing quick, deep, painful press-ups, wearing just his black boxers. Either he hadn't noticed her or he had chosen not to acknowledge her presence, grunting with each rise of his body. As she watched him push his body harder and harder, almost as if he was punishing himself, she got a better look at the scars and marks across his body. She could only imagine the fights and confrontations that caused such wounds to materialise and realised that she was alone with a very dangerous man.

Gasping for breath and covered in sweat, Matthew finally stopped. Sitting back against the sofa, he sat on the floor for a moment calming his breathing.

"Morning," he said between breaths, not looking towards Zoe.

"Morning," she answered back, jumping slightly as he spoke, "daily workout routine?"

"Something like that," he replied, pulling himself to his feet. He turned his back to her and walked across the room and into the kitchen. "Coffee?" he called out, flicking on the basic white kettle.

"Yes thanks," Zoe answered. She hesitated then started following him across the room, her defences were on full alert, wondering if he was waiting in there with a weapon. She slowly stepped forward towards the kitchen, keeping her steps light as she identified the sounds of mugs being placed on the worktop as the kettle started to boil. By the time she reached the doorway, Matthew was pouring water into the two mugs, holding the cup by the handle and keeping his thumb bent inside the cup so as to make sure the water didn't spill over.

"No milk I'm afraid," he said sliding a cup across the counter not looking in her direction as he sipped his own savouring the strong flavour as it woke his soul with each bitter taste.

"Not a problem," replied Zoe, picking up the mug and taking a sip.

"We need to talk," Matthew stated plainly, "I'm going to get dressed and then you're going to answer my questions." He didn't wait for her reply and made his way out of the kitchen, sliding his free hand along the countertop as he went.

"What's to stop me leaving while you're in the shower?" she asked, leaning on the door frame watching him make his way across the room.

"By all means leave," he said moving into the bedroom and out of sight, pushing the door closed as he passed through calling out. "Just remember that you have Berkant's entire organisation, except for me, after you – as well as a mole in your own police force. Also, you left your clothes in here." He stepped into the bathroom, closing the door and locking it. Pulling off his boxers, he stepped into the shower, turning it on as he did so, letting the freezing water hit his body like a thousand icy bullets.

Back in the living room, Zoe had nothing to do except sit on the sofa sipping her coffee. She told herself that if this man was going to kill her, he'd have done so by now. She debated with herself whether she could really trust him, but right now she felt like she didn't have much of a choice. Frustration was starting to build in her as she sat there; with no phone and no computer, she had no way to contact her superiors and update them on the situation and to tell them that there was a traitor in the ranks. A surge of anger rushed through her at that thought; anger and questions. *Who could it be? Why would they do this? Money? Were they perhaps under duress and had no choice?* Zoe could feel a headache start to form as she turned these questions over in her mind. She looked over to the bedroom, wondering how much longer Matthew was going to take.

"He takes longer than a woman," Zoe muttered to herself finishing her coffee. As if in cue, the door to the bedroom opened and Matthew stepped out. He was dressed, shaved and wearing a light grey suit with a matching tie and white shirt. From the inside pocket of his jacket, he pulled out a pair of sunglasses and slipped them over his eyes. He moved across the room, stepping in front of Zoe as he passed to sit down next to her on the sofa.

"The bathroom is free if you want to get showered," he said, reaching down under the sofa carefully and pulling out a Samsung tablet with earphones plugged in. He ran his finger across the unlock button making the screen light up. Like his phone, it reacted to his touch vibrating in different ways to signal what applications he was using.

"How does a blind man use a tablet?" Zoe asked, watching him operate the device.

"The same way you do," he answered, the tablet on his lap as he looked straight ahead, slipping an earphone into his ear as he opened up a news app.

"What are you doing?" she asked, as he quickly flicked through news story after news story. She could make out the quick mumblings of the headlines as the app read out the headlines in his ear.

"Checking to see if there's any mention of last night. Are you going to get dressed?" he asked, a hint of impatience in is voice as he tried to concentrate on the news.

"I haven't got anything to wear and I think if I walked around London with blood on my outfit people would notice," she replied, aggressively putting her cup down on the coffee table in front of them and returning his tones of impatience. Turning to him, feeling herself become more annoyed with this man as he looked ahead, instead of looking at her. Blind or not, it was incredibly frustrating to not have eye contact as she spoke to him.

Matthew sighed. Yanking the earphone out, he tossed the tablet across the coffee table where it slid off the other side onto the floor. Without saying a word, he got to his feet and stormed out of the living room and back into the bedroom. Zoe could hear him slamming drawers and cupboard doors. Concerned for her safety, she grabbed the coffee cup back up and held it over the edge of the table, ready to break it so as to us the jagged edge as a weapon. She'd done it before and she could do it again against this man.

Matthew came storming out of the bedroom roughly forcing a wallet into his suit pocket, a white walking cane tucked under his arm. Zoe sat there watching as he moved across the living room, faster than he normally did. In his frustration, he caught his leg on the edge of the table, nearly falling over. Matthew caught himself and swore loudly, kicking the table and causing it to flip over, making Zoe pull her legs to her chest to avoid them being hit. As he reached the door Matthew paused, his hand resting on the door handle, he took a breath to calm himself. He turned his head back towards her, opening the door slowly.

"Sorry, I don't usually let myself get angry." He struggled to say the words. Without waiting for an answer, he opened the door. "Lock this door behind me I'll knock three times when I get back." He stepped out of the flat, closing the door behind him. As soon as it was shut, Zoe was up and locking the door. She leant with her back to the door, listening to the sounds of his footsteps descending the stairs growing quieter and quieter.

"Shit," she cursed, banging the back of her head against the door. Looking around the flat, she felt more trapped than she had when she was undercover. At least then she could contact the outside world. She spotted the tablet lying on the floor. Sighing she remembered she couldn't use it even if she wanted to; it was fingerprint protected. Zoe ran her fingers through her hair, trying to calm herself as she processed her situation. She slammed her fist against the door, cursing this mess she had gotten herself into. She walked into the kitchen and decided the only thing she could do now was to eat something and wait for her blind would-be-hero to return.

He returned half an hour later. Zoe heard the three knocks and got up from the sofa, grabbing the large kitchen knife she had picked up and kept with her since he had left. She opened the door a fraction, looking through the gap carefully, keeping the knife out of sight behind her back. She saw him standing there waiting patiently with a white plastic bag held in one hand, his cane in the other. Zoe opened the door, stepping aside to let him in.

"I was starting to wonder whether you'd run off," she said as he stepped over the threshold. He said nothing as he dropped the plastic bag at her feet.

"Not just yet," he said, tucking his cane into his jacket pocket. He stood in the space between the sofa and the kitchen door, sniffing at the air, "been cooking?" he asked, turning his head around the room and picking up the different scents in the air.

"Porridge. Is that all right?" asked Zoe, sounding more like a sulking teenager than she meant to. She picked up the bag and looked inside, finding some newly bought clothes: blue jeans; a couple of tops; a black zip up hoodie;

some underwear and some toiletries. "Thank you for getting me all of this, are you sure it will fit me?" she asked sceptically looking through her options. Matthew had moved into the kitchen moving his hands over the countertop feeling her discarded bowl, coffee cup and some porridge oats that Zoe had spilt while making her breakfast.

"When you were helping me up and dragging me to the car, I got a good idea of your measurements, they should all fit okay." He returned from the kitchen moving over to the sofa to sit down. "I hope you're going to clean all that up in there?" He sat up straight, resting his hands on his knees, looking straight ahead and waiting for her response.

"Once I'm dressed, we'll see," she said heading over to the bedroom.

"When you're dressed, we need to have that talk we spoke about last night." Matthew didn't turn his head as he spoke, keeping his focus straight ahead of him. Zoe looked at him for a moment. To her it looked as if he were meditating silently. She said nothing and slipped into the bedroom, closing the door behind her.

Matthew didn't move the entire time she was away from him. He kept his body straight, rigid and on constant alert. His hands gripped his knees tightly as he took in his surroundings, his ears picking up every sound and his nose every scent. From outside he could hear the sounds of passing cars and buses, honking horns, cyclists shouting at pedestrians and police sirens wailing across the city. Inside he could smell the remnants of Zoe's breakfast; she had put sugar in the porridge. There were still traces of the perfume she had been wearing floating around the flat but these were being slowly replaced by the fragrances of the shower gel and shampoo he had bought her.

His ears and nose kept him alert to everything around him, allowing him to clear his mind of all unneeded thoughts. Like deleting unwanted files from a computer, Matthew searched through his brain, reviewing the last week: re-running events over and over; forgetting the unnecessary information and keeping whatever he felt might be useful to his current predicament. He spent several minutes going over the conversation with Simon O'Neill the night before. *Could he be completely certain that what that man said was true? Was it all a bluff to try and get him to lower his guard and take him out first? But then why would they have both been sent there to kill each other?* Matthew considered every option he could think of but always came back to the same answer. Berkant had betrayed him and had tried to have him killed.

This thought sent a jolt through him breaking his concentration for a moment. Matthew had not had an easy life, but he had never experienced betrayal before and it did not sit well with him. Rage started to grow in the pit of his stomach, like a pot of boiling water that could spill over any minute. He needed to calm himself. Emotions are a killer's worst enemy. Berkant had told him that. Matthew's hands gripped his knees tighter at the thought of that man. Taking long slow breaths in and then exhaling slowly, he tried to relax his body. If he let his anger get the better of him, he wouldn't survive this.

The anger he was attempting to dissipate had distracted him, his ears had not picked up the sounds of the person walking up behind him. He felt the hand press on his shoulder, as soon as the skin touched him, he reacted on instinct. Matthew leapt up, kicking the coffee table in front of him across the room with a loud crash. He spun around, his hand grabbing the wrist of the hand touching him, his other reaching into his jacket and grabbing the gun he'd found in the bedroom. In one fluid motion, his attacker's arm was forced behind their back, almost to breaking point, his weapon pressed against their head and ready to fire.

"Get off of me you fucking Psycho! It's me! It's Zoe you blind freak!" Zoe struggled against his grip. Matthew held her tightly, pushing his gun harder against her skull. It took him several moments before he realised what he was doing. He released her and stepped back from her abruptly, tucking the gun back into its holster under his jacket. Zoe spun around quickly, anger erupting in her eyes as she stared up at him. She shook her arm to regain a sense of feeling in it and then slapped him across the face as hard as she could, sending his glasses flying into the wall where the black lenses cracked.

"What the hell is wrong with you?" she screamed, raising her hand to hit him again. She stopped, her hand in mid-air as she looked at him. He hadn't reacted at all to her strike but his cheek was glowing red from where she had hit him. He stood there, looking straight over her head, his face expressionless. "Answer me, you robot!" she demanded. Lowering her hand and instead choosing to shove him backwards roughly, she stormed past him to sit in the lone arm chair opposite the sofa. "Are you going to talk or are you still meditating?" she asked calming herself down slowly, stroking her shoulder where a new pain had started to grow.

Matthew stood there motionless for a moment, then rubbed his hand over his face where she had hit him and walked away from her to where he knew a window was. It overlooked the alley where they had left the car the night before.

He placed both hands on the windowsill and rested his head against the cool glass.

"I'm not sorry and don't expect me to turn the other cheek," he said, enjoying the sensation of the smooth surface against his forehead.

Zoe scoffed behind him and folded her arms to stop herself from throwing the first thing she could grab at him, "I don't doubt that; you don't seem like a very good Catholic."

"Church of England actually," he replied, taking his face off the window and standing up straight, keeping his back to her as he spoke. "You and I are in a real mess here, I've been thinking it over and our options are extremely limited, if, non-existent."

"Well thank you, Captain Obvious."

"My point is," he carried on, trying to keep his voice calm and ignore her insubordination, "is that if our first move is the wrong one, then we're both dead and I have no intention of dying just yet."

Zoe said nothing, she looked at him, standing before her and began to really see the calculated killer, the killer that she had heard so many stories about during her time undercover, start to form in front of her eyes. "So what's the plan?" she asked, keeping herself on edge as she sat up, feeling the need to be able to move at a moment's notice. Matthew shook his head, finally turning around to face her. His blank white eyes seem to lock on hers like a magnet and it made her extremely uncomfortable.

"There is no plan. Not yet. We don't start planning till you tell me everything that you know and everything that you have on Berkant and his group. You've spooked them now by getting caught and that was stupid and sloppy." Zoe opened her mouth to throw an angry retort at his suggestion that she was 'stupid and sloppy' in her work, but he held up his hand silencing her immediately. "I don't like sloppy," he continued, pronouncing each syllable clearly as he spoke to emphasize his point, "I like detail and facts. That's how I work and that is why I am good at what I do. So if we're going to be the ones walking away from this, I need you to tell me everything that you have learnt while you were sneaking around undercover." He stepped forward, resting his hands on the back of the sofa in front of him. "That is our only plan right now." He continued to look at her, his eyes burning into hers so much that she started to wonder again whether he was actually blind or not, but she didn't break her gaze. Zoe looked right back at him standing up slowly.

"So your plan is to hole up in this tiny little safe house of yours, listen to me read you my notes and the information I stole from Berkant's people. Is that right?"

"You'll be telling me everything," Matthew scoffed, "unless you had the courtesy to print your notes in braille?"

"I don't care if I have to tap it out to you in Morse code, we can't just sit here going over my notes like we're revising for an exam." Her frustration was growing by the second, she began to pace back and forth, trying to keep calm and not lose focus. "While we're here, Berkant and his people could be fleeing the country."

"Unlikely, Berkant isn't a runner. If he could leave the country so quickly, he would have done so long ago," Matthew interjected. "He won't leave until he's sure every loose end is tied up and sealed. He won't risk anything being traced back to him."

"Alright fine then," Zoe's voice was growing louder, the statue-like way he held himself was irritating her more than it should. "So he's not going anywhere yet. Then his people will be looking for us, or going after our families in order to get us to come out of hiding."

"I'm an orphan and I'm assuming if the department had any sense, they would have kept all personal information regarding their agents' families off record am I right? Seeing as you're so worried about your family, I assume your parents don't know what you do for a living?" Matthew held himself as still as he could, listening to her move across the room. She was getting angry and could lash out again. He wanted to be ready this time.

"Doesn't matter anyway, I'm in the same boat as you," she replied, waving him away, annoyed that he seemed to have an answer to all her suggestions. She paused for a moment, considering him. "My files and records were locked away when I joined the undercover department. There's nothing on there that can be used against me. My grandfather was fully aware I work for the police; he was an officer himself. He put his life at risk against people like you for years. He even volunteered to help out during the miner's strikes in the eighties. He passed away not long after I graduated."

"Then what's the problem?" he asked, his head turning slightly so he could listen to the sounds outside as they spoke.

"The problem is I don't like being held prisoner and forced to read to a blind murderer like I'm Hannibal Lecter's carer." She burst out, letting her frustrations boil over as she slammed her hand against the wall. "We can't stay here forever."

"You're right. We can't." Matthew's voice grew as well, not to her level, but his tone silenced her quickly. "If you want to leave, I am not stopping you. But trust me when I tell you that you will not make it back to your HQ. Berkant clearly has people everywhere and they are looking for us. The dirt you have on them and the info that proves there is a mole inside the police has put a huge target on your back. I don't know you and you don't know a damn thing about me. However, I am the only person who can keep you alive and if that means tying you to a chair and forcing you to talk, then I will have no hesitation to do so. If it comes to that, believe me when I tell you that I will get every bit of information out of you if I have to." He moved around from the back of the sofa and walked towards her, each step definite and precise. His body seemed to grow as he moved, making her back away from him, "I am a murderer, yes, I won't deny that. I am a bloody good one actually and I have other skills as well. Such as keeping people alive while causing them an immense amount of pain. Like Chakra but without the fancy tools. I'll rip your fingernails out one by one with my teeth if I have to." He towered over her as she backed into the wall. He held his hands by his sides and he made no effort to trap her, just intimidate. "So if you want to leave, leave. You're not my responsibility. But you leave everything you have, and I'll do this on my own. I don't like to be double crossed and I'll be damned if I'm going to die by their hands." He let out a quick huff through his nostrils like a bull ready to charge and turned away from her quickly, storming into the kitchen to give her time to think.

Zoe stood there leaning against the wall as she watched him walk into the kitchen. She turned to the door of the flat and for a fleeting moment she considered running. She could handle herself, she could get to her superiors and update them on the situation, get the right people involved and bring down London's largest organised crime family. She made a move to leave but stopped before she'd taken her second step. *He's right,* she told herself. No matter how good she was at keeping a low profile or hiding in plain sight, she had no idea who or how many people in the police force had betrayed her. All it took was her being spotted or revealing herself to the wrong person and she could end up like O'Neill.

"Fuck it," she muttered to herself turning back and following Matthew into the kitchen where she found him putting the dirty cups and bowl into the sink. "What do you want to know first?"

Chapter Six

Charles sat at his desk typing on his laptop as he struggled to keep awake and finish his report. By the time he had been able to leave the scene at the mechanic's, it had been morning and he had seen no point in going home to sleep. Part of him was beginning to regret that decision. No one had questioned how he had arrived so quickly and luckily no one had found the rifle he had hidden in the vent on the roof. He moved his hands from the keyboard and rubbed his eyes slowly. *What a mess this is becoming,* he thought to himself. The words on the screen in front of him started to blur and shake, he needed sleep, perhaps he could head into the staff room and grab a short nap on the old sofa in there? His hopes were dashed as he spotted William walking across the crowded room, weaving between desks and other officers, clearly heading in his direction, a number of files and papers under his arm.

"Charles, what are you doing?" he asked without introduction, he was clearly in a hurry.

"Nothing I can't drop, what do you need?" Charles asked, keen to get away from this paperwork.

"You were in charge of the murder investigation last night at that motor bike shop, weren't you?"

"I was on sight coordinating operations, yes," Charles replied, carefully choosing his words. He had no reason to think William suspected him, but with everything that has happened recently he couldn't afford to be careless.

"Good, then you're with me. Grab your jacket and let's go." William turned and was already heading for the exit without waiting for a response. Charles scrambled to get his things together, calling over the heads of the team around him.

"Where are we going?"

"The garage, come on," William called back with a quick glance over his shoulder, and he was out the door.

They drove in silence, William behind the wheel looking straight ahead, eyes focused on the road. The files he had had back in the office sat on Charles' lap unopened. He looked across at William, drumming his fingers on the top file then looked out of his own window.

"Care to tell me what this is all about? Why have you dragged me from my desk to come all the way out here?"

"You hate sitting at your desk and you hate doing paperwork. If anything, I'm doing you a favour," William replied, not taking his eyes off the road.

"Okay then, why are we heading back to the crime scene? Forensics has already done the once over, what more is there to look at?" Charles asked, his nerves coming out in his frustration.

"Open the report that came back: third page, second paragraph," William replied, reaching across and tapping his index finger hard on top of the files that sat on Charles' lap. Charles reluctantly opened the file to the desired page and began reading.

"The victim found on the scene was shot twice in the head and body. What's your point? I could have told you that." Charles looked at his old friend, the annoyance clear in his voice. William shot him a look and darted his eyes down to the report.

"Well, no shit, Sherlock. What I'm interested in is the fact that the bullets found embedded in the walls were from a different gun, a military grade sniper rifle from the looks of it."

Charles said nothing and pretended to read the open report on his lap, his mind racing. *Those bullets were meant for bodies not walls,* he thought to himself. Keeping his cool, he pretended to flick through the file, not wanting his face to give away his growing sense of worry.

"So there was another shooter? Is that what you're saying?" he asked, keeping his face directed towards the paperwork in front of him.

"Looks that way, yeah." William glanced across at him, seeing his face buried in the paperwork before him. *That's unusual.* "Forensics say there are traces of three people inside the building at the time of the shooting. The dead one we know, Simon O'Neill, he has connections to the Berkant group. Too bad he's dead. The other two escaped so we don't know where they are."

Charles flicked through the pages and came across the same photograph he had passed on to Berkant's people and saw the girl that he had tried to kill the night before. He bit his tongue hard to stop himself from cursing out loud. *This was supposed to be quick and easy!* he screamed in his head.

"I want to have a look around myself, check inside and get a better idea of what might have happened. Words on paper just aren't the same as seeing it for yourself." William continued, turning the wheel carefully with both hands as he followed the traffic through the city.

"So what do you need me for? I can't exactly give you a play-by-play commentary, can I?" Charles asked, wanting more and more to get away and make contact with Berkant and try to clean up this mess. He could do it better than any of the thugs he used and Berkant knew this he told himself, clenching his fist out of sight of William by the passenger door.

"You were on the scene. You saw it before Forensics took the body away and checked the scene. You've seen things in person – whereas I've only seen them in photos, and you've always had a good eye on crime scenes." William briefly let his mind drift back to memories of past cases with Charles in their younger days when they used to comb through crime scenes together, going through the evidence and inspecting it from different perspectives. Charles sighed as if giving up and closed the file on his lap. Sitting back in the car seat, he rubbed his eyes again, perhaps rougher than he meant to.

"Late night?" William asked him, trying to lighten the tense mood of the car, watching his old friend rub his eyes. He didn't want to bring up his talk with the old Landlord of The Admiral's Arms, not yet anyway. He had his questions, yes, and perhaps he could call them suspicious, but he didn't want to accuse Charles of anything until he was absolutely sure. Charles said nothing nor did he look at William, he looked ahead waving a hand airily and thinking of how he was going to get through this inspection without giving anything away. They drove on in silence, both lost in their own thoughts as the car made its way through the city traffic to the shop.

*

Matthew and Zoe were sitting in the living room of the small flat, him in the armchair and her on the sofa surrounded by the files, photos and documents that she had either written or stolen. The papers spilled onto the coffee table in front of her as she talked, telling Matthew everything she knew. He sat in silence, upright in his chair with his elbows placed on the armrests either side of him as he listened intently, his focus solely on her voice as she spoke.

"I'd known about this drop off site for a while. Simon had had me watch it a couple of times and when I'd started to get more evidence, I figured I should start seeing if there was anything worth stealing." She'd been explaining to Matthew about how she had acquired all the information laid out before them.

"And what did you steal from this drop site?" he asked, gently scratching his chin as she spoke.

"I didn't get long to look before Simon caught me," she explained looking through the papers that surrounded the sofa and table. She found a collection of papers and photos held together with a rubber band. "But these are copies of my personal files and the work I've been doing since going undercover." Matthew leant closer, resting his elbows on his knees and his chin against his fists.

"So that confirms there's someone on Berkant's payroll inside your department."

"It will have to be someone who works in the undercover department, this information is held in secure files that only registered users have codes for."

"How many people have those access codes?" Matthew asked, a plan of action starting to form in the back of his mind. Zoe shrugged tossing the file onto the desk in front of her.

"Give or take no more than ten. But I've been out of the office for nearly a year now, for all I know people have transferred and there could be new starters."

"Or our rat doesn't even work there and is forcing someone who does to get the files?" Matthew chipped in. The size of the job seemed to grow bigger and bigger and this was going to take more time than they had.

"It's possible, yeah," agreed Zoe, running a hand through her hair and pushing it out of her face.

"Probable more like."

"Do we have any options to try and find out?" Zoe asked, flopping back on the sofa, they'd barely been at it an hour, but her brain was already feeling exhausted.

"Not really," said Matthew standing up to stretch and move. The scale of their problem was starting to feel like a weight on his shoulders and he needed to get it off quickly. He walked slowly back and forth in front of the coffee table, Zoe's eyes on him the whole time, sliding side to side as if she was watching a tennis match. "Normally, I would do several walkbys and spend a couple of hours outside your building to see what I can pick up. But the risk of being spotted by our traitor is too great. They might see me and run or be stupid enough to try and kill me."

"Not a great start to our plan, is it?"

"No, it isn't." Matthew stopped pacing and ran his hands through his hair, trying to calm the whirlwind of thoughts spinning through his head like a hurricane, "We're going to have to expose ourselves in order to try and draw out Berkant's man. The risk with that though, is that we could have all of them crashing down on us."

Zoe sighed, leaning her head back over the sofa. He was right, they had to flush out the betrayer but doing so would be putting themselves at risk of being killed.

"I should call William," she said, more to herself than to Matthew. She stood up slowly, turning to face him, placing her hands on her hips, "He's the head of my department, if he's the inside man then he'll come meet us. He'll want to silence us to keep himself out of trouble. If he's not, which I'm sure he isn't, then he's the best person to help us."

Matthew stood still, giving her idea some thought. It wasn't great but it was the best idea they had and based on what they knew so far, he was the best person to start with.

"Okay, let's meet this William. But I'm going to be the one to make contact," he said, pulling his phone out of his pocket and preparing to dial.

"Why you?" Zoe asked, she raised her hand and held it out in front of her, waiting to accept the phone. "Surely, I should be the one to call, he'll be wanting to speak to me."

"Exactly," replied Matthew, keeping his phone tightly in his hand, "if I make the call, he will assume I'm with Berkant's team. If he's the man we're looking for, he'll either reveal himself intentionally or he'll say something to give himself away. If he's straight, then we can arrange a safe meeting place, keeping you out of sight until I'm sure he can be trusted." There was a silence between them while Zoe contemplated the plan set before her.

"I suppose you'll want his number?" she asked, accepting that his plan was the best that they had.

"It would help," he replied simply, his thumb hovering over the first digit.

*

William and Charles hadn't been on the scene long. They had walked under the police tape and headed inside quickly. William had followed the drops of blood that lead to the back.

"Forensics are still trying to get an ID on whose blood this is," he explained, gesturing to the many spots marking the dark floor in the main shop that they had followed from the outside. Inside the mechanic's repair room, the body had been taken away and in its place was a large dry puddle of blood and a chalk outline. Police marks scattered the floor, highlighting the key areas that had been photographed and studied by the forensic team the night before. Charles hung back as William walked in, leaning against the door frame, watching him look around slowly, taking in every detail of the room.

"What do you think?" William asked, making Charles jump a little, waking him up out of his tired stupor.

"What do you mean?" he asked, covering his mouth to hide his yawn. "You've read the report and I'll be submitting mine when we get back to base."

"Not the events, the reasons?" continued William, hands in his coat pockets as he slowly walked around the room; looking across and under the broken machines, looking for he didn't know what. "Why were these people here? Who sent them? Why was there another shooter?"

Charles shrugged. "Insurance perhaps? Make sure the person who died was definitely dead? The extra shooter could have come with the one who escaped as back up?" William didn't look at Charles as he listened, instead he looked up through the shattered window on the ceiling.

"Perhaps. But then who shot first? We know the bullets that killed O'Neill came from a handgun and the ones that hit the wall came from a sniper rifle."

"Could have been a bluff," suggested Charles stepping forward to stand next to William looking up at the window with him. "Send a man inside, threaten him with the gun, then take him out by surprise from above? Perhaps the shooter missed, either on purpose or by accident and it was up to the man inside to finish the job?"

William said nothing but kept looking up at the window. Charles could see the wheels in his head spinning nonstop as he processed the scene around him.

"Let's go on the roof," he said and without waiting for a response, he was already making his way back through the shop to the front door. Charles moved quickly, keeping behind him as they walked outside, following the side of the building towards the back where the ladder to the roof was attached. Charles had to make a decision fast. If William found the gun, then it would have to be taken in as evidence and checked. Charles couldn't risk that, he hadn't had time to wipe it down; his prints were all over it.

William was already halfway up the ladder as Charles put his foot on the first step, if he had to, he'd have to kill him right here and now or risk getting caught. Charles had put plenty of dangerous people in prison and tough as he was, he knew he wouldn't survive inside. He stepped onto the roof. William was already by the window looking down into the shop, his hands holding an invisible rifle as he acted out the shooting in his head.

Charles stepped closer. Reaching into his coat pockets, he wrapped his fingers around a flick knife, ready to pull it out if he needed to. William let his hands fall to his side and began to walk around the roof, kicking aside discarded Coke cans and dirty dry leaves. Charles watched, staying back against the ladder, relieved that he had at least had the good sense to pick up the ejected casings of the bullets he'd fired before he'd descended from the roof.

"What are you thinking, mate?" he asked gently, sliding his thumb over the handle of the knife in his pocket as he watched William walk a full circle around the roof and back towards him. William looked up at him and shrugged, a bored expression on his face. He turned away from Charles, looking around at the surrounding buildings and street.

"Not sure really, not many escape points off this roof unless they were one of those free running enthusiasts." He shook his head at his own idea. "Can't have been, not with the gun they were using, not exactly the kind of weapon you can do backflips with." Charles shrugged watching him. Keeping his eyes on William, he didn't dare look towards the old, rusted vent in the corner where he knew the gun was still hiding.

"Probably left before they knew what was going on downstairs and drove away," he suggested hoping that would be satisfactory to get them off this roof. He turned, putting his hands on the rails of the ladder. "Come on, I need some coffee." He raised his foot and began to pull himself up. He looked back over his shoulder, William had not moved. He was moving towards the vent.

Charles stopped on the ledge of the roof, watching him closely, his hand slipping back into his pocket around the knife. "Will, come on. There's nothing new here." He stepped slowly away from the ladder and back onto the roof, his body tensing as he watched William get closer to the rifle's hiding place.

"Just a second," William called back over his shoulder, his interest clearly on the rusted, unused vent. He moved towards it, unaware that Charles was getting closer behind him. "Did anyone check in here?" he asked, almost within touching distance of the brown dirty metal casing.

"Yeah, I'm sure," was all Charles could say. His hand tight around the knife, he took a quick look around him, checking to see if they were being watched. He couldn't see anyone. He slowly pulled the knife from his pocket, the blade clean and razor sharp. As William bent closer towards the vent, about to expose what was inside, Charles reached out, preparing to wrap a hand around his mouth and plunge the knife into his throat. His fingertips could brush the skin on William's cheek as he reached out when a loud ringing from William's pocket caused him to pull his hand back as quickly as possible, the knife roughly pushed into his pocket. William jumped as the phone's ringtone awoke him from his concentration. He pulled the chipped and scuffed Samsung smartphone from his pocket, looking at the withheld number appearing on the screen.

"Someone trying to sell me something." He pressed the red circular button on the screen ending the call, "Sorry about that," he said turning to Charles. "Hearing isn't what it used to be." He began to put the phone back into his pocket, looking at Charles. "You okay, mate?" he asked furrowing his brow. "Seen a ghost or something?" Charles kept his hand in his pocket, the phone ringing had caught him by surprise and for a brief moment he had been sure William was going to catch him in the act.

"Phone caught me off guard," he said, forcing a laugh, "you need to put that on silent mode." William laughed at his friend.

"You're getting jumpy in your old age; it's just a phone." His smile vanished instantly as the phone began to ring again making them both jump. "Jesus, hold on." He raised his hand to request a moment as he walked away from the vent and past Charles towards the ladder. He answered the call, preparing to give this sales-person a piece of his mind. "Whatever you're selling, I'm not interested and you need to stop calling me or so help me God, I will have you arrested for—"

"If you don't stop talking, I will slit Zoe Garland's throat," came the gravelly deep voice of Matthew, cutting him off mid-sentence. "Do I have your attention?"

William froze as the silence grew between him and the mystery caller on the phone. He kept his back to Charles, not wanting him to see his face. He hadn't heard from Zoe in days and now someone was threatening to kill her.

"Who is this?" he asked, stepping away further from Charles not wanting him to overhear this. "Where is Zoe? Let me speak to her."

"You'll speak to her when I say so," came the reply, simple and to the point. "We need to meet face to face."

William looked back. Charles had moved closer but not within ear shot. William gave him a weak smile and rolled his eyes, mouthing silently 'trying to upgrade me' and shook his head in a dismissive gesture. Charles returned the smile and nodded towards the ladder, making his way slowly towards it. William pointed to it and nodded to let Charles know he would be right behind him. Charles pulled himself up onto the ladder and began to climb down until he was out of sight. Unbeknownst to William, he waited on the ladder, listening, trying to pick up as much as he could. Believing he was alone, William returned to the phone call.

"How do I know Zoe is alive?"

"You don't, but I need answers and she believes you're the right man to ask."

"When and where?" William didn't have time for this, nor did he feel he had a choice: he needed to protect his people, even if that meant putting himself in danger.

"Go to Rossodisera on Neal Street near the Cambridge theatre. Do you know where I mean?" Matthew asked, his ears listening to every breath and the tone of the old officer's replies.

"Rossodisera? I know that place yes," William repeated, picturing the establishment in his head.

"You have one hour. You will come alone; take a seat outside; order a coffee and wait for me to make contact. If I feel that you are not alone or you are being watched, I will leave and you will never find Zoe's body."

The call ended with a definitive beep. William kept the phone to his ear, the last sentence running through his mind on repeat like a skipping vinyl. What kind of mess had Zoe gotten herself into? His thoughts were interrupted by Charles' voice as he pulled himself back to the top of the ladder.

"Are you done yet?" he asked, feigning ignorance to the conversation that he had just eavesdropped on. He had only heard William's side but he was certain that this was connected to the night before. Wherever William was going, he needed to be there. "Come on, I need a drink and so do you. What did they sign you up for, a two-year contract?" He climbed back down knowing that he had convinced William he heard nothing.

"No, no nothing like that." William shook his head and put the phone away, his mind clearly elsewhere as he headed over to the ladder to climb down.

Chapter Seven

William made his way up Neal Street, towards the Italian restaurant, as instructed. The street was full of people heading towards the nearby theatres for the matinee performances or going into the many shops and restaurants that covered the surrounding streets. He had told Charles to take the car and go back to HQ, telling him he needed a walk to go over the case. Charles had been happy to oblige and had driven off, giving a wave out of the open window as he did.

William reached the restaurant, took a seat outside and waited to be served. He sat looking across the street at the grey and dated flats opposite him. There was no one else outside, he felt exposed. A surly looking waitress took his order and brought him a questionable cup of coffee in a dirty white mug. He sipped it begrudgingly, looking around and trying to pick out the would-be killer amongst the growing crowd of shoppers and theatre goers.

"Keep drinking your coffee and check the messages on your phone."

William jumped in his seat nearly sending his coffee over the floor. He turned to his right and saw in the corner of his eye a man in a grey suit with sunglasses reading a newspaper at the table next to his. "Don't look at me, just check your phone," the stranger instructed again, turning the page of the paper to continue reading. William picked up his mug tighter than he meant to, cursing himself for not spotting this man sooner: he had snuck up on him like a ghost. Sipping the coffee, he pulled his phone out and pretended to go through his messages aimlessly, flicking his index finger up and down the screen.

"So, we spoke on the phone?" he asked keeping his head down trying to get another look at this man out the corner of his eye.

"That's right. Pleasure to meet you, sir."

William stole a glance across at this new man as he flicked through the paper with such conviction and ease, he thought he might have the wrong person.

"You're surprisingly polite for a kidnapper," William replied, ignoring the coffee on the table and letting it go cold. "Where's Zoe?" He felt it was time to start asking the questions now.

"All in good time, William."

"How do I know you're telling me the truth? For all I know, she's already dead?"

"Before he died, Simon O'Neill had discovered she was an undercover officer in your department, but he had told Berkant. So Berkant had him killed and tried to kill Zoe and me." Matthew explained, flicking the paper straight as he pretended to read.

"Not a great plan, was it? What does this have to do with me? I'm not with that scumbag Berkant. I'm trying to have him locked up."

"Berkant is packing up. He's ready to leave the country and go home."

This revelation sent a rush of electricity through William, shocking him awake. How could he have not known this?

"He's leaving? You're certain about that?" he asked, keeping his voice as calm as possible.

"Very sure. He tried to have me killed. I was a loose end that he couldn't afford to leave behind."

"If he's leaving London, why is it so important that you keep Zoe?" William asked. His phone had been showing the same message on its screen for the last couple of minutes, all pretence was gone now. "Surely you can release her and I can get her into police protection?"

"No," Matthew replied, snapping the paper hard with a flick of his wrists, "Berkant has someone on the inside. They've been leaking information and not just your department, as much as they can get. We suspect Berkant knows that we know he has an insider. Zoe intercepted a drop off point and stole information meant for him. It's from your department: files on her and your other undercover officers."

William sat there squeezing his phone so tightly he felt the flimsy plastic casing would snap any second.

"Berkant has someone inside. You're sure?"

"Very sure and I'd like to find out who tried to shoot me," replied Matthew keeping his face hidden behind the newspaper.

"Then it seems you and I have a common enemy," said William, locking his phone and putting it into his pocket. He folded his arms across his chest looking across the street.

"The enemy of my enemy?" Matthew asked closing the newspaper and placing it folded on the table in front of him.

"Something like that. What's the plan then?" William asked, his eyes following the passing cars as the well-dressed stranger stood up, leaving two five-pound notes on the table.

"Follow me."

William got to his feet, following Matthew's example by scattering a couple of pound coins across the table. He turned to follow but stopped in his tracks when his new accomplice pulled out a white walking cane and began to make his way down the street, tapping it left and right as he went. William watched with a growing sense of disbelief. '*This has to be a joke,* he thought to himself. He stayed by his table, looking around, certain he was being watched. The blind man stopped and turned his head over his shoulder.

"Coming then?" he asked.

William shook his head and questioned his own sanity as he walked down the street to catch up with this stranger. They began walking together. The blind man grabbed his right arm and held it tightly around the wrist. William tried to pull away.

"What the hell are you doing?" he asked keeping his voice low so as not to attract attention.

"You're guiding me down the busy street or how else do you explain why we're talking together?" Matthew asked, keeping a firm grip on William's wrist, his fingertips feeling the pulse in his veins. They walked down the street together. To other pedestrians, William appeared to be guiding Matthew through the crowded street, but it was Matthew who was taking the lead as they walked together.

"I'd like to ask you a few questions please?" asked Matthew as they moved up the street towards the theatre.

"I have some for you as well but I'm guessing you're not about to let me?" William replied looking towards Matthew.

"You can ask one to start if you'd like?" replied Matthew, using his cane to create an open path ahead of them as they walked.

"Who are you and how do you know Zoe?" William blurted out, studying Matthew's face, trying to see behind the black sunglasses. He was finding it hard to believe that this man really was blind.

"That was two," replied Matthew. They had reached a point in the road where it split into seven different streets. In the middle was a War Memorial with seats around it. Matthew led them over to it and sat down, never removing his hand from William's wrist. "My name is Matthew Bartimaeus but please just call me Matthew. I used to work for Berkant. Coming across Zoe was just a result of circumstance. Now, my questions." Matthew tightened his grip on William's wrist. If he needed to, he could break it with one twist of his hand. "Did you leak information to Berkant and his associates?"

"Absolutely not," replied William, feeling his blood boil at such an accusation.

Matthew's fingers pressed tightly against William's veins as he spoke, he could feel his blood pumping through his body; the rhythm did not change. Satisfied, he released William from his vice like grip.

"Okay, I believe you."

"Just like that?" William asked, surprised, but grateful to be released. He rubbed his wrist where Matthew's fingers had been pressing tightly, leaving small marks on his flesh. "Jesus, are you some sort of human lie detector?" he asked sceptically.

"Pretty much yes. But you can call me Matthew."

"I might like to check your profile against my database."

"You won't find anything on me," replied Matthew, his head slowly moving side to side turning as he listened to the passing people; his senses on alert for a surprise attack.

"And why is that?" asked William, his interest in this strange man was growing with each passing second.

"Berkant had all traces of my existence erased from every government database when I was eighteen. As far as the government and your databases are concerned, I don't exist."

"Why did he do that?"

"You're better at killing people if you don't exist," Matthew replied simply, tilting his head towards a passing group of men. They walked past noisily but were of no threat to him.

William leant forwards, holding his hands tightly together, trying to process all this information. This, along with everything that had happened to him over the last couple of days, was making him think he should apply for an early retirement. He sat up slowly and followed Matthew's gaze straight ahead. Keeping his voice low, he leaned closer to him.

"I should have you arrested right here and now. Threatening an officer, a confession of murder and you're clearly in with Berkant."

"I *was*," growled Matthew, his grip around his cane tightening at the sound of Berkant's name. "He tried to have me killed. As far as I'm concerned, he's as good as dead."

William turned away and looked around at the crowds of people walking past, giving them no attention. He worried about the potential danger this man could bring to the area and all these innocent people.

"Just like that?" he asked, his tone becoming softer and more fatherly as he turned back to Matthew. "Sounds like you've known Berkant for a long time. You're willing to go after him after one murder attempt? Why not try to go with him?"

"I've killed for much less. If he wanted me to go with him, he'd have asked. It's clear I was nothing more than a tool for him. A weapon he could use to carry out his dirty work."

"You didn't think of this before?" William asked. A sense of pity was growing inside him for this man and he wanted to learn more. Clearly, there was a past to him that involved Berkant and his cruelty.

"Perhaps I chose not to think about that?" Matthew replied, more to himself than to William. "Berkant and his people were the closest thing I had to a family growing up. I guess I was kidding myself."

"Our emotions can blind us to the truth," said William without thinking. He covered his mouth with his hand as if to pull back the words. "Sorry," he said feeling more embarrassed than he should.

"Emotions get you killed. God blinds you," replied Matthew looking away from William towards the street they had walked up earlier.

"Not a praying man then?" asked William, turning away as he looked around them, thinking about how exposed they were sitting in the centre of the seven streets. His hand absentmindedly drifting over the breast pocket of his suit jacket, feeling the small red Gideon's New Testament he kept with him at all times.

"No," said Matthew definitely. Faith was not something that agreed with him at all.

"Perhaps God is what you need in your life?" suggested William.

"God doesn't want me," replied Matthew, reaching into his pocket and extracting a new Samsung smartphone. "If he did, I wouldn't be very good at my job, would I?"

William said nothing, he knew this topic of conversation was over. He shook his head bringing back his focus to the matter at hand. He had let himself get distracted and all the time they had spent talking, Zoe was somewhere and for all he knew, in danger.

"I suppose we should meet with Ms Garland and decide our next steps with her?" asked Matthew, sliding his thumb over the dial pad and typing in the number of the new phone he had bought her earlier.

"I suppose we should," said William, watching him carefully as Matthew put the phone to his ear. William could hear the phone ring as he waited for the call to be answered. The ringing stopped and Matthew spoke first.

"Zoe, head to the rendezvous point. William has—"

"Zoe can't come to the phone right now, can I take a message?" came a male voice Matthew did not recognise. He sat up straight, his knuckles white as he gripped his cane even tighter.

"Who is this?" he demanded. William could tell something was wrong. He jumped to his feet, looking around at the surrounding buildings. He was certain they were being watched, possibly by a gunman.

"Meet me at the mechanic's where you killed O'Neill at midnight. Bring your new police friend with you. Just the two of you, no one else. I'll keep Zoe safe until then."

The line went dead. Matthew tucked the phone back into his pocket. He tried to remain calm. Holding his cane with both hands in front of his chest, he listened carefully to everyone around him, making sure there wasn't an assailant about to attack. He turned his head towards William, hearing his fast nervous breathing.

"We have a problem; we need to go now."

*

Charles ended the call and put the burner phone Matthew had given Zoe into his pocket. He smiled down at Zoe, whom he had handcuffed to the radiator of the hotel room he had found her in, his tie forced roughly into her mouth to stop her from calling for help.

"Well, now that your friend knows I have you, we better get going," he said, taking a quick look out of the window onto the street below. He turned away from it and moved over to the bed where his coat lay. Pulling it on he looked back at Zoe as she sat on the floor shooting daggers at him from her eyes.

Charles had never left William after their trip to the mechanics that afternoon. As he drove off, he had kept his eyes on the rear-view mirror, watching William turn and walk away. Charles had immediately pulled over, parking the car on the street and rushing to catch him up. He had kept his distance the whole time, hanging back behind other pedestrians, ducking behind cars and vans but always keeping William in his line of sight. Charles recognised the street that William was going to meet this mysterious contact so had made sure to avoid it. Instead, he looped around until he was at the other end of the long road where he could watch William without being seen. He didn't have to wait long. He saw the blind man in the suit and with the cane, he had folded it up and slipped it into his jacket pocket before sitting down and pulling out a newspaper to hide behind. From his hiding spot, Charles had watched William take out his phone. Charles had watched William's lips moving and made the correct assumption he was speaking to this newcomer. Charles took the gamble, it was likely that his new man had a base nearby where Zoe, or at least the police files were being hidden. He had made his way down the street staying on the far side of the road away from them. William's focus had been on pretending to look at his phone and he had not noticed Charles slip by him.

Charles had seen the street the new man had come from and assumed that it would lead to the hiding place. Around him were shops and flats, he glanced up at the windows, looking for any sign of Zoe or an obvious hiding place. Either it was blind luck or her ineptitude, but he had managed to spot her at the window of a small, ancient hotel on his side of the road, looking the other way. He ducked into a doorway out of sight in case she turned to look back down the street from whence he came. He waited and slipped his hand into his coat pocket, feeling the knife there. Charles pulled off his tie and put it into the other pocket. He had a rough idea of which floor she was on and where her room was.

Keeping his head down, he stepped quickly back onto the street and headed straight into the hotel. He made his way past the unmanned reception desk and straight up the stairs. The worn carpets felt hard and thin under his feet and the peeling wallpaper was dusty and water damaged. He reached the second floor where he was sure Zoe's room was. There were a handful of doors on this floor with some missing numbers. He crept silently down the corridor, counting the rooms as he went. He knocked on one door twice and waited, keeping out of sight of the viewing hole and listening for any movement. He moved on to the next door and tried again, keeping to the wall out of sight.

He heard footsteps approach, he grabbed the tie in his pocket, crumpling it into a ball. He heard a lock turn as the door opened a fraction; he rushed forward throwing his weight against the door; ripping the lock chain off the wall; letting the door fly open and crash against the wall. Zoe had fallen back with a scream, and he quickly grabbed her as she moved backwards and forced the tie into her open mouth. Before she could pull it out, he punched her hard in the stomach and slapped her face with the back of his hand. She fell to the floor against the wall clutching her stomach. Moving faster than he looked capable of, Charles pulled out his handcuffs and slipped them around the pipe connected to an old broken metal radiator. He grabbed her arms and attached the metal cuffs to each wrist, keeping her from escaping. He was on his feet again in a moment, closing the door behind him and locking it with the key. He took a moment to catch his breath and then turned back to her on the floor.

"Good afternoon, Ruby, or should I call you Zoe now?"

Chapter Eight

Matthew started to run before William had even registered what he had said to him. Matthew knew roughly where he was going, but in his panic for Zoe and their evidence, his sense of sound and smell were not working to their full potential. As he charged blindly down the street with William struggling to keep up, he pushed people over, sending them tumbling to the ground like bowling pins. Shouts from angry pedestrians mixed with blaring car horns as he charged across the busy roads. If he could get to her before they left, he could move her to a safer location. *How did they find her?* he asked himself as he ran. He was starting to lose his sense of direction when a horn exploded in his ears and he felt the hard steel of a car bonnet slam into his legs, sending him flying up onto the car and over the bonnet, before crashing against the windshield, cracking the glass with his head and then sliding back down the car and landing on the road in a heap.

He lay there for a moment before trying to get back to his feet, but the pain in his side was greater than he expected. He ran his hand over his hip and thigh, feeling for any broken bones, so far he couldn't find one. He could hear the car engine still running, mixed with the sounds of worried voices as people crowded round him, checking if he was okay.

"Get back, get back, give him some air, I'm Police." William's voice carried over the crowd who parted to let him through. The old man knelt down next to Matthew, placing his hand gently against his chest. "You all right son?" he asked, as his hands moved over him checking for damage as well. Matthew managed to get himself into a sitting position, wincing with pain as he moved.

"We need to go; she's in danger," he groaned, trying to get himself to his feet. He felt William's strong hands force him back to the floor.

"They'll be gone by now boy. Lie down. You're no good to her or to me in this state."

Matthew sank down and a new sense of defeat grew in him. He could hear sirens growing louder as an ambulance approached.

"We can't afford to go to a hospital," he said quietly to William, his strength and pride leaving him as he sat there in the middle of the road.

"Don't worry, lad, you won't. Just follow my lead." William assured him as an ambulance charged down the street, the sirens drowning out all other sounds around them. Matthew sat there feeling the pain in his leg spread through the left side of his body, distracting him from other thoughts, such as how did an ambulance reach him so quickly? The sirens stopped and Matthew heard the sound of doors opening as the paramedics leapt out and rushed over to him.

The first paramedic began to examine Matthew, removing his glasses. He held his head and checked the bump that was slowly growing from where he had cracked the windshield of the car. Matthew answered the paramedic's questions regarding what happened, but his attention was on William who he could hear was talking to the other ambulance attendant.

"He was being mugged. I was passing just as they tried to take his phone, they ran and this one thought he could catch them himself. I don't think I need to point out the issue there?"

Matthew said nothing and clenched his fists tightly, passing it off as dealing with the pain in his body. He was not enjoying William's version of events. A snapping of fingers brought his focus back to the paramedic in front of him.

"Sir, sir? Listen to me. Does it hurt here?" The paramedic squeezed Matthew's arms with his hands, sliding down and checking for breaks as he did. Matthew shook his head saying nothing. He could hear William's voice growing fainter; he had obviously taken the other paramedic to one side to talk. Matthew felt his paramedic touch the bump on his head, making him wince slightly.

"Ow," he said sternly turning his head away from the paramedic.

"Sorry," he replied.

"You got here quickly," Matthew commented, letting the paramedic do his job.

"Luckily, we were in the area when we got the call." His hands moved down to Matthew's legs feeling down his thighs, then to his ankles. "Can you feel your legs, sir?" Matthew felt his toes being squeezed.

"I'm fine, thanks," he said, trying to get up. The paramedic pushed him down gently.

"Sir please, you shouldn't move. You've been in a serious accident. We need to get you on the gurney."

"I'm fine really." Matthew tried to move again but the paramedic's surprisingly strong hands kept him down.

"I must insist, sir," he said.

"It's fine, young man," came William's slightly patronising voice as he returned with the other paramedic. "I need to take this one with me for questioning. I can get him checked over back at base, as long as he can walk, he'll be fine." He reached down and grabbed Matthew's hand and pulled him to his feet slowly, making him groan as his joints and muscles screamed for him to stop.

"We should really take him with us. He's just been hit by a car so there could be all sorts of internal damage," countered Matthew's paramedic, still crouching on the floor and looking up at the three of them.

"He'll be fine," said William, pulling Matthew away. Placing his hand on his arm he coaxed, "Come on, son. If you need a statement this is my number." He reached into his pocket and handed the paramedics his card. Matthew moved slowly, limping as he went, clutching William's arm tightly as they walked. The crowd parted to let them pass as William led him down the road leading towards the Cambridge Theatre.

"Where are we going?" Matthew asked quietly, grinding his teeth as he grimaced with each step. "We need to get Zoe."

"Firstly, we need to get somewhere safe and then you can tell me what was on that phone call, lad. Let's find a hotel to get you put back together."

"No. Clearly, they aren't safe. I've got a place we can go to, we need a taxi," groaned Matthew, reaching into his pocket and pulling out his cane for the sake of appearances as they walked together.

"All right, I'll get us a cab," said William. Looking around for signs of a Black Cab, he saw the ambulance team packing up behind them. He made eye contact with one of them and gave a small nod and smile to signify everything was okay.

The paramedics slammed the rear doors closed and then leapt into the front and pulled away, turning the lights off as the mingling crowd moved aside to let them pass. The passenger pulled a phone out of the glove box and pressed the redial button on the keypad. He placed the call on loudspeaker as the phone rang, looking across at his partner as they made their way out of London. After several rings, the call was answered by the recognisable tones of Arif.

"Give me an update," he demanded.

"We were first on the scene. Luckily, he'd been hit by a car, so we had a cast iron excuse to get to him. He'd been hit pretty badly, but we couldn't take him."

"Why not?" Arif's anger was almost as instant as his father's.

"There was someone with him. A police officer, detective actually," the passenger continued, holding the phone tightly in front of him.

"What detective?" Arif was doing his best to keep his voice calm.

"Let's see." The passenger snapped his fingers for the card, the driver held out William's card for him without saying a word. "William Blaine."

"He's not one of ours. What happened to them?" asked Arif, he was already grabbing his jacket and gun ready to move out.

"They walked away. We couldn't grab them because there were too many people."

"So you've lost them?" Arif's words screamed out of the handset at them.

"I put a tracker on the blind one. Slipped it under his trouser leg during the examination," the passenger replied, keeping his own voice calm. "We should be able to get an idea of their location before he finds it."

"He shouldn't find it at all," said Arif. "Find them and let me know where you are. Observe them only. Don't do anything until I get there, you understand?"

"We'll be in touch." The passenger ended the call and immediately opened an app that brought up a map of London, a small dot flickering on the screen indicating where Matthew and William were. "Left here." He instructed the driver, keeping his eyes on the phone as they drove together in silence.

William had managed to call a taxi down; he helped Matthew into the back, letting him give the driver the street name of where they were heading to. They said nothing as the car made its way through the streets. Matthew clutched his hip where he had taken most of the impact, the pain increasing more and more.

"I should check in and update my team, we'll need back up," said William, pulling his own phone out of his pocket. Matthew made to grab it, but in his pain and discomfort he missed, his fingertips brushing against the smooth plastic.

"No phones, get rid of—"

"Don't be stupid, boy," William said, pushing his hand away. "You don't think I've already got a ghost sim in this thing; you can't track this phone."

"Don't call anyone," ordered Matthew, grabbing his hip again. "We don't know how many people in your team are working for Berkant."

William considered it for a moment, then reluctantly slipped the phone back into his pocket; turning it off, as he did.

"You're right." He sat back watching the streets go by. "So who was on the phone?" he asked looking out of the window.

"Not here," said Matthew leaning back resting his head on the seat. "Where are my glasses?" he asked, realising his face was exposed, his hand reaching up to touch his face.

"Oh sorry, here you go," said William, placing the expensive sunglasses in his hand.

Matthew slipped them back over his eyes, feeling more like himself as he did. He sank back into his seat, trying to relax himself and deal with the pain in his body: unaware of the small, button sized device, tracking their movements through the city.

*

Arif tucked his gun into the back of his trousers, keeping it out of sight. After his night of searching, he had returned home to rest for a couple of hours and changed into his combat boots, jeans and a black t-shirt. Throwing his leather jacket around his body to hide his weapon, he left his private quarters and walked quickly down the corridor. His heavy footsteps were absorbed by the thick expensive Turkish rug that ran the length of the hallway. He reached the dark wooden door that led to his father's office, knocking twice with his strong scarred hand. The door was flung open, and Arif was met with the angry face of Berkant.

"It's about bloody time." He turned away from his son and stomped into his office, running his hand through his hair and pulling several out as he did. "I sent you out hours ago. Where have you been?" he demanded of his son, grabbing a cigarette out of his ashtray and taking a long drag, ash falling to the floor. "I see you've changed. Been putting your feet up, have you?"

"We have, Matthew," answered Arif, ignoring his father's angry outburst. Berkant looked at him, he took the cigarette out of his mouth but said nothing. "I've had several teams driving around London. One of those teams has been driving around the city disguised as paramedics in an Ambulance looking out for him. Luckily for us, Matthew got himself into a car accident and they intercepted the call," Arif explained looking straight into Berkant's eyes.

"So they're bringing him here now?" Berkant asked, a sense of relief coursing through him. Arif hesitated before answering, being only too familiar with his father's rath.

"No, sir." Berkant crushed the cigarette in the palm of his hand still saying nothing, his hand shaking with a mixture of pain and rage. "He had a detective with him; they couldn't snatch Matt with him and so many people there. They've put a tracker on him and are following him as we speak."

This news seemed to satisfy Berkant slightly. He looked at his son and slowly brushed his hands together letting ash and the remains of his cigarette fall to the floor.

"It's a start, boy," he said. Turning to his son, he stepped closer and placed his hands firmly on Arif's shoulders. "Don't let me down though, we need this cleaned up."

"I'll take care of it, sir," answered Arif, straightening up like a soldier.

"I know you will," said Berkant, giving his son a stern look, "because if you don't, I'll have to get involved and I don't want to get involved."

Arif nodded and left the room quickly, a new sense of determination rushed through him like adrenalin. As he walked, he pulled out his phone to send a text to his team downstairs, telling them to be ready for him by the time he arrived. Arif reached the lift at the end of the luxurious corridor that would take him to the underground car park below. As he waited for the doors to open, he checked his pockets: feeling the spare ammo cartridges, a knife and a set of brass knuckle-dusters.

"I'm coming, Matt," he said to himself, stepping into the lift before the doors had finished opening.

*

The taxi had dropped Matthew and William around the corner from an alley entrance at Matthew's request. They stood on the pavement waiting for the taxi to disappear out of sight before they moved.

"He's gone," William informed Matthew, watching the black London cab turn a corner, seeking its next fare. Matthew said nothing and turned away from William, leading him towards the alley that led to their destination. He moved as fast as he could with his limp, still clutching his hip as he walked. He had put his cane back into his pocket as he had climbed out of the taxi. William said nothing as he followed Matthew. He was constantly looking around them, up at the surrounding buildings and back up to the entrance of the alley, looking for signs that they were being followed or about to be ambushed. He stopped and kept his distance as Matthew reached a damaged and graffitied covered door. He stood in front of it and began to slide his hand over it. William assumed he knew what he was doing and turned his back on him, checking around again feeling certain that they were being watched. His head turned at the sound of a lock clicking and saw Matthew stepping inside into a dark room, through the door he was touching a moment ago.

"Hurry up," he said to William, aware that he was hanging back because he had not felt his presence follow him inside. William quickly slipped inside, sliding past Matthew, his arm brushing his chest as he moved into the small room that only had a flight of stairs leading upwards.

Matthew closed the door. The sound of several locks turning echoed around them. He ignored them and began climbing the stairs slowly, gripping the handrail tightly as he did. "What is this place?" William asked, keeping close to Matthew in case he fell. "Your home?"

"My home doesn't exist anymore. Berkant knew where I lived," Matthew replied through gritted teeth. William nodded to himself, understanding, as they climbed towards a single door.

"Safe house?" he enquired as they reached the door.

"We'll see," said Matthew. He pulled his gun out of its holster under his jacket and held it in front of him as he slowly pushed open the door. He let the door swing open slowly, tilting his head slightly he put his finger to his lips, signalling to William for silence, as he stepped into the room with swift silent footsteps. Standing in the middle of the living room, Matthew held his gun with both hands close to his body, turning slowly around, his ears on alert as he listened for any sign of life other than himself and William. Stepping towards the bedroom, he sniffed the air, the scent of Zoe still lingering from the morning.

"We're alone," he said, slipping his gun back into the holster under his jacket. William stepped into the room looking around, the place was Spartan and recently cleaned. Matthew stepped across the room and opened the window, letting the air flow inside to cool his injured face.

"Was Zoe here?" William asked, surprising himself with how paternal his voice sounded.

"Yes," Matthew said, falling into the armchair. He groaned as he slipped off his jacket and ran his hands down the side of his body, flinching slightly where he could feel the large bruises that had begun to grow and spread. "Nothing happened," he continued, feeling William's wizened eyes boring into him.

"I wasn't implying anything."

"Good because there's nothing to say."

William slipped off his own jacket and tossed it onto the sofa, looking around the small space.

"How long have you had this place?" he asked with hands on hips as he turned back to Matthew, watching him test his injuries.

"Long enough," he replied. One hand still feeling his bruises, the other pulling his gun out of the holster wrapped around him and placing it on the armrest of his chair. He groaned against the strain it caused his body.

"Not much of a talker, are you?" asked William. He moved over to one of the windows in the living room and opened it, looking down onto the alley below him looking for signs of life.

"There's some food in the kitchen, if you're hungry?" Matthew rose slowly to his feet and started to make his way over to the kitchen. "I'm going to have a coffee." He was about to pass over the threshold of the kitchen when a strong arm caught him in the chest, taking him by surprise. Instinctively, he pushed it away roughly, his defences on alert. "What the hell are you doing?" he demanded of William.

"You're going to sit down right now and fill me in on everything that's been going on. Starting with how a blind man ended up becoming Berkant's go to killer."

Matthew sighed and turned away from William, his shoulders sinking a little, realising he wasn't going to let this drop till he had answered. He felt he'd better get it over with.

"Sit down," he said, patting the sofa as he walked past it, heading to the armchair he had occupied a moment ago. William moved away from the kitchen and sat down, resting his elbows on his knees as he leant forward ready to listen to what Matthew had to say.

"I was raised in an orphanage in the city. I was found abandoned on the doorstep. I was only a few days old. I was born blind and so the religious woman who ran the orphanage felt it would be clever to give me the surname Bartimaeus."

"The blind beggar Jesus cured?" William asked, thinking back to the passage.

"If you say so," Matthew continued. "Perhaps they thought it would be a positive influence on me; quite frankly I have no time for God." Matthew paused, choosing his words carefully; he had rarely, if at all, spoken about his past. "Long story short, no one wants to adopt a disabled child and no one wants to be his friend. I spent most of my childhood alone, training myself to use my other senses to help me get by, in the hope that someone might want to take me home. I was fourteen when I started to realise that I was never going to have a family. I made a choice, I didn't need anyone so I hid myself away and spent most of my days away from the home getting to know London... that's how I met Berkant."

"He saw me walking alone and realised that no one was paying attention to me. He approached me, at the time I didn't know any better but he was the closest thing I had to a caring adult and part of me still yearned for the father figure. It started small. He asked me to deliver packages for him, by then I knew the streets pretty well. If I was unsure, he found me a map in braille and taught me the way. He never officially adopted me but when I turned eighteen, he took me in."

He paused and sat back in the armchair, running a hand over his hair. He then slammed it down against the dusty fabric, making William jump. Talking about his past was bringing up some dark memories that he had thought he had pushed aside years ago.

"When Berkant took me in, I met his son Arif. I think Berkant wanted us to become like brothers but Arif never took to me. Berkant had us both trained to fight; sent us to boxing, karate, judo, whatever he could think of to make us better and stronger. I always felt I had to prove myself due to the blindness and I thought that I owed Berkant for all his generosity. I pushed myself harder and harder at every form of fighting he put us through and every bit of weapons training he made us do. As we got older, he made us fight each other for the entertainment of his gang or guests from abroad. They were close, we came very close to killing each other regularly: most fights we had to be pulled apart. Berkant loved it. He'd made us into two lethal killing machines."

"So you and his son didn't get along at all?" William asked, taking in every word. Matthew shrugged, growing up he and Arif had become bitter rivals, each trying to claim Berkant's parentage; Arif as his natural son and Matthew as his unofficially adopted child. Matthew thought back to the thousands of fights he and Arif had had. Each feeling that victory would earn the respect and admiration of Berkant. He shook his head, realising that William was watching him, waiting for some sort of response.

"I completed my first kill not long after I was eighteen. Berkant had me kill a drug dealer who had stopped paying him his cut. It was a quick amateurish job, but I got it done. I strangled him with an extension cable and then hung him from the ceiling to make it appear like suicide."

"How original," scoffed William thinking back to how many 'suicide' cases he had come across in his time moving up the ranks. Matthew ignored him.

"Over the years, I have improved. I became Berkant's number one contract killer. Not only for him, but for his associates, being regularly hired out to do jobs for them as well."

"So how did you get involved with Zoe and me?" William asked slowly, sitting back against the sofa.

"I had completed my job and had collected my pay when I was given another for the next night."

"And that was unusual?"

"For a contract the next day? Yes," said Matthew, unable to hide the impatience in his voice. "Most jobs I get a minimum of seven days to prepare, I should have known something was wrong straight away."

"Why do you think you didn't spot it?" William asked, more and more questions growing inside him.

"I guess I didn't want to believe anything was wrong, why would I?"

"So this new job led you to Zoe?" asked William.

"Yes, I was told there were two targets; it should have been easy. When I got there, Zoe was tied up. O'Neill had discovered who she was and tried to convince me not to kill him. I thought it was a bluff and killed him first. I went to speak to Zoe and she saved my life. She spotted the laser sight of the sniper rifle. Berkant had sent someone to make sure we were all dead."

"So you two came here and she told you everything? Where is all the data she stole and collected?"

"It's with her, and now with her kidnapper," said Matthew hitting the armrest of his chair again. "I should have left it here, but I didn't think she would get caught so easily. It felt safer to keep it with us."

91

"We all make mistakes, son," said William watching the frustration grow in Matthew.

"I don't."

"Nothing we can do about it now though. So what happened on the phone? What did they say?"

"We are to meet them on the roof of the mechanics where all this started. At midnight tonight," answered Matthew, getting to his feet slowly, the left side of his body ached and was going stiff.

"Always midnight." William sighed, slouching on the sofa, his interlocked hands resting on his stomach. "We might as well get some rest then before tonight."

"We need a strategy," said Matthew, limping slightly as he moved towards the kitchen. "We can't just turn up and expect everything to go smoothly, we need a plan of action and then a backup plan should the first one fail." He made it to the kitchen, flicking the kettle as he passed it to get himself a cup. William groaned, realising he might not get a chance to rest. He pulled himself slowly out of the sofa and followed Matthew into the kitchen.

"Mind making me one as well while you're there?" he asked, standing in the doorway and watching Matthew move around the kitchen with ease, his hands knowing exactly where to reach out to.

"How do you take it?" Matthew asked pulling out a second cup.

"Black and some sugar please."

"I knew there was something I liked about you. Zoe takes it in a similar way," said Matthew, granting William a small smile as he placed the coffee and sugar into each cup. Keeping his back to William, he poured the hot water into each cup, keeping his thumb inside each one to tell him when to stop. He slid one over the counter towards William and picked up his own, sipping the hot liquid slowly, letting its strong flavour soothe and calm him. William stepped into the small kitchen and stood next to Matthew, picking up his own cup and blowing on it gently before sipping as well.

"Thank you," he said, looking out of the small dirty window in front of them that opened onto a brick wall opposite them, "not much of a view here."

"I wouldn't know," said Matthew looking straight ahead, slowly enjoying his drink.

"Sorry, I shouldn't have said that. It's just, well, it's easy to forget with you."

"Thanks," said Matthew, shrugging. They stood in silence for a moment, each sipping his coffee, thoughts elsewhere. "Are you and Zoe close?"

"Only through work," said William, making his stance clear. "She's an exceptional officer and when she joined my department, she threw herself into her work. I liked her work ethic and took her under my wing. I wanted her to do well."

"Was she ready when she started working with O'Neill? The daughter of the two police officers? Probably grew up rather protected from the *dangerous world* I imagine?" asked Matthew, his voice full of scepticism. William turned his head to look at him.

"What are you talking about?" William asked, surprised and almost dropping his cup. "She was raised by her elderly grandfather after her parents ran off together to live a carefree life in Asia. She has more arrests on her record than most of Berkant's people. She straightened herself out and joined the Service. And yes, of course she was ready. I wouldn't have sent her if she wasn't. She went deeper than she was meant to, that's all. Once she started getting what we needed, she tried to get more and got herself caught. It would have happened to anyone who's as brave as her."

There was silence between them again. Matthew considered what William had said. He agreed Zoe had been very brave. He still was considering her predicament. He took a sip of his coffee and tried to organise his thoughts and emotions. He had never had anyone in his life he would call a friend. Yet his feelings towards Zoe were becoming that of friendship. He shook his head, annoyed with himself. *You're not a robot,* he told himself. Matthew gulped down the rest of his coffee and placed the cup on the counter harder than he meant to. *Emotions get you killed,* he reminded himself; he didn't need friends. This was about his life and Berkant's betrayal. Once that arsehole was dead and the files and Zoe were returned to the police, he would be gone.

William had been watching him and placed his own cup down gently, stepping back slightly in case Matthew lashed out at him.

"Everything okay there?" he asked.

"Fine," replied Matthew. He gripped the edge of the countertop with both hands, holding it tightly. "We need to start thinking about what we're going to do tonight."

"I think you're right, let's go sit down and talk this—"

William's words were cut short. Matthew had grabbed him by the collar of his shirt and dragged him to the ground as hard and fast as he could. As they hit the laminate floor, bullets came crashing through the walls, issued from silenced machine guns. The wall and cabinets shattered and splintered, sending debris everywhere. Matthew lay across William, waiting for his moment.

*

When William and Matthew had walked down the alley towards the entrance to the safe house, neither had noticed the ambulance drive past and pull up on the pavement around the corner. The two paramedics who had attended to Matthew earlier watched him and William make their way inside. Sat behind the wheel, Jason Church pulled out a pair of binoculars and scanned the building, looking for a sign of life to give him an idea of where they were inside.

"Give Arif the address," he told his partner, still looking towards the old grey building. The man next to him said nothing as he grabbed his phone and typed in the address, before slipping the phone onto the dashboard as he pressed the send button.

"Can you see them?" he asked, looking through the windshield and leaning forward.

"Nothing yet. Get the guns ready, Malcolm," ordered Jason pulling the binoculars from his face and nodding towards the back.

"We have orders to wait," Malcolm replied, not moving from his seat.

"Fuck our orders. We can handle those two and probably get a hefty reward from Berkant for finishing the job first."

Malcolm considered his options and climbed into the back of the ambulance. Where medical equipment would usually be stored, weapons sat instead. Inside the cabinets and drawers were a range of handguns and machine guns, spare ammunition and a selection of combat knives. Malcolm Rook pulled out two MP5SD submachine guns and inspected them carefully. Integrated suppressors made these guns perfect for a job such as this. He carefully placed the ammunition cartridges into the weapons, each one loaded with subsonic bullets that made the gunfire extremely quiet when in combat.

Jason and Malcolm had met in the British army and had completed several tours of Iraq and Afghanistan during their time together. Like so many former soldiers, after their service, work had been hard to come by or to keep and both men had fallen into financial difficulty. Arif had approached them in a small pub in the East End of London as they both nursed pints of lager, contemplating their futures. With an offer of regular large amounts of money and work that fulfilled their desires for action and danger, how could they refuse? For the last three years, they had been part of Berkant's group, working under Arif. The ambulance had been a recent addition to their repertoire, and it had proven to be very useful in their line of work; people died in the back of ambulances every day.

Weapons loaded and ready, Malcolm climbed back into the front, holding the guns in his hands, placing them out of sight between the two men in the footwell.

"Anything?" he asked.

"Yes," replied Jason, putting the binoculars in the driver's side door. "Third floor up, they've opened a window for us. Drainpipe looks strong enough. In and out nice and quick?"

Malcolm nodded, picking up the weapons and handing one to Jason. The two men climbed out of the large vehicle; Jason leaving the keys in the ignition as they would need to get away quickly. They walked together in silence, the guns tucked neatly under the fluorescent jackets of their paramedic disguises. Jason reached the drainpipe first. Gripping it tightly with both hands, he placed his first foot firmly on the wall and began to climb slowly and silently. Malcolm took one last look around the alleyway and then began to follow up the black metal pipe.

Jason eventually reached the open window, lifting his head up slowly, looking inside as he gripped the windowsill. All he could see inside was the small empty living room. To his right, he could hear voices talking in the small kitchen. Smiling to himself, he climbed silently into the building, crouching slightly as he stepped away from the window to give Malcolm room to get in. Once inside the room, the two men slipped off the heavy jackets that concealed their weapons, placing them carefully on the floor to minimise sound. A nod was exchanged as they lifted their weapons, holding them tightly against their shoulders both flicking the safety switch off together with a clear unisoned *click.* This was what alerted Matthew to their presence.

*

Inside the kitchen, Matthew lay next to William, his arm still gripping the old man tightly as he held him to the floor. Plates shattered, cups and glasses disintegrated and his cupboards and cabinets were quickly turning into kindling. William put his hands over his head in a vain attempt to protect himself from the debris. Adrenaline rushed through Matthew, blocking out the pain that he had been feeling in his body. He became intensely focused as chaos ruled everything else. He listened as best he could, there was almost no sound coming from the firearms in the other room; military grade hardware, he told himself. The bullets kept coming but they would run out soon enough, giving him only a few seconds to make his move before they reloaded. The moment came. As the gunfire halted, the only sound now was the tinkling of broken crockery dropping to the floor. Matthew was on his feet instantly; without hesitating, he rushed out of the kitchen and into his living room.

"There!" shouted Jason, throwing himself over the sofa out of the way of the charging man.

Malcolm wasn't fast enough to act; he was ejecting the empty ammunition cartridge when Matthew ran out of the kitchen. Moving quickly, he made out the sounds of metal sliding against metal as Malcolm released the cartridge. The noise helped Matthew plot where his attacker was. Using his whole body weight, Matthew threw himself into the strong body, raising his knee as he did, striking Malcolm in the chest and breaking his rib cage. As the man cried out in pain, dropping his gun, Matthew grabbed him with one hand and with the other punched him hard in the face, breaking his jaw and sending teeth and blood flying out of his mouth.

Between the muffled cries of agony, Matthew could hear another gun being prepared to fire. Grabbing his opponent with both hands, he pulled him in front of him as bullets shot across the room, pummelling Malcolm over and over while Matthew used him as a human shield. As the dead body became limp in his hands, he pushed him forwards over the sofa and dived behind it, planning his next move.

Before he could move, there was a shout of pain and the sound of a body hitting the deck. William had joined the fray. Stepping out from the kitchen, he had thrown a metal pan across the room, catching Jason in the face. While Jason clutched his face in pain, Matthew leapt up and over the sofa, moving to the sounds of William's heavy feet as he staggered forward. As he rose over the sofa, he kicked out at William, knocking him to the floor. Matthew hit the deck and rolled to his feet. He found William with his hands and pushed him away, back towards the kitchen. He bent down and rolled forwards, quickly finding the other attacker. He pulled him towards him and in one quick movement snapped his left arm cleanly. As Jason cried out in pain, Matthew grabbed his head in both hands and roughly slammed his forehead against the nose of his unknown attacker, breaking it instantly. Matthew felt warm blood hit his face and his struggling opponent fell backwards from the impact of the headbutt. Matthew held on with a tight grip, keeping him on his feet. In a quick fluid movement, he pulled out the right arm of this man and broke it with a hard strike from his hand. The sound of cracking bone mixed with the yells of agony and Matthew let him fall to the floor. He stood over the heap before him, his body tense and alert as he caught his breath.

William got back to his feet and took a step closer. What he had seen Matthew do, filled him with a mixture of impressed amazement and intense fear. *How dangerous is this man?* he thought to himself. He looked around the room. The wall leading to the kitchen was completely destroyed. The plaster had been damaged beyond repair by the gunfire, creating large craters in the wall, showing the now demolished kitchen. William turned to the windows where the men must have entered the flat. The walls were covered with bullet holes and blood, the sofa that he had been sitting on mere moments ago was a ripped and torn shell of its former self.

"Jesus," he exclaimed, turning back to Matthew and the whimpering man on the floor. It took him a moment before he recognised the man on the floor who was clutching his bent and broken arms against his body. "He's one of the ambulance crew who had treated you," he said. "Who the hell are these guys?"

Matthew hadn't moved since he had dropped Jason to the floor but the question from William seemed to awaken him from his angry meditation. Taking a deep breath, he flexed his fingers in preparation for what was about to come.

"Let's find out."

Chapter Nine

Matthew slowly crouched down next to the man on the floor. Ignoring his cries of pain, Matthew reached out and slid his hands across the broken and bruised body until he found what he was looking for; the gun that had been fired at him. Pulling it roughly out of his attacker's grasp, he held it in his hands and inspected it. One hand holding the trigger, the other moving over the smooth black metal feeling its shape and size. He pulled out the cartridge and tossed it over his shoulder before dropping the gun at his feet.

"Search him," he ordered William, staying crouched down and tentatively taking the broken arm in his hands. Once again, he moved his hands carefully over what he was inspecting. He could feel the unnatural angle the arm was bent into, smiling a little at his own handy work. William walked over and knelt down on Jason's other side. He quickly patted him down, searching for any other weapons and anything that might help them identify this man. All he found was another ammunition cartridge, otherwise the man had nothing on him.

"This is it," William explained, placing the cartridge on the man's body near Matthew's fingers.

"Former soldiers," Matthew explained, ignoring the additional ammunition. "Ex British army?" he asked, directing his voice towards the man on the floor still held in his hands. Jason said nothing, gritting his teeth and attempting weakly to free himself of the blind man's grip. "Answer me," Matthew said more loudly, squeezing the broken arm hard making Jason shout out as well in pain.

"Yes! Four tours!" he shouted, trying harder to free his broken arm. William watched, his sense of worry growing as he considered where this could be going.

"That's better," continued Matthew, loosening his grip slightly on the arm.

"How can you tell he's a former soldier?" asked William, looking down at the man that had been taken down with surprising ease.

"These weapons are military grade and think about how they surprised us. Came up the drainpipe and through the window?" he asked Jason, turning his head slightly towards him. Jason nodded in reply. When he didn't hear anything, Matthew squeezed his broken arm again, harder this time making Jason scream in pain again.

"You're going to have to speak up, friend. I'm not good with visual clues," he said calmly, holding tightly as Jason tried to pull away.

"Yes! Yes! Let me go, you psycho!" he shouted.

"Why should I?" Matthew asked, a sense of purpose rushing through him as an evil grin spread across his lips. "We've only just started." He stood up pulling Jason to his feet by his broken arms, causing him to shout out again. Once he was on his feet, Matthew wasted no time in getting to work. With all his strength, he pushed Jason back against the wall, making his skull slam hard against the surface. Before Jason could register the stars in front of his eyes, Matthew punched him hard in the face, causing more blood to pour out of his broken nose. As blood flowed out of his nostrils, Jason tried to cover his blood-soaked face with his injured hands.

Matthew had no plans to stop now. He was in his element and finding his flow. Punches rained down on Jason's face and stomach with such speed that the hands were a blur as they flew back and forth. Jason's cries of pain mixed with the loud thumps of Matthew's fists. Jason could barely stand but when his legs gave way and he tried to fall to the floor, Matthew grabbed him and forced him back to his feet to resume his attack.

"On your feet, soldier!" he shouted in a mocking tone, increasing the speed and force of his punches. Jason's face was becoming a mess. His eyes began to swell, the floor was covered in his blood and broken teeth. Matthew grabbed his broken arm and slapped his hand onto it with a hard karate chop forcing the broken bone to pierce the skin. Jason was on the verge of passing out and he had stopped screaming with pain, his mouth so swollen he could barely move it. Holding up his other arm in protest to try and protect himself. He dropped to the floor, his back against the wall gasping for breath. He was unrecognisable now; his face a bruised and bloody mess. The bone of his broken arm ripping through his flesh, forced his arm into an unnatural angle. William had seen enough, rushing forward he grabbed Matthew's arm and pulled him back.

"Stop! We need him alive. What's gotten into you?"

But the rage that had been growing in Matthew since that night in the mechanic's had burst out of him like an explosion. He ripped his arm out of William's grip, giving Jason a hard kick in the stomach as he did.

"Get off me!" he shouted towards William as he kicked again, catching Jason's face and causing his head to crash into the wall again.

Before he could kick again, Matthew felt pain slam into the side of his head and he was sent crashing into the armchair, falling over it as he failed to catch himself. His head was spinning; before he could get to his feet, he heard the sound of an ammo cartridge being slammed into a gun.

"Make one more move and I'll shoot you in your own home, boy." William had grabbed the gun as soon as he had struck Matthew with a punch that had caught him by surprise. He held the gun tightly, his eyes firmly on Matthew "Calm down," he ordered.

Matthew got himself into a sitting position, rubbing his head as he leant against the armchair.

"That was a low blow," he groaned, shaking his head to get rid of the dizziness he was feeling.

William kept the rifle aimed at him but kept his distance in case there was an attempt to attack him.

"We need this man to talk," he continued. "We need any information he may know on who sent him and why."

"He tried to kill us," Matthew reasoned, slowly getting to his feet and raising both his hands feeling that the gun was still being pointed at him.

"So?" asked William, his own anger starting to rise as he quickly looked towards the semi unconscious man on the floor. "You kill him, you're no better than he is."

"I'm already better than him," replied Matthew coolly. "If it had been me, you'd have been dead without even knowing I was there."

"Your skills at killing aside, you know damn well we need to question this man and then we need to get him to a hospital where the proper authorities can deal with him."

Matthew scoffed as he straightened his back, rubbing his bloody knuckles. He could feel the pain in the side of his body begin to return now that his adrenaline was subsiding.

"We take him to a hospital. Someone belonging to Berkant will find him and probably kill him anyway so what difference is it that we do it?"

"We are not killing anyone if we can avoid it." William made his orders clear. "Now calm yourself down while we try and get something out of this man that might save our own lives."

William stepped towards Jason and knelt down next to him, keeping the gun pointed at him. He was struggling to breath; blood was dripping from the corner of his mouth and from his nose; both his eyes had become purple and puffy. William wondered whether he could even see. He clicked his fingers next to Jason's ear to get his attention.

"If you can hear and understand me, nod you head," he ordered.

There was a pause before Jason slowly nodded in acknowledgement. Even this simple act appeared to cause him pain after Matthew's attack.

"Good, now how about you start by telling us who sent you?"

It was a futile question. Jason tried to open his mouth but all that came out was more blood. He groaned and rested his head against the wall. He raised his broken arm and pointed towards Matthew and made his hand into a gun gesture, miming as if to shoot him.

"Sent to kill my friend there?" William asked. "Did Berkant or someone from his people send you?"

Jason managed another nod to confirm and William sighed. "Do they know where we are?" he asked, sure he already knew the answer. Jason gave another nod before sliding further down the wall as all his strength left him. William was on his feet straight away, slinging the weapon over his shoulder.

"We should move."

Matthew was already on his feet and slipping on his jacket. He reached down onto the armchair and slid his hands across the armrest and cushion searching for his gun. William spotted it had fallen to the floor when he had punched him into the chair and quickly bent down to grab it. He thrust it into Matthew's outstretched hands.

"Thanks," he muttered as he tucked the gun into his shoulder holster, buttoning his jacket as he made to go to the door. William grabbed his own jacket and hid the rifle under it.

"We need a car," he exclaimed, rushing to the window to look out for any more intruders.

"There's one outside," Matthew said, opening the door and heading down the stairs. "I've got the keys," he called back, moving as quickly as he could.

"What about this guy?" William called after him, heading towards the door but stopping at the threshold to look back at the now unconscious Jason.

"Carry him if you want but I'm not waiting for you," Matthew shouted up the stairs.

"You can't drive a car," William shouted back. He was torn between helping the dying man in front of him or escaping with his life. Looking at the bloodied and beaten fake paramedic on the floor, William made up his mind and rushed down the stairs after Matthew. Bursting through the door outside, he saw Matthew unlocking the car with the black plastic key in his hand. Matthew turned his head towards the noise of the door slamming against the wall, he tossed the key towards William who caught it with both hands.

"Hurry. They'll be here soon." Matthew's mindset had changed from explosive rage to quiet, concentrated focus. He climbed into the car, plotting a route for them to take to get away quickly. William ran over to the driver's side and climbed into the car, pulling the gun over his head and placing it on Matthew's lap.

"Hold this," he ordered, turning the key in the ignition, firing up the engine with a loud roar. He pulled the gear lever into reverse and pressed his foot hard into the accelerator pedal, sending the car up the alleyway with increasing speed.

"Head to the right when we get to the top," Matthew instructed, pulling his seatbelt across his chest.

"Do you know where we're going?" William asked as he spun the wheel at the mouth of the alleyway, throwing the car round to face the right direction. As he forced the car into first gear, he froze as something in the rear-view mirror caught his attention. William spun around in his seat to see two black Land Rovers, each with blacked out windows, speeding down the road towards them, "Shit! They've found us," he said, slamming his foot on the accelerator, throwing himself and Matthew back into their leather seats.

"How many?" Matthew asked, as he grabbed the gun on his lap. He pulled out the ammo cartridge, quickly running his fingers over it to feel how many bullets were inside. He slammed it back into the weapon.

"Two cars," William said, checking his mirrors again as he pushed the car as hard as he could, "no wait, one has gone into the alleyway."

"Good," replied Matthew, he rolled the passenger window down. Undoing his seatbelt, he leant out the window. Feeling the air rush past him, he turned away from the direction of travel and fired the gun, aiming towards the sound of the roaring engine behind them. William looked back to see a hailstorm of bullets hit the large black vehicle behind them, cracking the windshield in multiple places and obscuring the driver's field of vision.

"Great shooting," William called out as he drove straight through a set of red lights. Horns blared and cars skidded to avoid them and the closely following Land Rover. "Get back in the car!" William grabbed Matthew and pulled him back inside the car, flicking the driver's side control to roll the window back up.

"What are you doing?" Matthew asked, his hand sliding over the door handle for the control, "I can get them."

"There's more people here. I won't increase the risk of innocent bystanders being shot."

Matthew kept hold of the gun and reluctantly gave in to William's instructions as he pulled his seatbelt back across his chest. He sat back into the seat, gripping the door handle for support. As soon as he sat back in the seat, the wing mirror next to him exploded as several bullets caught it. The rear window soon followed, making William and Matthew both duck down in their seats. Behind them, two gunmen were leaning out of the passenger windows and firing at them with small Uzi machine guns. Passing people screamed and dropped to the floor as bullets flew in all directions.

William threw the car left and right across the road to try and avoid the gunfire. They sped down a small street. Cars ahead of them could hear the gunfire. Their drivers saw the speeding cars race towards them and mounted the pavement to get out of the way, causing more pedestrians to dive for cover. William went as fast as he dared, scared that at any second someone would step out in front of him, not paying attention, or a cyclist would fly out of a side street with their headphones on full volume. The wing mirror next to him took a bullet, glass and plastic bounced off the window, leaving William with only one mirror to check on their trigger-happy friends. Looking ahead, William could see the main road approaching quickly, cars were already starting to build as it was approaching rush hour.

"Hold on!" he shouted at Matthew over the sound of screeching tyres and bullet fire.

William took the corner sharply at speed, causing the BMW to skid across the tarmac into a main road. Cars flooded the street in both directions. Lights flashed, horns screamed and fingers were raised as he cut across the traffic, speeding away from their pursuers. The chasing Land Rover skidded behind them, following them into the road. As it turned, it smashed into the side of a black cab that had turned to avoid William and Matthew. The Land Rover's rear wheels skidded as the driver forced the car away from the resulting crash and into the rush hour traffic of London.

Ahead of them, the BMW wove in and out of the traffic, speeding down the road, avoiding cars, vans, cyclists and pedestrians. The car's engine roared with power as the car gained more speed. William attempted to get away and pushed the car to its limits. The engine began to scream in protest. His eyes darted from the road ahead into the rear-view mirror to check on the location of the Land Rover. Every time he looked, the car had gained more distance on them as it darted between other vehicles. Clearly the driver was better at high speed than he was. William switched between gears nonstop as he kept the car going as fast as the increasing traffic would allow him. It was becoming harder for him to weave the car between other vehicles as they began to cluster closer and closer together. He forced his way through wherever he could, breaking off wing mirrors and scratching paintwork.

"We're running out of room here," he called out, searching for an opening as fast as he could.

"Pavement?" Matthew suggested. "They'll get out of the way."

William held the steering wheel tightly, his knuckles turning white as he did so. He looked back in the mirror; the Land Rover was almost on top of them. He slammed his hand against the wheel and pushed his foot so hard onto the accelerator pedal that he thought it would go through the floor. He spun the wheel in his hand, turning the car towards the pavement. The BMW scraped past other cars, scratching more paint work and damaging body work as they went. Pedestrians watched in amazement, many taking pictures or filming on their phones as the car bounced onto the pavement and began speeding down it, away from the bullet damaged Land Rover. The pavement was very narrow and many of the people who were on it had to throw themselves into shop doorways or across the bonnets of cars in the road to avoid being run over. The car's paint work became more and more damaged as sparks exploded around the car with every moment of contact with streetlamps and road signs.

"They won't be able to follow us down here," said William, his voice was a mixture of relief and tension. He looked back in the only remaining mirror. He could make out the Land Rover attempting to get onto the pavement but had almost instantly become wedged between the buildings and the other cars that had pulled up to avoid being hit by it in the first place. The men inside had leapt out of the car and looked down the pavement where the many pedestrians were getting back to their feet, watching the speeding BMW disappear down the street. The three men said nothing to each other, but instead turned away from the ensuing chaos and began to run towards the nearest tube station, the sound of police sirens could be heard in the distance, approaching the scene of destruction.

William looked back in the mirror, keeping his foot down on the pedal as the car sped down the pavement, sending more pedestrians and tourists running to avoid being hit. He couldn't see anyone following them so he loosened his grip on the steering wheel and re-joined the road, cutting across a white van as he did so, ignoring the sound of the van's horn.

"Looks like we've got away," he said, relaxing a little as he slowed the car down. He could hear the sirens in the distance growing fainter as he looked around for a place to leave the car. Matthew sat up in his seat, rubbing his head gently. He had taken a few knocks against the door as William had thrown the car around the road.

"For now, we have. I get the impression this car has been shot to pieces?" Air was rushing through the car through the smashed rear window and the many bullet holes that lined the vehicle.

"Yes, even I couldn't talk us out of the shit storm we would get into if we got pulled over."

"We need to get rid of the car and go on foot," explained Matthew.

"What about the bullet casings? Our prints are all over this car."

"Worry about that later," continued Matthew. "Right now, they know the car and probably have noted the registration plate. When it comes to why you were in this car, I will tell your superiors I was holding you hostage."

William looked across at Matthew. For someone who had just been shot at, he was remarkably calm.

"Are you sure about that?" he asked, turning the car down a small empty side street. Pulling up on the pavement, he immediately turned off the engine. Matthew said nothing as he tossed the gun into the back seat and opened his car door.

"Come on, we need to find somewhere to stay until midnight."

William watched him climb out the car and then did likewise, leaving the key in the ignition. He caught up with Matthew at the mouth of the street, letting him take hold of his arm as they walked together, slipping into the crowds. Matthew pulled out his cane, letting William take the lead as they left the ruined car behind.

As Arif's car had approached the address his contacts had given him, he hadn't expected a car to come flying out of an alleyway backwards. His first instinct had been to ignore it, kids stealing cars were very common around here, but then he saw him. Matthew in the passenger seat. Something had clearly gone wrong inside and he had to find out. Grabbing the walkie talkie on his belt, he called out orders to the team in the car behind him.

"Black BMW. They're both in there. Kill them if you have to." He grabbed the wheel of his car, turning it into the alleyway. "We need to get inside." His car drove down to the end of the alley. He looked behind him through the rear window and saw the two cars speed away. "Don't fuck this up," he said to himself.

The car came to a halt at the end of the road. Arif was already opening his door before the car had completely stopped. Ahead of him was an open door. Arif rushed inside before his team had got out of the car, his weapon loaded and ready for whatever was inside. Arif took the stairs two at a time, bursting into the bullet strewn living room. He took in his surroundings, disappointment and anger building quickly inside him.

As his team joined him in the room, Arif caught sight of Malcolm's dead body and Jason on the floor, sitting in a small pool of his own blood. Bullet holes covered the walls, plaster was still crumbling away and trickling like a stream to the floor. Arif looked through the doorway to his left and saw the destroyed kitchen; it was pretty obvious what had happened here.

"Check him," he ordered, turning away from Jason's disfigured and bloodied body. His two accomplices moved over to him. The first one checked Jason's pulse, putting two fingers on his neck while the other the opened his eyes and slapped his cheek gently.

"He's alive," confirmed the first, stepping away from him to go and check the bedroom next to them. Arif stepped across the debris covering the floor, over to Jason. He crouched down in front of him, next to his comrade.

Arif slapped Jason's cheek hard, attempting to wake him up. When he got no reaction, he slapped him a second time. Jason's eyes flickered as he came round, groaning as his pain returned with his consciousness.

"What happened?" Arif asked simply, looking straight into Jason's swollen, bruised eyes.

"We...entered...thought we...we could take them..." Jason could barely speak and his words were barely coherent through his bleeding broken mouth.

Arif tightened his fists in anger, doing his best to resist hitting this man in the face.

"I told you to wait till we arrived," he said. His team stepped back, sensing the anger getting ready to burst from him.

"Thought…we…" Jason didn't finish his sentence, Arif punched him hard in the face, more blood spurted out of his nose when his knuckles made contact. Jason's head was slammed against the wall just as hard as when Matthew had hit him. More blood stained the wall as his skull cracked. Arif wasn't done. He grabbed Jason's head with both hands and began to repeatedly slam it against the wall, causing more plaster to fall away and more blood to spread across it. Arif was on his feet, throwing all his strength into destroying this man's head. When he finally released it, there was little left of Jason's head. His face had practically disappeared, fragments of his skull mixed with his blood and brain across the wall and floor. Slowing his breath as he calmed himself down, Arif pulled a handkerchief out of his pocket and cleaned his bloody hands. Without a second glance at his team or the mess that was once a pair of former soldiers of the British Army, he walked out of the flat, heading down the stairs to the outside.

"Burn this place to the ground," he called back to his team.

Obediently, the two men began to break the remaining furniture for kindling, one of them found a couple of liquor bottles that had survived the earlier gunfight and began to splash the liquid across the room. A match was lit and tossed into the mess that was once Matthew's safe house. The alcohol caught instantly and soon the small flat was in flames that would eventually spread to the rest of the old building. The two men ran down the stairs quickly to escape the flames and climbed into the car where Arif was waiting for them patiently, his phone in his hand as he called the other team who, he had sent to chase Matthew and his companion.

Chapter Ten

Matthew and William made slow progress through the city. Matthew's earlier injuries were still causing him pain and resulted in him limping as he walked. William was doing his best to remain inconspicuous as they walked, but his head was constantly turning left and right – on the lookout for any police officers who might recognise him.

"Will you stop looking around? You're drawing more attention to us." Matthew said quietly through clenched teeth, his grip on William's arm tightening with each step.

"I can't be seen with you, especially after that car chase. How do I explain all this to my superiors?"

"More than likely they probably already know," Matthew replied, doing his best to ignore the pain and plot a route based on the street names William had been giving him as they walked. "We're in the most watched country in the world, you've probably been ID'd on a security camera by now. We need to keep moving."

"Get rid of that limp then and we might be able to go faster," replied William, doing his best not to drop his injured companion.

"I could break your leg right now if you like and we can limp together like some sad three-legged race, how does that sound?"

"Just shut up and find us somewhere to hide."

Matthew said nothing and focused on where he was. The noise on the street was starting to increase, making it harder for him to concentrate. People in suits were leaving their offices, either to finally go home or go out for a drink after a long day of meetings and presentations or climbing into black cabs to go on to another meeting. Tourist numbers were also beginning to increase, many were either looking at the street maps to lead them back to their hotel or they were looking for a place to have dinner. He could hear voices calling out names, pointing out places or signs leading to the next landmark for a photo opportunity.

Matthew focused on clearing his head and tuned his hearing, like an old-fashioned radio, to drown out the surrounding useless noise and use his mind's eye to find them somewhere to hide. He hated hiding. Hiding was what cowards did, like William next to him. He wanted to keep going, to keep fighting and be the one doing the hunting, not be the hunted. But between his injuries and William's need to not be discovered in such a compromising position, they really had no choice. Matthew continued to limp down the street, his cane ahead of him clearing a path as they walked. In his mind's eye, he finally plotted where they were and began to focus his attention on getting them off the street.

"Take a left at the end of this road," he instructed William, keeping a firm grip on his arm. William duly followed the instructions and pulled Matthew left around the corner of the stone building.

"Where next 'Sat-nav'?"

"Take the third side street, there should be an old hotel halfway down."

"Another one of your safe houses?" William asked, looking ahead for the street in question.

"No. Just an old establishment no one who could see would notice," Matthew replied, doing his best to control his temper. Having William with him felt like an anchor around his neck, on his own he could move quickly, disappear in large crowds, even when he was injured. But now, with his new accomplice, he felt exposed, as if he was carrying a large target on his back. If he could, he would have separated himself from him as soon as he got out his safe house, but he knew that however he felt, he needed him if he was going to get out of this mess alive and stay out of prison.

They turned down the third street together, William looking around for anything that resembled a hotel. There were rubbish bags everywhere, most had been ripped open by foxes with their contents spread across the road. William carefully stepped over the strewn rubbish as he followed Matthew's guidance. Eventually, his eyes rested on what he thought was just another derelict building, until he noticed the small broken sign above the door stating '**Hotel**'. He looked at Matthew as he stopped outside the building before looking it over. At least half of the windows were boarded up or broken. Several bricks had fallen away, leaving holes in the side of the building. The entrance was covered in more litter and bin bags. Matthew was right, anyone who could see would avoid this place like the plague. As he stood there giving the hotel a once over, Matthew let go of his arm and stepped forward, putting his cane back inside his jacket.

"Told you," he said over his shoulder to William, as if he had been reading his mind. Matthew walked over to what was left of a door; it looked as though a small breeze could knock it off its hinges. It squeaked loudly as he pushed it open and stepped inside. William took one last look up and down the street, checking they were not being followed, before following Matthew inside.

The inside of the hotel was only slightly better than the outside; what was left of the red carpet was either stained or water damaged and wallpaper was peeling off the walls or missing completely. The lone armchair that made up the reception waiting room was missing a leg and was being propped up by a stack of old newspapers. The reception area was an old wooden desk, hidden behind a rusting cage to protect its occupant, which consisted of an overweight, grey-haired excuse of a man. He was wearing a trilby with a feather in it. He greeted the new arrivals with a look that showed a complete lack of interest. Matthew walked straight up to the desk, resting both hands on the dirty, splintered wood.

"Good evening, Mick."

"Evenin'," Mick replied, looking down at the newspaper laid on the desk before him. "Usual room, is it?" His hand already sliding for the box in front of him that held the room keys.

"Yes please," said Matthew, pulling several notes out of his pocket. "Same rate I assume?"

"No," stated Mick simply, his eyes still down on the pages before him.

"I beg your pardon?" asked Matthew, the danger in his voice was already clear. This did nothing to Mick's demeanour; he carried on reading.

"There's two of you. Price is doubled, I've got bills to pay."

"What's her name?" asked Matthew sourly, sliding additional notes under the cage which Mick snatched at quickly, giving Matthew an equally sour look as his thrust the key towards him.

"Upstairs, Stevie Wonder."

"You're a prick, Mick," said Matthew, taking the key and heading towards the stairs, sliding his hand off the wooden table and shaking the dirt off as he went.

"Clear up after yourself this time. This place is filthy enough as it is," Mick called out. He gave William a quick look over before lowering his face back to the newspaper. William began to follow Matthew towards the stairs, his feet stuck to different parts of the floor as he walked. He gave the overweight receptionist a look of deep disgust as he passed him. He was tempted to pull out his badge and, for the first time in his career, abuse his authority to scare some sense into him. As his hand moved to his coat pocket, he thought better of it. Looking at this pathetic creature, William could tell he was a person who cared more about money than loyalty and would most likely sell them out for the best price, if he wasn't planning to already.

Matthew and William made their way up the stairs slowly. Every step creaked and groaned under their weight and several were on the verge of breaking point. As they walked down the hallway towards their room, small clouds of dust rose around their feet with every step on the thin, worn carpet. When they reached the room, William was surprised they even needed a key, the door was broken in several places and the lock was brown from years of rust. Matthew pushed the key into the lock, he turned it slowly with a loud click.

Extracting the key, he walked into the room with William close behind him, who turned, closing the door and applying every lock the room had to offer. Turning around, William looked around the room, taking it all in. It was a small basic space: an old double bed sat against the wall with a broken bed side table next to it holding an old lamp with no bulb; the lone window was covered in dirt and had bars across it; the two wires hanging from the ceiling indicated the fire alarm had been taken out long ago; there was no television, radio or telephone. William grimaced at the sight of his temporary base, wondering whether the alley outside would be more comfortable.

"Good God what a dump," he exclaimed, not daring to go near the ensuite for fear of what could be inside.

"There are worse places to hide out," replied Matthew, sitting down on the end of the bed and slipping off his jacket slowly as his limbs stiffened slightly.

"Easy for you to say, you can't see it."

Matthew said nothing. Kicking his shoes off, he climbed back onto the bed and fell back, resting his head on the small pillows. William watched him for a moment, rolling his eyes as he turned to check if the door was definitely locked before moving across the room to the hard armchair in the corner. He made himself as comfortable as he could, assuming Matthew was taking a nap. He figured he might as well do the same and save his strength for what he was sure was going to be a rough night.

*

Arif and his men drove for ten minutes before they had contact from the other members of their team. The men had jumped on the first train that had arrived at the underground station they had run into after abandoning their car. They had ridden for two stops, then left walking amongst the growing crowds, keeping apart from each other, but making sure they were in each other's sight line at all times. When they emerged out of the underground back onto the streets, a phone buzzed and the leader of the group answered. It was Arif.

"Do you have them?" he demanded, as soon as the call was connected.

"No, sir," came the reply. The crowd was thinning out now as people parted across the street, allowing the three-man team to slowly come together as they kept moving quickly down the street. The team leader could hear Arif slam his hand on the dashboard of his car through the phone.

"What happened?" he asked, giving the dashboard another strike with his hand.

"They got to the main road before we could get to them. Between the traffic and the police, they got away from us and we couldn't follow them. We had to abandon the car."

Back in his car, Arif slammed his foot to the floor, his anger overflowing at the incompetence of his team.

"So you let them get away and left a car in the middle of the road for the police to find?"

"They're being tracked and the car and its contents are untraceable back to us," answered the team leader, feeling braver than he should. There was silence on the other end as Arif considered his options.

"Where are you now?" he asked, his voice calmer now. The team leader gave their current street name to Arif as his partners joined him, waiting at a nearby bus stop for cover.

Back in the car, Arif gave his driver the street name. The driver made a sudden U turn in the road, causing other cars to swerve and blast their horns. The driver ignored them all and sped off down the street to get to the pickup spot as quickly as possible.

"Do we have them on the tracker?" Arif asked, turning his head to the back of the car. His other team member was sat in the back, holding the phone that Jason and Malcolm had used to track Matthew and William.

"It's pretty weak but we should be able to find them as long as they don't discover the tracker first."

"Good, keep an eye on them. We'll get the others and then finish this."

Arif sat back in his seat, pulling his gun out from under his jacket. He double checked the magazine and flipped off the safety. Looking straight ahead as his driver wove the car in and out of the traffic, he rested the gun on his leg, out of sight, as he began to make his plan. Closing his eyes, he carefully considered every step and scenario. Like a champion chess player, he played out the scenes of attack for Matthew, going over every possible outcome until he felt he had the right strategy for victory.

A few minutes later, the car was approaching his waiting team.

"There they are," informed the driver, pointing ahead as he slowed down the car.

"I see them," Arif replied, spotting the three-man team waiting amongst the large crowd at the bus stop.

Each of the three waiting men spotted the car as soon as it came round the corner. Moving slowly and carefully, they each slipped through the waiting crowd to the front, standing at the edge of the pavement. The leader nodded at the car to signal he had seen them and saw the car move into the bus lane, slowing down to a crawl as it got closer to them. It would be a quick pick up, the car would barely stop, any second the rear door would open and the three men would leap into the back and squash into the rear seat, while the car would pull away at speed and rejoin the flowing traffic. All three of them bounced gently on their feet ready to spring into action and leap into the car. It was almost upon them: any second now.

Inside the car, Arif and the others watched the other team as they got closer, the rear passenger moved across the back seat to the street side by the door. The car was about to be level with them.

"Now," ordered Arif.

Instead of the door opening, the front and rear passenger tinted windows rolled down, Arif and his two companions each picked out a target and all fired in unison while the car was still moving.

The team at the bus stop realised what was happening, but it was too late for them. Instead of the door opening, the windows rolled down a fraction, keeping the passengers inside the vehicle out of sight from the other people on the street. Before they could move, duck or draw their own weapons, they had each received a bullet to the head. All three of them fell to the floor as their heads snapped back from the impact of the bullets. People around them screamed, ran for cover or dived to the floor to avoid any further gunfire. Those who had been standing behind them were now covered in blood, skull fragments and brain matter. In all the panic, no one paid too much attention to the car speeding away up the street through the traffic and out of sight, leaving three dead bodies and a street full of terrified pedestrians behind.

Back in the car, Arif and his men tucked their weapons away, what they had just done bore no effect on any of them. The other team had failed and they had had to pay the price for it. This was their job: this was their world. Do what is expected of you or prepare to take a bullet for your failures.

"Do you know where they are?" Arif asked, relaxing slightly in his seat and resting his head against the leather head rest of his seat.

"Yes, sir," came the reply from the back seat. The phone was passed forward towards Arif who took it quickly, looking at the screen and assessing where his target was.

"They're at the hotel. Easy pickings," he said, smiling at the screen. The finish line was in sight.

"I'll have us there in ten," said the driver, pressing his foot harder on the accelerator and pushing the car forward towards their destination.

*

Back at the hotel, William couldn't sleep. His mind wouldn't switch off and Matthew's breathing was distracting. He looked across the room, inspecting the unconscious murderer in front of him on the bed. How could he rest so easily? They were being chased across the city. *Hunted down more like*, William thought to himself. He leapt to his feet and paced the room, every step made the floor creak and squeak loudly. William could feel his pulse quickening as he moved around the room. He was trying not to panic but he felt completely useless right now. He couldn't just sit here waiting, but he didn't have anywhere to go either. The meeting with Zoe and her captive wasn't until midnight and he knew he should be resting, calling his wife to let her know where he was or letting his superiors know what was going on and requesting back up. This whole situation was infuriating to him. He wanted to get moving, make a plan, do something, anything.

He looked over at Matthew sleeping on the bed and clenched his fists. This whole mess was all his fault as far as William was concerned and yet, there he was, taking a nap as if this was an everyday occurrence for him. Feeling like he had to do something to relieve his stress and tension, he kicked the bed as hard as he could, making it jump and bang against the wall. Matthew was awake instantly; he sat bolt upright, his gun, from under the pillow, in his hand and held out in front of him, scanning the room. William ducked out of the line of fire, crouching on the floor at the end of the bed.

"Put it away, boy! It's me!"

"Don't wake me up like that again," Matthew replied, relaxing his body and slowly slipping his weapon back under the pillow.

"Need to catch up on some beauty sleep?" William asked, returning to his chair in the corner, watching Matthew yawn and sit up on the bed.

"We need to rest. We don't know what we're going up against tonight."

"Well forgive me, Princess, but I can't just put my feet up and relax after the day I've had."

"If you can't sleep, then at least shut up and let me," Matthew demanded, lying back down on the bed and slipping his hand under the pillow to hold his gun.

His frustration returning again, William slammed his hands on the arm rests of the chair as he sat back and slouched, getting himself into a more comfortable position.

William had barely closed his eyes when the room exploded with the sound of gunfire. Throwing himself to the floor, William turned to the outer wall. It was rapidly disintegrating as endless bullets crashed through the old bricks and dirty window. He lay face down on the dirty carpet, his hands over his head to protect himself from the raining glass and stone. The gunfire seemed endless.

He could hear other parts of the building smashing and breaking along with the screams of whoever else was inside the building as bullets continued to crash through the walls. William knew that whoever was out there firing the guns was looking for them both. He started to crawl across the floor towards the bed, Matthew had vanished from sight. *Had he been caught by a bullet, had he already fled the room?* William made it round to the far side of the bed and he saw Matthew on the floor, gun in hand.

"Are you okay?" William shouted over the gunfire and falling debris.

"Yeah, you?" Matthew asked, keeping as flat to the floor as he could.

"We need to get out of here."

"Grab my shoes and come on," he called back over his shoulder as he started to crawl towards the door. His gun in one hand, the other sliding along the wall to guide him through the room.

"Your shoes?" William asked, flabbergasted. He couldn't believe it, with all the gunfire around them, this man wanted his shoes.

"Just grab them!" Matthew shouted. He reached for the door handle, pulling his hand away quickly as bullets missed his fingers by inches. More bullets hit the door. Matthew hit it with his fist causing it to fall forward out of its rotten frame into the hall. Not waiting for William, he crawled out into the hallway where the gunfire was less damaging.

As he pulled himself up into a low crouching position, Matthew felt William brush against him and his shoes thrust into his chest.

"Here are your bloody shoes," he said, keeping close as he too pulled himself into a low crouch. Matthew said nothing in reply. Taking the left shoe, he flipped it over and pressed the edge of his heel. The heel compressed slightly and then a small rubber handle ejected from inside the heel, Matthew grabbed the handle and pulled it out, revealing a small knife.

"Take this," he ordered, pressing the knife into William's body for him to take. William took the small, sharp knife and held it tightly in his hand. He wasn't sure how effective this weapon would be in a gunfight, but it was better than no weapon at all.

"Now what?" he asked. The hailstorm of bullets had stopped as the shooters had paused to reload their weapons.

"We need to move, now." Matthew didn't wait for William's answer. He slipped his shoes on in an instant and was on his feet. He raced down the hall as fast as he could. His free hand grazed the wall as he ran to guide him. William scrambled to his feet as fast as he could and ran after Matthew, keeping pace and waiting for the inevitable barrage of bullets.

They made it to the top of the staircase when the gunfire resumed. Hundreds of bullets pounded through the walls: William ducked, covering his head as the walls around him exploded. Matthew threw himself forward, diving down the stairs and into a forward roll as he hit the stairs halfway down. He crashed to the floor at the bottom of the stairs, his momentum carrying him forward as he stumbled and fell forward, landing amongst the broken furniture and building debris.

Brushing several large pieces of plaster out of his hair, Matthew was back on his feet in seconds and crouching low to avoid the deadly bullets crashing through the walls. Holding his gun in both hands tightly, Matthew took several deep breaths, slowing his heart rate down to prepare for battle. With the destruction and noise around him, it was hard for him to picture his own or the shooters' positions. Keeping low, he began to crawl over to where the front door used to be. Behind him he could hear William stumbling his way down the stairs as the bullets crashed around him. Matthew pressed himself against the wall, waiting for his chance. He heard William let out a cry of pain behind him.

"You been hit?" he shouted out over his shoulder.

"Just a graze!" William shouted back. He clutched his arm tightly where a bullet had caught him. He slumped down and took the last couple of steps on his knees. He slid down to the floor and began to make his way over Matthew.

By the door, Matthew fired several shots randomly outside, towards the shooters, in the hope of taking them by surprise.

"There he is!" someone outside shouted out. Matthew could just make out the voice over the gunfire. He recognised it instantly as Arif's. He clutched his gun tighter, preparing for Arif's inevitable brutality that could only be matched by his own. Matthew fired one more round out of the doorway, into the alley; he didn't expect to hit any of them as he couldn't clearly pinpoint their positions. The gunfire stopped. Matthew had achieved what he wanted. The men outside scattered, searching for cover.

Matthew listened intently, keeping close to the wall. The alley outside was small with limited cover. Matthew knew time was of the essence: the gunfire wouldn't go unnoticed and it was only a matter of minutes before hundreds of armed police arrived, blocking them in. For his own and Zoe's sake, Matthew couldn't allow that to happen. He could hear the footsteps of the men outside moving quickly for cover, Matthew counted three. Preparing to fire, Matthew hoped that he would hit Arif. Exposing himself briefly, Matthew pointed his gun out through the doorway and fired towards the sound of running feet. The resulting scream and sound of metal hitting the floor confirmed he'd hit his first target; whether or not they were dead was not his main concern. He turned to the sound of running footsteps towards his left and fired again. Another scream confirmed his second target was down.

"Holy shit," William exclaimed, more to himself than to anyone else. In all his years, he had never seen such accuracy before and to see it from a blind man was just overwhelming. William's momentary amazement was costly though, instead of watching for the other shooter his eyes were locked on Matthew and his shooting prowess. This allowed the third man outside to charge forward with such speed that he reached Matthew before William could warn him.

Matthew had turned towards the sound of charging footsteps in time to take a knee in the centre of his face. He fell back with a shout of pain, clutching his bleeding nose with his free hand. He could feel his blood pouring down his face, staining his face and shirt. He'd been tricked, he realised that now as he tried to get back to his feet. It was Arif. While the other two shooters had scattered, Arif had stayed where he was, exposed, out in the open because he knew that Matthew would be choosing his target based on sound and movement. As he had fired his second shot, Arif had charged forward to make his attack and finally end this mess and Matthew's life.

Arif stepped forward towards Matthew, swinging his fist towards his face. Matthew blocked it and threw his own fist back towards Arif's jaw. But he wasn't quick enough. With his head still spinning, he couldn't focus. Arif blocked him and struck back harder than before. His hard, clenched fist striking Matthew's chest, almost cracking a rib as Matthew fell back to the floor, letting out a cry of pain. Matthew tried to get to his feet as fast as he could, his face covered in blood, his chest screaming out in agony but he just couldn't get to his feet in time. As he pushed himself up, Arif's foot met his face, sending him crashing backwards onto the floor where he lay amongst the broken furniture and rubble.

"You have no idea how long I've waited for this moment," Arif said, pulling a long combat knife out of its sheaf on his waist. He stepped closer to Matthew, placing his foot on his chest and pressing gently on the spot where he knew a rib was about to crack. Matthew let out a roar of pain, grabbing Arif's foot, trying to push it off—he couldn't move it.

William moved towards the two men quickly, the knife Matthew had given him in his hand. His intention was to push the blade into Arif's side, aiming to wound rather than kill. Unlike Matthew and Arif though, he couldn't move as quickly or as quietly as them. Arif knew he was coming by the time he had taken his second step. Stepping away from Matthew, Arif turned, grabbing William's arm and striking him across the face with the other. William dropped the knife and staggered backwards, his feet stumbling over the crumbling reception. Shaking his head to clear it, he rushed back towards Arif, showing no fear. He was quicker than Arif had expected and landed a blow, striking upwards and catching Arif's chin, sending him stumbling backwards over Matthew who was still on the floor. William raised his hands, ready to continue when Arif found his footing. Ignoring Matthew, he stepped closer to William with the combat knife still in his hand. In the distance, the sound of police sirens was beginning to grow louder.

"Come on, old man," Arif taunted, faking a swing to intimidate William. William didn't flinch, he'd been in plenty of fights in his time and had taken punches from bigger men. Ignoring Arif's taunts, he moved slowly around the destroyed room until his back was facing the entrance to the hotel.

"Only one way out of here," he said, eyes locked on Arif as he prepared himself for the blows that were coming his way.

Arif flashed him a confident smile as he moved forward towards William, his arms raised for combat. He swung with his weaker, left hand at William's face. He blocked it, which was what Arif wanted. As William moved to block the first punch, Arif struck with his right, catching William on the side of his face, knocking him sidewise so that he stumbled into the destroyed armchair. William righted himself briefly, arms raised ready to fight back.

The sirens were getting louder. The police were almost upon them. William swung low, aiming for Arif's stomach. Arif blocked with both hands, pushing William's down. William caught Arif by surprise, striking his nose with his forehead, sending him stumbling backwards clutching his now broken nose. The headbutt earnt him some ground but it also cost him. William clutched his own head, wincing as stars flashed around his head.

Both men staggered, holding their heads, but Arif was the first to react. Charging forward with a roar, he tackled William around the waist, throwing him backwards. They crashed through what was left of the door into the dirty alley outside. The momentum carried Arif over William as they hit the ground, sending him rolling across the floor. He was on his feet instantly. William slowly pulled himself up, looking up at Arif and clutching his stomach where Arif's shoulder had caught him in the tackle.

The sirens were now almost upon them. Arif quickly looked up to the mouth of the alley. When they arrived, he would be trapped. Although he had many police on his side, he couldn't risk being caught. With one last contemptuous look at William, he turned and ran out of the alley, disappearing around the corner and out of sight.

William stood there looking up to the place where Arif had disappeared, holding his stomach which was still sore from the tackle. He could feel bruises growing on his face from the punches and headbutt. Groaning, he turned and made his way back towards the hotel. He had to get Matthew out of here as well because even with his position within the police, he would have a hard time explaining the situation. More than likely, Matthew would be locked up and Berkant's people would get wind of what was going on. William didn't much fancy his odds of survival on his own after what had just happened. He'd have to get Matthew to run and meet him later. He could explain his presence to the police fairly easily, on his own, but with Matthew, it would be more difficult.

He climbed over the rubble that he had just crashed through. The sirens were louder now; he didn't have long. He stepped inside and looked around for Matthew: he wasn't there. He'd gone. William moved around the room tossing aside the broken furniture and brickwork in case something had landed on him during the fight: nothing. William looked towards the stairs, the sirens now at the entrance of the alley. The loud noise was painful against his sore head. Wincing with pain, William walked to the bottom of the staircase and looked up. It's possible that Matthew had gone upstairs during the fight to hide. William didn't have time to check, he could hear car doors opening and heavy footsteps of the riot police running towards him. He'd better come up with an explanation quickly.

Chapter Eleven

Back in her hotel room, Zoe struggled against the handcuffs around her wrists. Sat on the floor, she pulled and twisted her hands, desperately trying to slip herself free or break the chain to escape. In front of her, Charles was pacing back and forth, ignoring her, his phone in his hand. His thumbs danced across the screen as he wrote message after message, becoming more and more frustrated with the lack of a response from whoever he was texting.

Eventually he'd had enough, tossing the phone across the room onto the bed he let out a quick shout of frustration as he sat on the edge of the bed looking straight ahead at the wall.

"Something on your mind?" Zoe asked, stopping her own struggle to sit back against the radiator and watch her captor. She'd managed to spit out the rag in her mouth. Keeping quiet seemed like the best option rather than screaming for help. She wasn't sure how he would react and she needed to stay alive.

"You shut up," Charles replied, pointing his thick finger at her.

"Berkant not answering your calls?"

"I said shut up," said Charles, anger rising in his voice as he got back to his feet. Looking down at his phone on the bed, he saw that there had indeed been no replies.

Zoe sat still, her head resting against the back of the radiator, watching Charles. Even though she knew he needed her, she also knew that he could be dangerous and there was every chance he might not just leave her alone while they waited for their meeting.

Doing her best to cover her hands behind her back out of his sight, she began to try to make her hand as small as possible so she could try and slip it out of the handcuff. Compressing her hand as best as she could, she tried to pull it free. The handcuff was still tight but she could feel a little give. She couldn't give herself away. If she could get one hand free, it would be her first step to escaping.

Charles had returned to pacing around the room. This wasn't going the way he had expected. He was so sure that once he had Zoe, he'd have had Berkant's people racing to find him and reward him. He was now stuck in this troublesome situation with his hostage. He hadn't even begun to plan how he would get her out of here without her either escaping or arousing suspicion.

He looked at her, attached to the radiator with her hands cuffed behind her back. He was in the position of power, not her. Even if Berkant and his people didn't show or return his messages, he still had the information they needed. Had they forgotten he was a police officer? If they weren't going to help him, then he could at least use his authority and have them all arrested. Thanks to Zoe, he now had enough evidence to lock Berkant and his inner circle up for the rest of their lives. It would be his word against theirs. If they tried to take him down with them, he could make up some nonsense about working undercover secretly, believing there was a mole inside the police. It wouldn't be difficult for him to create false reports to build a fake trail of evidence to keep himself out of prison.

Charles smiled to himself as he concocted his plan. The only loose ends to tie up would be Zoe and whoever she was working with: that wouldn't be a problem. He had Zoe and she wasn't going anywhere. After tonight's meeting, he would deal with her easily: it was her partners that would be trouble. He continued to pace the room, planning out tonight's meeting in his head: mapping out where he and Zoe will be waiting and anticipating the others moves and how they might try to get to them both.

Zoe's eyes were locked on him moving back and forth across the small room. Her first hand was free, she managed to squeeze it out without giving herself away. Keeping her hand behind her back, she started to get her other hand out of its cuff. With her first hand free, she could use it to press her second hand at the joint of her thumb, making it as small as possible in order to get it out of the metal ring. Charles had made this hand cuff tighter. Zoe had to bite the inside of her cheek so she didn't make a sound as she almost dislocated her thumb in order to escape. Charles was so wrapped up in his own thoughts, he gave her no attention. Giving her hand one last tug, she slipped it out, freeing herself from the radiator. As it popped out, her wrist hit the metal radiator making a small 'clang' as her watch connected with the rusting metal. Charles turned his head sharply towards her when he heard the sound. Zoe kept her hands behind her back, pretending to struggle. Seeing Charles was looking at her, she returned his gaze, eyes locked on his.

"What?" she asked, doing her best to maintain her innocence.

Charles said nothing and stopped pacing the room. He turned towards her, looking down at her helpless figure on the floor.

"Comfortable?"

"I've stayed in better places," she replied, glancing around the room slowly.

"See I had you figured as the kind of girl who enjoyed being handcuffed," continued Charles with a sly smile on his face.

"It's usually with better looking men than you."

Charles stepped closer, crouching down in front of her, his face inches from hers.

"Now, now, Zoe, I think you might enjoy being handcuffed with me," he said, the smell of coffee and cigarettes on his breath flowing up her nostrils.

"I'm not exactly having much fun so far," Zoe replied, turning away from his face and the stench of his breath.

"What if I moved you to somewhere more comfortable?" Charles asked, looking towards the bed to his right. This was the opening Zoe needed. She whipped her hand out from behind her back, digging her nails hard into Charles' cheek. She dragged her hand down his face leaving deep red lines.

Charles let out a scream of pain, making to grab her hand and pull her off him. Zoe reacted first, kicking him in the chest, hard. He over-balanced, falling to his back and grabbing at his bleeding face. Zoe leapt to her feet, jumping over Charles as she ran for the door. Charles twisted himself on the floor, throwing his arm out; he just clipped Zoe's foot as she ran, causing her to lose her footing and fall to the floor.

She pushed herself up instantly, rushing forward: the door handle inches from her fingertips. As they brushed the cool smooth metal of the door knob, she felt Charles grab her hair, wrapping his fingers tightly into it and tugging her back hard. Zoe let out a scream of pain as he pulled her roughly, snapping her head back as she was thrown to the floor. She hit the floor with a loud thud, almost rolling backwards over herself with the force of Charles pulling her back.

Zoe tried to get back to her feet, but he was on top of her instantly. Wrapping his hands around her throat, he pinned her down, straddling her chest as he choked her. There was a crazed look in his eyes as red hot rage flooded his senses, blood flowing out of the deep wounds in his face. Zoe gasped and grabbed Charles' hands around her throat. She couldn't breathe.

Her legs kicked out, trying to catch Charles with her knees to try and get him off her but she couldn't reach him. She dug her nails into his hands to try and soften his grip but his hold around her throat remained firm. Charles looked down into her eyes as she began to lose consciousness. Her hands stopped struggling against his and her body was becoming limp: Charles had almost finished choking the life out of her. His full weight pressed on her chest and his hands firm around her windpipe, the troublesome bitch was almost dead.

Darkness began to envelope Zoe; she could no longer fight off Charles. Her hands fell to her sides as her body slowly gave in and fell limp. Just as the blackness swallowed her whole, she could breathe again. The weight on her chest was lifted and she rolled over, clutching her body as she gasped for breath. The room around her was blurry. As she lay on her side, she could just make out Charles reaching over the bed, grabbing at something, then pacing around the room quickly, now ignoring her completely.

"Who the hell is this?" Charles demanded, rubbing his sore bloody face.

"You're an eager man," came Arif's calm voice.

"I don't like being ignored."

"I believe we told you to stay out of this? We have this under control."

"And I believe that I have something you need," replied Charles, smirking down at the half-dead Zoe, nudging her with his foot as he walked past her.

"What are you talking about?" came the reply. Charles smiled to himself, he finally had their attention.

"Maybe I didn't make myself clear, I have someone you want." Charles looked back at Zoe on the floor. She was slowly collecting herself and had managed to pull herself to her knees on the edge of the bed. Deep, dark bruises were already forming around her neck. Charles slowly placed his foot on her shoulder and pushed her back down to the floor.

"Do you have Matthew?" Arif did his best to keep his voice calm. His car was moving through the streets of London at the legal limit to remain as inconspicuous as possible.

"I have Zoe and I've arranged a meeting later tonight."

"Where?"

"That's for me to know. You'll find out when I'm ready to tell you," Charles replied, sitting down on the corner of the bed, pushing his foot against Zoe as she sat on the floor, keeping her pressed against the wall.

"I don't think you are in a position to be making such demands," replied Arif, the danger in his voice growing more and more.

"Actually, I am," said Charles, giving Zoe a wink as she watched him, her face emanating hatred and loathing. "As I now have Zoe, I also have all the information she had been collecting on you all. Foolish really of her new friend to leave it all with her." Shaking his head disapprovingly at Zoe, he smiled as he did so. He continued talking down the phone, "So right now I have everything: her, soon her new friend and enough information to put you and your dear old Daddy away until the day you die. Did you forget I am a Police Officer?"

"A crooked one," Arif reminded him. His anger rising, much like his father's. "We have dirt on you as well, did you forget that?"

"It's my word against yours. You've tried to cut me out before. Don't do it again. I'll be in touch." Charles hung up the phone and tossed it over his shoulder onto the bed. "Time to get some rest." He punched Zoe hard in the face, causing her head to hit against the wall behind her and knocking her unconscious. He dragged her body across the floor. He handcuffed her hands again, wrapping the chain around the pipe of the radiator once more but this time keeping them in front where he could see them. Satisfied she wasn't going anywhere, Charles climbed onto the bed. He lay on his back, exhaling as he relaxed his body and tried to get some sleep.

*

Back at the crumbling mess that was once a hideaway for criminals, drug dealers and prostitutes, William was leaning against a squad car having his injuries checked over by a doctor.

"Will you please stop? I'm fine," he said to the young paramedic, waving her away with his hand. The paramedic stepped away, rolling her eyes as she peeled off her latex gloves and headed back to the ambulance. William watched her go, annoyed at himself for being so short with her. He needed to get away from here and find Matthew. Officers were everywhere and forensics were on their way.

"Inspector Blaine?" William looked up. A man in a dark suit and a long brown overcoat was making his way slowly towards him through the crowd of police and scattered cars. "Can I have a moment?"

"Depends who's asking?" William replied, watching this man suspiciously. He wasn't familiar; this wasn't a man he knew.

"My name is Thomas Foy. I'm with the Special Investigations Unit. Dealing with organised crime both home and abroad."

"I don't see a badge or ID," said William. His arms folded, he looked this man over. He looked over Thomas' shoulder, checking behind him for any partners or aides who might be with him.

"And you won't, sir," Thomas continued, giving William a small smile. "I am alone and I am not with Berkant or any of his people so please don't worry."

"It's not a matter of worrying son, it's a matter of trust."

"If you want to be trusted, be honest."

"You shouldn't trust everything you see; even salt looks like sugar."

"And the Devil was once an Angel," replied Thomas, stopping just out of arm's reach of William and smiling, "but I'm only here to ask a few questions; nothing more."

"Ask away then, sunshine. Then be on your way."

Thomas stepped towards the crumbling ruins of the Hotel, hands clasped behind his back.

"So what happened here?"

"Gang violence?" William suggested, shrugging as he watched Thomas walk away from him.

"Possibly?" replied Thomas turning back to look at William. "Or perhaps something involving Berkant, his son, you and a wanted professional killer?" Thomas looked William in the eye as he faced him. William stared straight back.

"Possible."

"What's going on here, Inspector?" Thomas asked moving closer to William, who remained against the car.

"You seem like a bright young man. You tell me."

"Seems to me like you're involved in something," replied Thomas, pulling a crumpled packet of cigarettes out of his pocket, along with a silver Zippo lighter, "care to fill me in?" He put a cigarette between his lips before flicking open the lighter. He took a long drag, exhaling the smoke slowly as he held the packet out towards William, offering him one.

"No thanks," answered William, shaking his head at the offered packet. He sighed, thinking how best to answer, "There is something going on, something big. However, it's better if I don't tell you anymore. I don't know how many people are involved, who's on who's side. How much do you know?"

"Nothing that isn't common knowledge," Thomas replied, taking another drag and stepping closer to William again, "we've been watching Berkant and his people for several years now. We knew you had an undercover on the inside and we know that Berkant has started to clean up. We assume he's planning on leaving the country. You only just came up on our radar recently though."

"I like to keep a low profile and I agree with you about Berkant. The information we'd been collecting led us to believe that he's planning to go home." William paused, looking Thomas over slowly, "So how come I don't know that my people are being watched by your people?" he asked standing up straighter, keeping his arms folded across his chest.

"It's better I don't tell you anymore." Thomas looked around at the passing police officers as he took another drag of his cigarette. "But what does Matthew Bartimaeus have to do with all this?"

"He was in the wrong place at the wrong time," answered William.

"And what about you Inspector, same thing?"

"I'm just trying to get one of my own out of danger."

"Well then I better stop taking up your time." Thomas stepped to one side, finishing his cigarette before flicking it away. William nodded at Thomas, who returned the gesture. William started to make his way up the alley towards the main street where a crowd of curious people had gathered to see what had caused so much commotion. He looked back at Thomas over his shoulder, asking himself if he had made a new enemy or ally.

From inside his pocket, he felt his phone vibrate. He ignored it and kept walking, taking his time. He knew Thomas was watching him and didn't want to give anything away just yet. His phone kept ringing as he slipped under the police tape and made his way through the crowd who were straining over each other for a better look and taking photos on their phones. Feeling like all eyes were on him, he pulled his phone out of his pocket. An unknown number was calling him.

"Hello, Matthew. Where are you?"

Chapter Twelve

Matthew was waiting for William outside Waterloo Station. He had changed into a new clean black suit with a matching shirt and tie. William spotted him from across the road, standing outside the main entrance like a statue, his cane in both hands down the front of his body. William had taken a black cab across London and had stopped a street away as per Matthew's instructions. Jogging across the road to avoid passing cars, he slowed down as he reached the pavement, slipping in amongst the passing crowds as he walked towards Matthew.

"I see you scrub up well," said William, giving Matthew a once over. His suit fit perfectly and Matthew's short hair was tidy and clean looking. The bruises on his face were pronounced and there was a cut on his lower lip, but otherwise he looked great. Matthew gave a small sneer as he sniffed the air.

"You need a shower, Inspector."

"So where did you run off to?" William asked, ignoring Matthew's reply. He stepped closer, allowing Matthew to rest his hand on his shoulder. They moved inside the busy station, walking slowly as the other passengers brushed and ran past them, trying to make their trains home. Matthew said nothing. Instead, he looked away, listening to the people around them.

"So why bring me here, are we going somewhere?" William asked as they walked together; Matthew swaying his cane out ahead of them as they walked, clearing the path through the crowds.

"Large crowds provide amazing privacy."

"They also come with a lot of surveillance cameras," replied William, looking around the station and counting half a dozen CCTV cameras as they walked.

"Feeling paranoid, Detective?" Matthew asked, leaning his head closer to William as they walked to better hear him over the surrounding crowd.

"Something like that," William answered, his head turning back and forth as they made their way up one side of the long station.

"Stop moving your head; it's hard to hear you and you're going to attract attention to us." Matthew's hand gripped William's shoulder tightly, giving him a firm tug to straighten him out. William snapped his head back and gave his shoulder a rough shrug to loosen Matthew's grip.

"We already have plenty of attention."

"Nothing I can't handle."

"Oh yes, you really proved that to me," replied William sarcastically. "The way you handled that beating and then disappeared, leaving me to fight that psycho on my own."

"You're still standing, aren't you?" asked Matthew.

"Yes, well, things got more complicated while you went off to get a new suit."

"Don't you like it?" asked Matthew with the smallest of smirks, "The last one had a bug problem."

"I didn't know you had a sense of humour?" said William, almost tripping over his own feet as he looked across at Matthew.

"There's a lot you don't know about me."

"I thought you were a better fighter," said William, glad to finally have something to put Matthew down with. Matthew's grip on his shoulder became suddenly tight.

"What did you just say, Inspector?" he asked, stopping in his tracks. William had struck a nerve and he wasn't about to stop.

"You heard me," he replied, slipping out from under Matthew's grip, stepping in front of him and bringing his face close to Matthew's. They stood so close that their noses were almost touching in the middle of the crowded station. "I've seen some pretty amazing things from you today. But you took one hell of a beating today, all things considered."

"All things considered?" Matthew asked. His knuckles were white as he held his cane tightly.

"For a blind man, you can take a lot more than people who have eyesight ever could."

"What is your point?" asked Matthew, doing his best to keep his temper. Every word was pronounced clearly, slowly and dangerously.

"The way Berkant's son dealt with you back there was like watching a Heavyweight Champion take on a schoolboy." Matthew grabbed William's shirt pulling him roughly towards him so that their noses squashed against each other. Passing people gave curious glances, unsure whether or not to step in.

"Now you listen to me," Matthew said quietly, but with clear anger in his voice, "What happened back there was a one off. In case you don't remember, we had just been running through gunfire. Now as I see it." He paused, aware that what he just said might lead to a comment or eye roll from William. "Arif and his people are still at large, which tells me that you didn't exactly get a knockout either so why are you giving me shit?"

"I'm giving you shit, boy," continued William, holding Matthew's cane between them in case Matthew attempted to use it as a weapon, "because when I needed backup, you decided to run off and go pamper yourself while I took a beating and then got interrogated by someone from the Special Investigations Unit, who I am pretty sure are watching us right now.

"Before you came along, I was happy doing paperwork at my desk and planning my retirement. Now I'm running around London, being chased by one of the most dangerous organised crime gangs in the country with a blind murderer as my sidekick and guide. So I'm giving you shit because I am having a particularly bad day." He let go of Matthew's cane and brushed his hand roughly off his shirt, taking a small step back but keeping close enough to hear his voice over the large crowd and regular announcements. Matthew stood there, almost frozen and looking straight ahead of him. A look that William returned even though he knew Matthew couldn't see it. Matthew opened his mouth to speak but stopped himself. Looking away for a moment, he took a deep breath to calm himself.

"Okay, William. I am sorry you're not enjoying yourself." He began with a heavy tone of sarcasm to his voice. "But the last couple of days haven't exactly been peachy for me either. I want this to be over just as much as you do. Right now, you and I have a common goal and a common enemy. So as much as neither of us likes it, we're working together." He paused, reaching forward slowly and gently wiped his hand down William's shirt, smoothing it out. "We still have several hours to kill before the meeting with Zoe and her kidnapper, so let's go find somewhere to lay low and you can get cleaned up." He stepped beside William and placed his hand gently on his shoulder, sticking his cane out ahead of them. William let out a long deep sigh, resigning himself to this unlikely partnership. He stepped forward with Matthew as he guided him towards the exit of the station.

"So another one of your secret criminal hotels?" William asked as they walked towards the exit, walking against the incoming crowds.

"Not this time," replied Matthew. "So you say we're being watched?" he asked carefully, walking down the stone steps with William as they stepped into the cool evening air.

"Possibly," said William, looking around slowly and carefully, trying to spot anyone who looked suspicious.

"With us or against us?"

"I haven't decided yet."

*

Half an hour later, Matthew and William had checked into a nearby Premier Inn. They had risked additional CCTV exposure by quickly slipping into a Primark to get William a clean shirt, trousers, underwear and socks. They had gone up to their room quickly and Matthew had sent William straight to the bathroom to clean up. While William locked himself in the bathroom to have a hot shower and dress, Matthew made his way slowly around the bedroom. Feeling the surfaces with his hand to memorise its lay out. He made a mental note of all the objects laid out on the tables; the lamps, the phone, the remote control, the kettle and the box of condiments. Apart from the gun under his jacket, the metal kettle was the best weapon in case of a surprise attack.

Hoping it wouldn't come to using a kettle in a fight, he moved quickly over to the door of the room, grabbing a wooden chair as he went. He wedged the chair against the door as hard as he could and double checked the locks. Satisfied that no one could get in through the door, Matthew made his way back to the bed. From the bathroom he could hear the sound of splashing water as William used the shower. Matthew took off his glasses and rubbed his eyes slowly. His body felt stiff and bruised. He felt his shoulder pop as he stretched his arms above his head; he groaned and gently massaged the joint. Matthew fell back on the bed, relaxing his body. As he lay still, he took in all the sounds around him. William had turned off the water and was now getting dressed. Matthew could hear him rummaging through the paper shopping bag, picking out his new clothes. Matthew focused his listening as he lay on the bed, picking out certain sounds and noises from the hotel around him. He could hear distant doors closing, voices muffled through the walls and the sound of traffic passing outside in the busy London streets.

Eventually, William stepped out of the bathroom, almost tripping over the chair Matthew had wedged against the door to the room. He stepped around it and stopped as he saw Matthew lying back on the bed in an almost meditation-like state. Keeping his distance, he took a moment to observe him before giving the edge of the bed a gentle kick.

"Are you awake?" he asked. He had changed into a pair of black trousers and a simple white buttoned shirt. Matthew slowly opened his eyes, revealing their blank whiteness to William. As he slowly sat up, he picked up his glasses and returned them to his face.

"Just about. You smell much better," he said, turning his head in William's direction.

"Thanks." William ran a hand through his damp hair and crossed the room to the small armchair in the corner. The two men resumed their places from the previous hotel once again. "So what now?" he asked Matthew.

"We still have a couple of hours to kill. I suggest we get something to eat and rest up."

"I doubt they offer room service here."

"We better go out and get something to eat then," said Matthew, slowly getting to his feet. William moved faster, placing a hand on Matthew's shoulder, he pushed him back down into a sitting position on the edge of the bed.

"You stay here. I'll find somewhere quicker." William stepped around the bed, removed the chair from the door and undid all the locks. "I'll knock twice to let you know it's me."

"Don't worry, I'll smell it first." Rolling his eyes, William left the room, closing the door firmly behind him. Once the door was shut, Matthew moved swiftly across the room, replacing the wooden chair under the door handle as before, then making sure all the locks were secure. With the room to himself, Matthew returned to the bed to lie down in peace.

*

William stepped out into the cool city streets, slipping into the passing crowds quickly. He knew there was a fast-food restaurant around the corner at the end of the street and aimed to get a quick meal from there. As he walked down the street, he felt like every eye and CCTV camera was following him. Telling himself he was being overly paranoid, he moved on. Keeping his head down, he walked swiftly through the crowds, looking around now and again, searching for anyone who may potentially be following him.

William should listen to his instincts more. Across the road, sitting parked in a loading only bay, was Arif's black Land Rover. He was sitting in the front watching William walk down the street, his two-man team occupying the driver and rear passenger seats. All three of them watched William closely, noting where he had come from and making mental notes of where he was heading.

After his conversation with Charles, Arif had become even more focused. He had no concerns about the men he had left dead in the street or back at the hotel: they knew the risks of the job and they had no markings or ID, so the police would never be able to prove they worked for him. Arif was sitting silently in the front seat, considering his options. With his contact in the police holding him ransom, he had very few choices ahead of him. He didn't want to head back to base and talk to his father, but he had felt like he had no other choice.

As he'd prepared to instruct his driver to head back, he had seen them. Coming out of Waterloo station were Matthew and the old Police Detective; he couldn't believe his luck. He was ready to reach into his jacket to retrieve his gun to kill them both, right there and then in the street and be done with them. Common sense had prevailed.

Taking his hand out from inside his jacket, he had instructed the driver to keep the car going and slip into regular traffic. His driver had automatically sent the car in a loop around the street to pick them up again without being spotted. Keeping back at a two-car length, they followed the two men through the city streets to a small Premier Inn hotel. Their car parked up beside the pavement in a loading only bay, ignoring the dirty looks from passing pedestrians and shop owners, the three men had watched the Premier Inn in silence. Unmoving and undeterred, they had kept their eyes forward, looking for any sign of the men exiting their new base.

When William finally emerged, Arif sat up in his seat to attention. The old man was walking on the opposite side of the road towards them, looking around nonstop as he walked. *He really makes himself obvious,* thought Arif as he watched William make his way down the street.

"Follow him, see where he goes," he ordered a man in the back. His operative, Adam, slipped out the back-passenger door without question. He walked to the back of the car and then casually down the pavement, watching William across the road, keeping behind his line of sight. Whereas William stood out looking like a sore thumb as he walked down the street, Adam blended into the crowd, making himself practically invisible. He was able to move upstream through the oncoming crowd, slipping between them smoothly, without bumping into any of them.

At the end of the street, William turned left around the corner, twisting his body to avoid hitting a couple who were arguing as they walked towards him. Adam took the opportunity to get across the road to William's side unseen. Now shadowing William at a two-person distance, he followed him along the pavement, making sure to remain as inconspicuous as possible. As William slowed down, so did he. Pulling a packet of cigarettes and a lighter out of his pocket he stopped to light it; suspecting William was about to stop or enter a building, he needed an excuse to stop in the street. Glancing up as he took a long drag of his cigarette, savouring the nicotine as it hit his system, he saw William step into a fast-food establishment. *Food run,* Adam thought to himself as he leant against a wall, enjoying his cigarette while he pulled out his phone to text Arif with an update. He spent ten minutes outside smoking his cigarette and watching the pedestrians pass him by, keeping a close eye on the passing traffic as well, looking out for any police cars or patrolling constables.

As he flicked his cigarette butt to be swept away by the rush of passing vehicles, William walked out of the restaurant carrying a paper bag that smelled strongly of burgers and chips in one hand and two drinks in the other. He headed back in the direction of the hotel he had come from. Adam gave him a twenty second gap before joining the throng of passing pedestrians to follow at a safe distance. Adam blended into the crowd easily, keeping couples in front of him as he walked to hide his presence, in case William looked back, but keeping him in his sightline as he walked, maintaining that twenty second gap.

When the hotel came into view, Adam stepped away from the crowd and jogged across the road. He slipped into the back of the car. Closing the door firmly, he looked out through the tinted glass to watch William head back inside the hotel and out of sight.

"He's up there. Someone is with him. Two drinks, a large bag. Could be another detective."

"No," interjected Arif, still looking out the window towards the hotel. "He's up there with Matthew." He clenched his fist at the thought of Matthew so close to him.

"What do you want to do?" Adam asked, his gun already in his hand as he started attaching the suppressor.

"We should wait," Arif admitted reluctantly.

"Do you think they're meeting that other detective tonight?" Adam asked, resting his gun on his lap.

"Even if they're not, I bet they will be there." Arif turned to the driver. "Get Berkant on the phone. We need to update him." His driver pulled out his phone. Dialling Berkant's number, he waited for the dial tone before handing the phone over to Arif.

*

Matthew was on his feet before the second knock, gun in hand. He had smelt the burgers as soon as William had stepped out of the lift, but anyone could buy fast food and he needed to be careful. He moved silently to the door. Pressing his ear against the wood, he listened as best he could. Through the thick door he could make out heavy breathing. The smell of the food was stronger now, masking the smell of the hotel shower gel and shampoo that William had used earlier. Matthew held his gun tightly in his hand, pressing the end against the door at body level. If it was William, he'd make himself known. If it was an enemy, they'd make themselves known another way; the way that Matthew was used to; the way that involved violence and death.

So far, Matthew was still alive and the men and women who had attacked him in the past were dead. Today was going to be no different. Matthew took slow deep breaths, preparing himself for a potential attack. Keeping his gun pressed against the door, he took a step back, ready to move away quickly in case the door was kicked down.

"Will you open the door?" came William's annoyed voice. Matthew pulled the chair away with one hand as he held his gun in the other. He unlocked the door, opening it slowly, keeping his gun out of sight behind the door. William stepped inside quickly, pushing Matthew aside. "For goodness' sake, boy," he said gruffly, kicking the door shut behind him. He turned the locks and added the chain. "Put that away you idiot," he ordered seeing the gun in Matthew's hand.

"In my experience, you can never be too careful," replied Matthew, slipping the gun back into the shoulder holster. He followed William towards the bed where he was already unpacking the food.

"In your experience? I'm guessing I'd already be dead. Is that right?" William asked, taking a bite out of his own burger. He was more hungry than he realised and relished the taste of the thick meat.

"Were we not working together, you'd have been dead before you finished knocking on the door," answered Matthew. He sat down on the edge of the bed and moved his hand slowly to find one of the drinks. A straw already through the lid, he took a sip, grateful for the thirst-quenching liquid.

"I don't doubt that. What would you have done with my body?" William continued eating his burger, curious to know more about Matthew's workings. Matthew, however, was aware of the direction his questioning was going. Putting his cup down on the bed, he picked up a chip and took a bite.

"I trust that this conversation stays between us?" he asked.

"What do you mean?"

"William. Despite everything that's going on, you are still a detective and I, am—"

"A killer?" William interjected.

"Professional killer," Matthew corrected, "and that's my point. I answer that and you have more information to use on me when you try to arrest me once this is all over."

"Try to arrest you?" William asked, putting down his burger and picking up his own drink.

"I'm not exactly going to turn myself in," Matthew continued, "so I want your word that everything that is spoken between us while we hide up in this cheap hotel room, stays between us?"

William said nothing. Considering his options, he tapped his drink against Matthew's in a toast-like gesture. "Stays between us," he confirmed with a reluctant smile.

"Well, if I wanted to kill you, I'd have two options. One would be to shoot you through the door, probably through the viewing hole as it would give me cover by anyone passing by, or I open the door to pull you inside by surprise. Both have their pros and cons."

"What are they?" William asked with great interest.

"If I shoot you through the door, it takes you by surprise. You're dead without entering the room and I don't have to worry about a fight, pro. Con; I then have a body to pull inside and dispose of it as well as the potential blood stains, not to mention the brain and skull fragments to clean up. There's also a chance that someone may walk out of their room while I'm dragging your corpse inside. Then I'd have more bodies to deal with."

"You'd kill innocent bystanders?" William asked, his burger halfway to his mouth as he listened.

"I'd try not to. If someone were to see me pulling your body inside, I'd do what I could to subdue them before they raised an alarm. But if I had to, yes, I would kill them as well. Now, pulling you inside the room," he continued, unfazed by the confession of killing the innocent if needed, "I could wait by the door as I did when you came back, then quickly pull you inside. This does allow for more privacy, a quicker and cleaner kill. Taking you by surprise, I could choke you to death or stab you in the heart or throat. The downside though is that if I stumble or you're a better fighter than I give you credit for, which rarely, if at all happens, a fight would be inevitable. A fight in such a small space would create noise which could lead to the police being called and that would increase the chances of me being caught or even killed because I would be distracted by their arrival.

"So even if both scenarios are successful, there's still the matter of disposing of the body. Now, amateurs would try to make it look like a suicide, tie around the neck, cut the wrists etc and leave a hastily written note. That's sloppy and I don't do sloppy. A fake suicide can work, I have done it in the past long ago, but I'm better than that now. I'd leave you tucked up in bed dressed to look like you're asleep with the 'Do not disturb' sign on the door."

"You'd just leave the body in the bed for some poor cleaner to find?"

"Gives me time to clean up any evidence that I was in the room and make a slow and inconspicuous exit out of the building."

"And you've done that before, left a body that you killed tucked up in bed as if they were asleep?" William was both impressed and horrified by Matthew's story.

"Longest was three days before they were discovered in the room."

"Good God," William exclaimed.

Matthew said nothing and continued to eat his food, enjoying the effect he'd had on the experienced policeman. William looked away as he ate, feeling disgusted with himself more and more for sitting in such company. He was quickly losing his appetite; he tossed his remaining burger back into the paper bag with contempt. He stood up and began to pace back and forth across the room.

"Have I upset you?" Matthew asked nonchalantly, continuing to eat his food before picking at the remains of William's, feeling across the bed for the remaining chips.

"You just described killing a person as if you were telling me about your plans to decorate your living room," William said, keeping his voice low, aware that these weren't the thickest walls.

"Does death frighten you, Inspector?" Matthew asked. He moved his hand across the bed, searching for the napkins. He found one and began to clean his greasy fingers.

"I've had plenty of experience with death, Matthew. What I don't like is knowing that the man in front of me has been responsible for most of the unsolved murder cases in London. Worse still, he doesn't seem to care."

"I don't care, William," Matthew replied, shrugging. He paused to take a long sip of his drink, letting the cold fizzy liquid cool his throat before continuing, "What I do is a job. A job that I am extremely good at. Now if you can't get your head around that, then you're not going to survive the night. I will not kill you, unless I have to. But if we are in a situation where we have guns aimed at us, I don't want you thinking about how many people have died at my hand. If your concentration isn't on the matter at hand, you will die. So make your peace with what I do and then get your head together. We'll need to make a move soon and as much as I don't want to admit it, I could use a pair of eyes tonight."

William said nothing as he looked down at Matthew sitting on the bed. Running his fingers through his hair, he turned away and headed into the bathroom. He felt like he could throw up, but more than anything he needed to get away from Matthew. He gripped the basin with both hands, taking long deep breaths. As he calmed himself down, he looked at his reflection in the mirror and suddenly felt a hundred years older.

Chapter Thirteen

As night crept over the city, a cool breeze picked up, pushing the clouds swiftly across the sky and turning the moonlight into a flickering light bulb over London. The crowds in the centre grew bigger outside the theatres, bars and clubs as the late-night revellers began making their way home. The outskirts of the city became a quieter wasteland, their only occupants scattered rubbish and the occasional fox or rat scavenging for food.

Charles and Zoe stood on the roof of the bike mechanics, his arm wrapped tightly around her neck and shoulders, keeping her pressed against his chest and using her as a human shield. His gun was pressed firmly against her head with his finger on the trigger. He had woken her just over an hour ago. They had walked out together arm in arm: Zoe's handcuffed wrists were hidden under a coat and her hair was brushed forward to hide the bruises across her face. His gun was hidden under his own jacket and pressed into the side of her body. The walk through London had been slow and tense. Zoe knew better than to attempt an escape and had cooperated without argument. They stood in silence, facing the ladder entrance to the roof. The silence was only broken by the rustling trees overhead. At their feet sat the bag containing all of Zoe's collected evidence and files of information.

Eventually, the sounds of feet against metal cracked the tense silence around them. Zoe looked towards the ladder that led to the roof. As the steps grew louder, a pair of hands appeared at the top, followed by William's cautious head. He stopped as his eye line came over the top and he froze at the scene before him. Below him, he felt Matthew's hand hold his ankle gently. The two men had agreed cues before arriving and Mathew knew to drop down if William moved his leg in a certain way. For a moment, all the codes and planning he and Matthew had done evacuated William's brain. He was still trying to process the sight before him; his old trusted friend, holding his protégé with a gun to her head. He shook his head, clearing his thoughts and reminding himself why he was there. Tapping his foot once against the rung of the ladder, he felt Matthew release his grip and continued to climb up and onto the roof. Keeping his distance, he stood still facing Charles and Zoe, his eyes slowly moving around the roof, trying to spot any additional gunmen. He felt Matthew step down onto the roof and brush against him as they stood shoulder to shoulder.

"Two people?" Matthew asked quietly, out of the corner of his mouth.

"One gunman, one hostage. That I can see," replied William, doing his best to hide his amazement at Matthew's analysis.

"Let's move slowly," Matthew advised. He placed his hand on William's shoulder. The pair of them walked slowly across the dirty roof towards Charles and Zoe.

"Evening, William," Charles called across to them as he tightened his grip around Zoe. "Doing some charity work?" William felt Matthew's hand tense up on his shoulder as they stopped two arms lengths away from Charles and his hostage.

"What do you call this then, Charles?" William asked as he brushed Matthew's hand off his shoulder.

"Insurance," Charles answered back, giving Zoe a small shake as he pressed the gun harder against her temple.

"Insurance? We're all on the same side, Charles."

"There are no sides, William. We're nothing more than cowboys out for hire to the highest bidder."

"We're officers of the law, Charles," William called out, doing his best to control his anger.

"He's not," Charles responded, with a nod of his head towards the silent Matthew.

"Maybe not, but out of the two of you, I'd trust him more. How long has this been going on for?"

"Long enough, William. Like I said, out for the highest bidder. It's amazing how much people will pay to get information I don't have access to."

"You son of a bitch!" shouted William. "You've been forcing my people to do your dirty work, haven't you?"

"Nothing that incriminates them William, calm down," said Charles, with an air of boredom to his voice. "I've always enjoyed pulling rank on the young 'uns. Something I think you've enjoyed with this one," he added giving Zoe a hard squeeze with his big arm.

William said nothing, but moved towards Charles ready to strike, his anger taking over his senses. Matthew grabbed his arm quickly, just as Charles turned his gun towards William.

"Ah, ah, stay where you are," he ordered, keeping a tight grip on Zoe now that his weapon was turned away from her. William froze mid step, seeing the barrel of the gun facing him and with Matthew's hand holding him tightly. "Now, that's better," continued Charles, returning the gun to Zoe's head.

"What do you want?" Matthew asked, keeping his hand on William's arm.

"I think it's best if you stay out of this and let the grown-ups talk," retorted Charles, not even looking towards Matthew.

"You're the one who needs to talk. Explain yourself," said William, shaking himself free of Matthew's grip.

"I'm just being realistic, William. The lines between criminals and the innocent are becoming more blurred by the day. Children 'borrow' their parents' debit cards to buy ridiculous accessories for computer characters everyday but we don't arrest them, do we? Thousands of people download movies illegally every day because cinema prices are too high. People commit crimes every day."

"Those are nothing more than petty crimes: you've committed a kidnapping today as well as God knows what else?" William called back. "You can't compare yourself to children who don't know any better. You're supposed to know better."

"Like I said, the lines are becoming blurry. They accused me of being a criminal back home when I'd done nothing wrong. I was nothing more than a scapegoat for those cunts covering their own arses for their mistakes. I made a choice after that and since I moved here, I realised something. We've been fighting a war we're never going to win, William. Criminals like your blind friend are beating us every day."

"If you can't beat them, join them?" asked William through clenched teeth.

"Something like that."

"So what happens now?"

"Now?" asked Charles with a careless shrug. "We wait. I'm pretty sure I've been followed by Berkant's people. They thought they could cut me out, but now I've brought them everything they need plus a few extras. We wait for them to show up and give me what is mine."

"What's that? A bullet in the head?" asked Matthew. He turned his head to the left slightly, listening and smelling his surroundings. The mention of

Berkant's name had put him on alert, the hairs on the back of his neck stood on end. He tried to attract William's attention by brushing his hand against his arm, certain they were being watched. Charles suddenly pointed the gun towards Matthew, his own anger starting to rise.

"You'll be the one with the bullet in the head if you don't keep your mouth shut. We wouldn't be in this mess if it wasn't for you."

"Good thing you're a terrible shot," Matthew replied. Charles kept the gun aimed at Matthew's calm face.

"Care to find out how good a shot I am from this distance?"

Zoe had her chance. With the gun pointed away from her head and Charles' anger drawing his focus away from her, she had to take her opportunity or miss it completely. In one fluid movement, she stamped her heel as hard as she could onto his foot, while simultaneously reaching behind her and dragging her nails down his face, retracing the wounds she had left earlier. The combined pain in his foot and face caused Charles to roar with pain. As Zoe struggled to free herself from his grip, she pushed his arm up into the air as he pulled the trigger. The gunshot exploded into the night air, echoing off the surrounding buildings.

William hit the floor, crashing to his front and ducking out of sight of any further gunfire. Matthew ducked and rolled forwards, towards the sounds of Zoe and Charles struggling. The echoing gunfire masking them for a moment and causing him to stumble as he got to his feet. Shaking his head to focus the sound, he rushed forwards to help Zoe.

She was trying to free herself from Charles' grip. She had managed to slip under his arm, but he had caught her hair and was pulling her back firmly. She kicked and punched him in his stomach and face but he held on tightly, yanking her back roughly. He turned the gun towards her ready to kill her there and then. Matthew ran across the roof towards them. Everything felt as though it was moving in slow motion, but his mind was on fast forward. Moving across the roof, he planned where he would strike Charles to free Zoe whilst disarming him safely at the same time. He had barely taken his second step when another gunshot shouted out, causing him to freeze.

He'd been caught off guard: was Zoe dead? Matthew regained his composure and began to run forward again. Matthew had barely gone two paces towards the sounds of struggling breath, when he felt a body slam into him. The force of his attacker sent him crashing to the ground onto his back. His instincts on high alert, Matthew prepared to defend himself.

"Stay down! There's a shooter!" Zoe shouted into his face as she landed on his chest.

"Get off me! Move!" Matthew shouted back, pushing Zoe as hard as he could off of him. Zoe rolled across the roof looking back at Charles who had dropped to his knees. During their struggle, the bullet from the mystery shooter had gone straight through his throat, sending blood all over Zoe's face as she escaped out of his tight grasp. While he choked and gasped, his blood gushing from his throat, Zoe had rushed forward to get Matthew out of the line of fire. Rolling across the roof, Zoe watched Charles fall to the floor as the last breaths of life left him. Now on his knees, he looked at her as he slowly fell to one side. He landed on top of the bag of evidence, his final breaths gargling out of the new hole in his throat before silencing as his deceased body lay still in a pool of his warm, spreading blood, soaking the bag and its contents underneath him.

Zoe started to get to her feet, along with Matthew. She grabbed his hand and pulled him forward as they ran across the roof towards William, who had already started to make his way to the ladder.

"Come on!" he shouted as he climbed onto the edge ready to climb down. Zoe and Matthew reached the ladder as William swung his leg up and over and began to descend. William stepped onto the first rung as Zoe reached up to join him on the ladder.

A shot rang out across the air. Zoe ducked her head instinctively as the gunshot screamed against her ears. Feeling no bullet hit her, she looked up to continue climbing up the ladder. She looked up just in time to see William fall from view over the roof.

"No!" she screamed. She looked down to see William lying still on the dirty wet concrete, a pool of blood growing beneath him. Zoe threw herself over the edge of the building in one fluid movement. Grabbing the sides of the ladder with her hands and feet, she slid down quickly to the ground leaving Matthew at the top. Another shot rang through the air as she slid out of view: she felt the wind of the passing bullet just miss her head as she sped down the ladder to the ground below.

With the wall of the building shielding her, Zoe rushed to William's twitching body. A bullet wound on his chest was ejecting blood at a steady rate and a pool of red was growing behind his head from his landing. Zoe knelt beside her fallen mentor, running her hands over his chest to try and somehow stop the bleeding. Over her panicked breaths, she heard Matthew land behind her after he had slid down the ladder as well.

"Help me," she said, turning back to him. "Please help me!"

Keeping low in case the shooter could still see them, Matthew stepped closer to the two police officers and knelt beside Zoe. Like her, he ran his hands slowly over William's body, feeling his wet shirt drenched in blood and eventually finding the bullet wound. His blood-soaked hands rested on William's chest, Matthew felt the rise and fall of his chest and his heartbeat beginning to decrease.

"There's nothing we can do for him," he said, simply sitting back and wiping his hands on a handkerchief he had pulled out of his suit pocket.

"Fuck you! We have to do something. We need to get him to a hospital."

"He'll be dead before we make it to the street. If we try to move him, we risk causing further blood loss or damage to his body. Plus, we could become exposed to the shooter carrying him and then we're all dead. I'm sorry, Zoe, we can't do anything for him."

Tears began to roll down Zoe's cheeks. Suddenly, she felt more vulnerable and alone than she ever had in her life. The closest person she had left in her life to a family member was dying in front of her and there was nothing she could do about it. She clung to William's shirt as her close friend passed away before her eyes.

"We need to go," said Matthew, reaching out to place his hand on Zoe's shoulder, pulling her gently.

"No, no we can't." She choked, doing her best to hold back the tears and emotions ready to burst out of her like a broken damn. William's shaking hands reached out to meet hers. Their blood-soaked hands held onto each other tightly, William's breath became choked and bloody as he coughed. He pulled Zoe closer to him as he felt his life begin to leave him.

"Admiral's...arms," he whispered to her, his hands became weaker and slipped away to his side. Zoe couldn't speak, the grief washed over as she began to break down even more. As she fell across her friend and began to cry, Matthew stepped away. Her sobs were distracting and the shooter wasn't finished. He listened as best as he could, trying to pick up any sounds of danger, but Zoe's cries of anguish were too loud. They had to get away. He stepped back towards her and grabbed her shoulder, pulling her away. She shook him off and returned to William's lifeless body.

"We have to go."

"Go then! If they want to come and finish me off, they can," Zoe replied, holding on to William's jacket even tighter than before. Matthew had had enough. Gripping her arm tightly, he pulled her away roughly, dragging her to her feet. She fought him off as best she could, hitting out at him and trying to release his grip as he staggered and dragged her away from William's corpse.

"Get off me. Get the fuck off me!" she shouted as she did her best to fight herself free of Matthew's grip, but he wouldn't let go.

"Shut up, will you? I can't concentrate," he ordered, doing his best to remember his steps back away from the building, all the while expecting a bullet to hit his head any second. They made slow progress up the road that led back to the main street. Matthew constantly having to tug and pull Zoe as she continued to fight him. A small breeze ruffled his hair, the air cool against his face. They were getting closer to the main road now, which meant they were more exposed. Could their shooter see them from here? Matthew didn't want to find out.

"Car?" he demanded of Zoe, turning his head towards her, doing his best to listen over her nonstop obscenities aimed in his direction. She raised her hand to slap his face. Matthew felt her body move and anticipated the strike. As she swung at him, he caught her by her wrist. Pushing her arm away, he struck her across her face with the back of his own hand. "Do not make me have to do that again," he said. The danger is his voice was cold and clear. "Car?" he repeated.

Ignoring the pain in her cheek, Zoe looked around for a getaway car. Matthew's slap seemed to have knocked some sense into her and awoken her from the trance of grief that had swept over her. She turned her head left and right looking for a vehicle, she spotted one down the road to her right.

"There's a motorbike half a metre across the road to our right. A one two five," she explained. Matthew didn't have time to curse their lack of options. A shot was fired. The sound of the bullet exploding from the rifle filled the air as it narrowly missed the pair of them. Zoe didn't need telling twice, grabbing Matthew's arm she began to run across the road, zigzagging slightly to avoid any more gunfire. Matthew matched her speed and did his best to move with her as she dodged left and right. More gunfire followed them across the road towards the bike; each bullet missing them by centimetres. Matthew knew their luck wouldn't last forever. Zoe led him behind the bike to give them some small cover from their shooter. It was a small bike; a baby racer, a mostly plastic body covering a small one-cylinder engine sat on two thin tyres.

"The shots came from behind us, at your two o'clock. At least three stories up, judging by the angle they're missing us," Zoe explained as she ripped away the plastic cover around the handlebars, exposing the wiring around the ignition. Matthew nodded, pulling his gun from under his jacket. He turned his body, aiming his gun in the direction Zoe described and letting off three quick shots. The suppressor on the weapon, covering the sound of each shot, helped Matthew to listen for a confirmed kill or return fire. After the third shot, he ducked back behind the bike next to Zoe who was striking two wires against each other with one hand while the other pressed the bike's electric starter button.

"How are you doing?" he asked, keeping low behind the bike as a shot hit its headlamp, sending glass and plastic across the pavement. The engine kicking into life answered his question, Zoe kept twisting the throttle to warm the engine and keep it running.

"There's a chain on the wheel," she called over the screeching engine. Matthew handed her his gun; it would be quicker for her to take the shot than for him to search for it himself and risk being shot. Zoe took the weapon, lined up her shot and fired. The small padlock broke away at the impact of the bullet. Keeping behind the bike, she reached out and pulled the remaining chain away out of the wheel so they could ride away. "Ready?" she asked, pressing the gun into Matthew's hand as she prepared to climb onto the bike. Another shot was fired, taking out one of the front indicators. Matthew leapt up and let off two more shots in quick succession as Zoe threw her leg over the seat and kicked the bike into first gear. Matthew grabbed her shoulder and took his place on the passenger seat. As Zoe twisted the throttle hard, he wrapped one arm around her waist and fired the remaining bullets, emptying his gun's cartridge, shooting in the direction of their attacker.

Sirens began to fill the air, there were no more shots but Matthew knew they weren't out of trouble yet. Zoe's hair whipped his face as she pushed the small bike as fast as it could, moving through the gears quickly and keeping the throttle open. Matthew tried to pinpoint the direction the sirens were coming from, but the bikes high pitched engine made it difficult to hear anything else.

"Can you see the police?" he shouted at the back of her head.

"No, but we're being followed," she replied, glancing in the remaining cracked wing mirror and spotting the headlights of a large SUV growing larger as it got closer. The black vehicle was much faster than the small bike and was closing the gap between them quickly.

Matthew tightened his grip on her waist as she pushed the bike to its limit, weaving between the few cars still on the road at this time of night. Horns blared and brakes squealed as the metal monster behind them stalked its prey. The little engine screamed in protest as Zoe pushed it as much as she could. Her thighs gripped the tiny body of the bike hard, her knuckles white as she held on for dear life. The traffic began to thin, leaving the roads empty for Zoe to weave the bike as much as she dared to avoid the gunshots issuing from their pursuers' side windows. Matthew held on to her waist harder, his fingers pressing into her stomach as he felt the bike rush across the road.

The car was almost within touching distance now, the noise of its engine drowned out the sound of the tiny bike. Holding on to Zoe's waist with a vice-like grip, Matthew strained his ears to make out any other sounds over the roaring engines. Apart from the obvious fact that he hadn't yet been shot in the back, Matthew noticed that the sound of gunfire had stopped.

"They're going to try to run us off the road!" he shouted in Zoe's ear. As she checked the mirror, the car hit the back of the bike, causing it to bounce and nearly topple over. Zoe gripped the handlebars tighter, preparing for a second shove from the black tank behind her. The car rammed them again, harder this time. Zoe had to slam her feet down onto the road to keep the bike upright. Her teeth bared, Zoe swerved the bike off the road and onto the pavement. The front wheel hit the curb at speed, forcing it into the air and nearly sending Matthew off the back as he was unprepared for the sudden change in direction and elevation.

"Let me know next time you're going to do that!"

"Shut up!" Zoe shouted back.

Parked cars blocked them from view of the chasing car so Zoe chanced a look across at them. The windows were rolling down and guns held in outstretched arms took aim at them once more.

"Keep your head down!" Zoe called back at Matthew as she bent down over the handlebars. She felt Matthew follow her down, pressing his chest into her back. Bullets flew at them once again. On the pavement, they were harder to avoid. Matthew felt bullets whip past him, narrowly missing his head and body. If they didn't get away soon, they were finished.

"We need to get away, cut across them!" Matthew called, his face pressed against Zoe's cheek, keeping them both as low as possible to hide behind the parked cars as they raced through the empty night streets.

"We'll be crushed!" Zoe shouted back, stealing another look at the pursuing car.

"We'll be shot to pieces if we don't!" Matthew shouted back, feeling another bullet fly past him.

Over the roar of the engines and constant gunfire, Matthew picked up a new sound; police sirens. Matthew cursed to himself. Either the police picked up the chase straight from the mechanics or someone had made a call to report the sounds of speeding vehicles and gunfire.

"Next opening, cut across the road to the other side. We need to get away before the police get involved!" Matthew ordered. He moved away from her as much as he dared to give her space to prepare to turn the bike.

Zoe looked ahead, searching for a gap in the parked cars along the pavement. She didn't have to look far, up ahead was a stretch of road with double yellow lines. There would be no cars to protect them from the bullets and it would be easier for the car to crush them.

"Hold on!" she called, her fingers twitching against the handlebars, preparing to send the bike into a sudden turn. She felt Matthew's hands tighten against her and his body press into her back again.

The last parked car was level with them. As the rear end passed her, Zoe threw the bike hard back into the road. The bike bounced off the pavement onto the tarmac, making the two riders bounce on the seat. As she sent the stolen bike across the road like a rocket, she looked over her shoulder at the black car. The driver had seen the opening the parking restrictions had offered and had clearly thought of mounting the pavement with the intention of attempting to run them over. As Zoe turned into the road, the car turned towards the pavement, the two vehicles cut across one another at high speed. She had taken the turn too quickly. As the bike hit the road, it slipped out from under them. The bike dropped too quickly for either of its two riders to react. Zoe and Matthew hit the road, both shouting out in fear and pain as their bodies slammed into the road, sliding and rolling as the bike bounced away from them, the plastic body disintegrating and sparks flying off the exposed metal work.

The front of the chasing car had passed the rear wheel of the bike, missing it by inches before it had sped away. The car was travelling too fast for the driver to change course. Turning the car at high speed and the surprise of the bike cutting across him had caught the driver off guard. He tried to correct the car's direction which caused it to swerve dangerously left and right across the road. It was too much for the heavy vehicle. As the driver fought to get it under control, the car tipped over and began to flip and roll down the road.

The crashing car bounced over the now stationary bodies of Matthew and Zoe. Matthew heard the fast approaching sound of crunching metal and flattened his body on the road as best he could, reaching out and trying to find Zoe to get her to do the same. The car crashed over him; he felt broken glass, plastic and metal rain down on him as the car passed over his body. He lay on the road on his back, catching his breath as he followed the sound of the crashing car moving away from him.

His body ached all over, the fall from the bike had left him battered and bruised. He quickly assessed his body. He couldn't feel any new breaks but his chest was hurting even more now. He wriggled his toes quickly, then slowly pulled himself into a sitting position. He ached all over. The car had stopped rolling and had come to rest somewhere down the road. Matthew knew that they had to move since the occupants of the car could still be alive and have some fight left in them. He and Zoe, however, were unarmed and the police sirens were getting closer.

"Zoe!" he called out, slowly getting to his feet. "Zoe?" he called again when she didn't answer. He couldn't hear her. He slowly got to his feet and stumbled when his injured legs gave way under him. Matthew managed to get back up and stayed on his feet, turning his head left and right, spinning around in the road trying to find her. A groan cut through the approaching sirens, Matthew turned in the direction of Zoe's voice and moved his aching body towards her. "Zoe?"

"Right here," she groaned, reaching out her hand towards Matthew as he got closer. They found each other; Matthew took Zoe's hand, holding it tightly as he helped her slowly to her feet.

"Can you walk?" he asked.

"Just about. Can you?" She could see the extent of Matthew's injuries from the crash. His suit was torn and dirty and she could see fresh cuts and wounds on his arms and legs from where he had rolled across the road.

"I'll be fine," he replied, his concern growing that it would only be a matter of minutes before the police arrived.

"I hope so," replied Zoe, looking down the road at the wrecked SUV. "I think our friends might not be so lucky."

"I'd rather not be around to find out. We need to leave here now."

"Do you know anywhere safe we can go?"

Matthew ran his mind through the city of London, thinking of the various hide outs and establishments he had used in the past to avoid capture or arrest. None of them felt safe anymore.

"Possibly," was all he said. Taking her arm, he let her lead him away from the wreckage splashed across the road. The two of them limped into the dark side streets, out of sight, as the blue lights of the approaching police cars lit up the street.

Chapter Fourteen

Arif's eyes snapped open at the sound of the sirens. He took in his surroundings slowly; his body was aching all over. He was in the front passenger seat of the car that had been chasing Matthew and Zoe and he was now upside down in his seat, held in place by his seatbelt. Broken glass littered the roof below him. He looked across to the driver: he was dead. Although the airbag had deployed, the crash had caused too much damage and he now hung upside down in a blood covered mess like meat in a slaughterhouse.

Slowly looking into the back of the car, Arif saw that his other accomplice was alive but unconscious, his limp body lying on the wrecked ceiling with his arms and legs at unnatural angles. Arif didn't have time to check how badly injured he was, he couldn't be around when the police arrived, regardless of his father's connections. He released his seat belt with one hand and caught himself with the other to stop his body slamming onto the glass covered surface below him. Arif slowly crawled out of the shattered window, doing his best not to cut himself further on the broken glass and jagged metal. Getting to his feet slowly, he cursed Matthew silently to himself. He didn't have time to dwell on his anger long for the first police car was almost on him.

Quickly reaching back into the wrecked car, he found his gun and efficiently put a bullet through the head of the rear passenger. Arif couldn't risk anyone talking. Stepping back from the car, he looked back down the road. The police were slowing down as they came upon the wreckage. Arif moved as fast as he could away from the scene and into the shadows, pulling out his phone as he did, calling his people to arrange a pickup.

*

Matthew and Zoe made slow progress through the dark streets. They kept to as many back streets and alleyways as they could to avoid the few passing night-time drivers and any other late-night walkers. Zoe led the way, keeping Matthew informed of the street names as they walked. Matthew's grip on Zoe's arm was beginning to get tighter. She looked across at him as they walked and realised he was hunched over, his free hand clutching his stomach where a pool of blood was spreading across his shirt.

"Jesus, you've been shot!" she exclaimed, stopping in her tracks to inspect his wound.

"Please don't bring him into this. It's nothing," he said as casually as he could, trying to push her hands away and keep walking. Zoe slapped his hands away from hers. Bending down, she carefully opened his shirt to see where the bullet had hit him. Blood was spilling out of his stomach, soaking his skin and clothes.

"How much blood have you lost? You can barely stand," she said, pressing his hand back against the wound to apply pressure.

"I'll be fine," Matthew replied sternly. His impatience and annoyance growing with each passing second, they stood in the middle of the street. He felt exposed, anyone could be watching them right now.

"You're not fine, you're bleeding out. You need to see a doctor."

"We can't go to a doctor. Doctors ask questions. Questions mean the police and the police mean Berkant." Matthew tried to step away from her to try and keep moving. He didn't have a set destination in his head yet but moving felt better than standing still. His blood loss was beginning to get to him though and he swayed on his feet, losing his balance as he tried to move. Zoe grabbed him, wrapping his arms around her shoulder to support him.

"If you won't see a doctor, what do you expect me to do? Should I let you bleed to death then spend the night dragging your corpse through London?" She demanded angrily. Matthew stopped in his tracks. She was right, he was losing blood, he was injured, weak and no good to her or himself in this state. Over his career, he'd been shot many times but then had access to Berkant's private doctors who would patch him up without a second thought. Now he had no such luxuries.

"We need to move," he said, coming to a decision. He let her support him as they began to continue their midnight walk. "I know a place that might help us," was all he told her as they made their way slowly up the street.

*

Thomas Foy walked slowly away from the mechanics which was now swarming with police and forensic teams who were investigating every inch of the crime scene. William's body was still on the ground, surrounded by several officers, some taking notes and photos while the rest were talking to each other quietly or looking down at the long-serving, respected officer.

Thomas looked back at the scene, over his shoulder, before leaving it for good. No one had paid him too much attention and he preferred it that way. This was a real mess. Two inspectors dead, one crooked, the other murdered. On top of that, the undercover was still missing, presumably with a wanted killer and most likely being hunted by one of the most dangerous criminal organisations in the country. He slipped away unnoticed, hidden under his jacket was a blood-soaked bag full of incriminating evidence. As he made his way back to his car, a black Audi parked alone, away from all the flashing lights of the police cars and ambulances, he patted his coat pockets, searching for his cigarettes. Finding the crumpled packet in his inside pocket, he pulled it out slowly. His last one.

"It's been a long day," he said to himself as he placed the white stick between his lips, cupping his hands around his silver zippo lighter. He took his time with the first drag, savouring the flavour as the smoke filled his lungs. Exhaling slowly, Thomas climbed into his car and placed the bloody bag in the footwell of the passenger seat. He pulled his car key out of his pocket and slipped it into the ignition in one quick smooth movement. The engine kicked into life and Thomas pulled away, putting as much distance between himself and the chaos behind him as he could.

As he moved into the city streets, with no clear destination in mind, he touched the car's dashboard, pressing the phone button and bringing up his contact list. There were only a handful of numbers saved to his phone and the one he needed was at the top of his list. Pressing the call button on the steering wheel, he only had to wait two rings before the call was answered by his superior.

"What happened?" asked a hard, cold voice. The man on the other end sounded tired and frustrated.

"It's a mess, sir," Thomas replied, keeping his eyes on the road, one hand occasionally tipping ash from his cigarette out the window.

"As we suspected?"

"It appears Inspector Blaine was working with his undercover and the blind man."

"And the other?" The man sounded bored with the conversation already, as if he knew the answers before he asked.

"Bought out by Berkant's people and a massive chip on his shoulder, looks like he may have killed Blaine before he was taken out by one of Berkant's gang. There was a gun fight and it looks like Zoe and the hitman escaped but were followed. I arrived on the scene before the local police so I have the evidence they've all been fighting over."

"That's a start. You will find these people, won't you?"

"Yes, sir," Thomas replied. It was asked as a question, but he knew it was an order.

"I know you will. Keep us posted. Try and get the undercover out first. Berkant and his people are expendable but try and bring them alive if you can."

"And the blind man, sir?"

"If you can't kill a man who can't see, then perhaps you're not as good as I thought."

The line went dead. Thomas flicked the stub of his cigarette out the window and pressed his foot to the floor of his car, sending the speedometer up as he began to form his next move.

*

Matthew and Zoe had been walking for twenty minutes. The only words between them were Matthew asking the street names and Zoe confirming them. He told her nothing of their destination, instead focusing on his wound. His free hand was pressed against his body, trying to stem the flow of blood. His other arm was wrapped around Zoe's shoulder to let her support him as they moved at a slow pace.

"How much further?" Zoe asked him, concerned that he might pass out at any moment, but equally, if not more concerned that any number of Berkant's people could appear and start a fight they couldn't win.

"Nearly there," Matthew grunted. He hated feeling like this; weak, exposed and needing someone's help. To be in this situation was a first for him. Hopefully it would be the last. The street they walked along was mapping out in his mind as they drew closer. He knew they would be there soon but whether they would receive any help was another question. Zoe led him around the corner and onto a street the same as any other they had walked down. On the opposite side of the road was a large factory building, the gates locked with a rusting chain and padlock. Clearly it had shut down many years before. On their side of the road, a few houses. Some had boarded windows and others were smashed. Towards the end of the road, some of the homes showed signs that people still lived inside. At the end of the street was a house larger than the rest, as if three houses had been converted into one.

"Last one on the left," was Matthew's only instruction. He was beginning to get weaker now. His hand was stained red with his blood, his clothes drenched. He was slowing down now, Zoe had to pull harder with each step as they moved towards their final destination.

"What is this place?" she asked, her grip tightening around his body as they walked. Matthew ignored her, instead focusing his attention on staying conscious. They approached the building slowly, all the windows were in darkness except for two on the ground floor either side of the door. Zoe was almost dragging Matthew as they reached the door. He reached up with his free hand and knocked twice. While they waited for an answer, Zoe noticed the small stone plaque on the wall next to the front door with one simple word, 'Orphanage'.

"This is where you grew up, isn't it?"

Matthew nodded in reply. He was ready to pass out. He could just make out the sound of approaching footsteps. His legs gave as he heard the door open and barely registered the gasp of shock before he passed out, landing at Zoe's feet.

Chapter Fifteen

Matthew could hear voices. They sounded distant and almost incomprehensible, as if they were speaking another language. He was lying down on a soft bed. His body felt stiff and tight. He twitched his fingers, feeling the rough cotton against his skin. He knew he'd been undressed. Matthew moved the fingers of his hand that lay on his chest and felt the many layers of bandages and medical wrappings over his bullet wound and other injuries.

The voices were getting louder and becoming clearer, more into focus for him now. There were two voices, both of them female. One was Zoe but the other he couldn't quite place. They were arguing about something, the tones of concern and anger filling the room, echoing off the walls and increasing Matthew's headache. He wanted to rub his head, a dull pain was growing in his temple thanks to the mixture of his injuries and the loud voices either side of him. He attempted to lift his arm, but more pain shot through his body like a current, making him wince with a sharp intake of breath between his teeth. He must have caught the attention of those around him. Their voices stopped and he felt his mattress shift as someone sat on the bed next to him.

"Matthew, are you okay?" Zoe asked, placing her hand next to his. Her cool fingers brushed against his skin. Matthew was surprised at how much he found himself appreciating her being there with him.

"Where am I?" he asked, turning his head left and right, trying to listen for clues.

"You're home," replied a stern, authoritative voice. A voice Matthew hadn't heard for many years. His memory was rebooting slowly and the voice brought back old memories from a different life. A life he had left behind long ago. He was beginning to question his decision to come here.

"You've been unconscious for just over an hour now," said Zoe.

"What brought you back here then?" asked the other woman's voice. Her contempt towards Matthew was obvious with every word she spoke.

"We needed a safe place to lay low and get him fixed up. Like I said to you earlier, Matthew thought this would be a good place for us."

"I'm starting to regret that thought," Matthew chimed in, slowly sitting up. His body throbbed all over as he moved, begging him to stay still.

"What are you doing? Sit down." Zoe's hands pressed against his shoulders, unintentionally inflicting more pain on him as she tried to keep him on his back. He brushed her hands away and pulled himself in a sitting position on the bed.

"I'm not going anywhere," he explained through gritted teeth, as more daggers of pain stabbed his body.

"You still haven't answered my question?" The stern voice seemed to command the room with each syllable.

"You're still alive?" asked Matthew wishing more than ever he had a stiff drink in his hand.

"More than you are by the looks of it, Matthew," she replied. She moved around the bed to his other side. Matthew followed the footsteps as she walked closer to him.

"I'm sorry to fall on your doorstep like this. But under the circumstances, I needed a place that no one would expect me to go to."

"What circumstances might those be?"

"The kind that if they find us, they will kill us, Mrs Wilkinson." Her name said with just as much bitterness and contempt as her voice when she spoke his.

"So I can see you two used to get along like a house of fire," said Zoe, looking back between them.

Neither replied to her. The tension between them took over the room like a tsunami of resentment and hatred. Zoe looked from one to the other, feeling more and more with each passing second that she wanted to be anywhere but here. She turned to Mrs Wilkinson.

"I am sorry to bring you into this mess, but we had no other option." She looked into the elderly woman's eyes, hoping to find a trace of pity. The returned look was as cold and unreadable as a champion poker player's. The tall slim woman before her gave away nothing. Professional in her work, she was a woman whom you could tell commanded respect and inspired fear with just one look. She paused before speaking, clearly choosing her words carefully.

"I have no doubt about that. From what has reached my ears, this one,"—she nodded her head towards Matthew—"has been nothing but trouble since he was

157

taken from us. I will keep an eye on him. But what are you planning on doing next? Moving in permanently?"

"Not bloody likely," Matthew said to himself but his words were not missed by his former matron.

"I need to go and find a place called the Admiral's Arms. I'm guessing it's a pub," Zoe explained, remembering the words of her now deceased mentor. Just the thought of him made her want to lash out and cry. She swallowed her grief, needing to stay strong. The thought of him lying dead on the concrete cut into her like a razor blade. She fought against the wave of grief that wanted to consume her, telling herself that there would be time for mourning later.

"Why there?" Matthew asked, inclining his head towards her slowly.

"William told me to go there before he died."

"I'm sure he said a lot of things, but you can't go out wandering the city looking for one random pub. Berkant will have his people everywhere looking for you."

"I don't hear you coming up with any better ideas. I don't need you. If anything, having you is holding me back."

"If it wasn't for me, you'd have been killed back when I first found you," Matthew retorted, attempting to get out of bed. Mrs Wilkinson stepped forward and pushed him back against the white pillow with one hand. Leaving her hand against his bandaged chest, she looked across the bed at Zoe. If any of this conversation confused or shocked her, she didn't let it show. She stood still, one hand against Matthew, the other resting against her hip. Her eyes bore into Zoe's as if reading her mind. It made Zoe feel exposed, almost naked. She folded her arms across her chest.

"Whatever is going on with the two of you, I don't need to know. I don't want to know. Frankly, for the safety of the children here and myself, the less I know the better." She removed her hand from Matthew and slowly made her way past the end of the bed and towards the door. "If you need to go somewhere, then go in the morning. From the looks of both of you, you've been through hell tonight. You will get some rest, eat something and then be on your way."

Neither Matthew nor Zoe spoke. Mrs Wilkinson stepped out into the dark corridor, beckoning Zoe to follow her. Zoe didn't speak to Matthew but as she stepped away, she gently brushed her fingertips against his bare arm. Without looking back, she stepped out of the room and followed her new chaperone.

Arif waited on the pavement at the agreed meeting spot. His body was aching in several places. He had checked for broken bones when he had fled the car and so far, he seemed okay. He slowly and gently stretched his right arm, lifting it over his head; his shoulder felt like it needed to 'pop'. He continued to lift and twist his arm, trying to achieve the necessary sensation of moving the air locked between his joints.

He heard a car approaching in the distance. Turning around he looked down the dark road. It was one of his father's; a black SUV, headlights blaring, blinding him. The car was approaching at speed. He slowly moved his arm, his hand moving towards the gun tucked into the back of his jeans. A new sensation of fear gripped him for a moment, had something changed? The black car screeched to a halt in front of him. Before he could reach out for the door handle, the passenger door was flung open with such force Arif was almost knocked backwards.

Berkant stepped out. Standing over his son, a look of fury to rival the devil himself on his face. He had left his jacket in the car. The sleeves of his shirt were rolled up to his elbows, revealing the thick black hair that covered his arms. He'd undone the top button of his white shirt, loosening his tie. He slammed the car door closed behind him as he looked into his son's eyes with such intensity that Arif was sure that fire would shoot out at any second, but he did not look away.

"I like to think of myself as a patient man," Berkant began, making sure to choose his words carefully before speaking, "but this little adventure has gone on long enough. We should have been out by now, heading home, halfway across Europe. Instead, because of your incompetence, we are now running around London like a group of amateurs. If you had just done what I had told you to do the first time—"

"Sir, I can explain," Arif began but Berkant slapped his face with the back of his large hand; the force of his strike sending Arif to the floor. Blood was flowing out of the corner of his mouth. He wiped it away with his hand, looking up at his father. The far side doors of the car opened and both Arif and Berkant listened to the sounds of footsteps walking around. Two bodyguards appeared and stood either side of Berkant, looking down at Arif.

"We are going to correct this. I thought you could handle this alone, but once again you need me to step in and tidy up your mistakes. Perhaps you'll never be ready to lead our organisation when I'm gone. We will find Matthew and his new friend and any other loose ends you may have created."

Arif didn't speak. Resting on his elbow, looking up at his father and the bodyguards. He kept looking up into Berkant's eyes, determined not to break eye contact.

"Do you have anything to say?" Berkant asked him.

"No, sir," Arif replied.

"No, you don't." Berkant raised his hand. A large combat knife was placed in his palm by the silent, obedient bodyguard on his right. He knelt in front of his son, holding his face with one hand and forcing Arif to open his mouth. Arif grabbed his father's hand with both his own. The bodyguards swept down on either side of Berkant, silently grabbing Arif's hands and legs with pincer-like grips to pull them away. "You'll never disobey me again," Berkant said gently. He slid the knife into his son's mouth. Arif's legs kicked out and he screamed as much as he could with a knife severing his tongue.

His father's strong hand held his face in place as he attempted to make the cut as clean as possible. The strong guards to his left and right helped keep Arif in place as Berkant slid the knife through Arif's mouth. As quickly as it had started, it was over. Berkant pulled out the severed tongue and tossed it onto the road in front of his car. He and his bodyguards released Arif.

As they rose to their feet, he rolled on to his stomach clutching his face, his bleeding mouth open in an agonising scream. Berkant gently kicked him over onto his back, wiping his hands with a white handkerchief from his pocket. He dropped the bloody handkerchief onto his mutilated son and climbed back into the car.

"Tidy him up and let's go."

Chapter Sixteen

Zoe sat at one end of a long, well-scrubbed, wooden table. A single light bulb hung over the centre of the table as she held her hands together, resting them in front of herself. Mrs Wilkinson moved smoothly around the dark kitchen. Soon a plate appeared in front of Zoe; sliced bread, some cheese, ham and an apple.

"It's not much but it's the best I could do at this time of night," the formidable woman informed Zoe. She stepped out of the light for a moment and returned with two cups of coffee. She placed one next to Zoe's plate and then took the seat across the table from her. Zoe took a sip from her cup; the coffee was as black as tar and strong enough to power a jet engine. She drank and ate gratefully, tearing apart the bread and gulping down the scolding coffee. Her last meal felt like a lifetime ago.

"Would it not be safer for you to go to the police?" Mrs Wilkinson asked, her own coffee cup held in both hands. In reply, Zoe shook her head, her mouth currently full of food.

"I am the police," she said eventually, "we don't know who we can trust."

"Why haven't you arrested him then?" Mrs Wilkinson asked, nodding towards the door they both came through.

"Perhaps I will when this is all over?" Zoe shrugged. "He's saved my life several times since we met."

"Matthew saving lives instead of taking them?" Mrs Wilkinson commented scornfully.

Once again, Zoe focused her attention on her food before speaking again. Mrs Wilkinson didn't seem to mind the silence. She sat very still, watching Zoe, only moving to sip her coffee.

"Did something happen when he was a child here?"

"Nothing at all. For a boy born without sight, he did as well as he could growing up. It was what happened to him after he left."

"Berkant?" asked Zoe and Mrs Wilkinson nodded.

"That man took that child and turned him into a monster. He started to refuse the social worker check-ups and after a while, they stopped wanting to go. We were told they were threatened with violence against themselves and their families."

"Why didn't you get the police involved?" Zoe asked in an almost mocking tone, fully aware of the answer. Mrs Wilkinson knew this by the look on her face and ignored the question.

"I hired a private investigator. He observed Berkant and his people from a distance. He sent me reports in the post every month telling me what they were doing to Matthew: training him to be a thief, then a bodyguard and then finally, a killer. These reports stopped though. I never heard from the PI again. I assumed Berkant or someone in his organisation became aware of his watching and scared him off."

"Just scared him?" Zoe asked sceptically.

"Scared him off," Mrs Wilkinson confirmed, perhaps more to herself than to Zoe. She took another sip of her coffee, "There are some things that happen to us in life that are better left unknown."

"I'm going to get him." The determination in Zoe's eyes was clear. Her coffee, food and the conversation with Mrs Wilkinson seemed to have lit a fire inside her and she felt the energy flood through her veins.

"Now do you mean, 'get him' as in bring him to justice? Or 'get him' in the other way?"

"Does it matter?" shrugged Zoe, pushing her now empty plate away from her on the table, eager to get going.

"It does." The elderly woman carefully put her cup down and looked straight into Zoe's eyes once more. "These people are criminals. You and I both know the things they have done. Do they deserve to die? Maybe, maybe not. It is not our place to decide that. But it is your place—" she pointed a finger towards Zoe's chest—"to have them locked up for their crimes."

"But the system doesn't always work. We know that Berkant has corrupted people inside every law enforcement office in the city. He may not even spend a single day in prison."

"Then you must do whatever you feel is right for you." Mrs Wilkinson rose to her feet. Collecting the empty coffee cups and plate, she took them over to a white sink behind where she had sat, placing them inside it to be cleaned later. "I cannot stop you from doing what you want to do. I will go and sleep in my study down the hall from Matthew's room. If you need any more food or drink, help yourself. I will check on Matthew in a while, but for now he needs to rest."

She left without another word, looking straight ahead as she did and leaving Zoe alone in the kitchen, sitting in silence which was broken only by the occasional car driving past the building and the dripping of the tap over the sink. Zoe struggled with the internal debate going on inside her head. She knew what her job required her to do, what she should do. But after what she had seen and been through over the last day, what Mrs Wilkinson had told her about Matthew and what had happened to him over the years, she felt that death was a more fitting punishment to Berkant's crimes.

*

The drive in Berkant's car had been a silent one, apart from the sounds of Arif's treatment. Berkant had sat in the front passenger seat next to his driver and in the back, his two bodyguards had begun their work on Arif's severed tongue. The back seats had been removed to create more space in the rear half of the large SUV. Arif had been laid on his back and one of the two men had intubated him while the second prepared to seal the wound and control the bleeding. The driver kept the car ride smooth as possible, to better aid them with their work.

They had given no pain killers to Arif for the repairs and as he lay there, he clenched his hands tight and did his best not to cry out in pain as the remains of his tongue were sealed shut. His two, would-be paramedics showed no emotion as they worked on him; they had their orders and that was enough. Berkant looked ahead in his seat, giving his son's medical treatment as much thought as he would to swatting a fly. He didn't need his son to speak; he needed him to listen.

Eventually the two bodyguards knelt up, peeling off their surgical gloves. One of them caught Berkant's eye in the rear-view mirror and nodded, signalling their work was done. Berkant looked away, satisfied with their work. Arif remained on his back, his hands by his sides and doing his best not to show any weakness in front of his father or his men. His thoughts quickly shifted from resentment to revenge towards his father for what he had just done to him. His grief and anger swirling and transforming rapidly in his mind like a mutating virus. He had his role, he had his job and he had his orders. But now, having had the ability to speak ripped from him, he began to question whether his loyalty should remain where it is.

As Berkant's car had sped away in a cloud of swirling exhaust fumes and dust, a cigarette butt flicked out from the shadows, bounced once on the wet tarmac and landed on the mangled remains of Arif's tongue. The still lit tip of the cigarette extinguished by the residue of blood and saliva. Thomas slowly stepped forwards out of the shadows of his hiding spot in a side street. Turning his head as he walked, his eyes followed the direction of the speeding car. He had been lucky in coming across this family spat; an almost forgotten tracker, that had been placed in Berkant's car by a now deceased informant, had proved useful. Thomas had taken a gamble on the route Berkant's driver might have taken and it had paid off.

Thomas nudged the remains of Arif's tongue with his foot while putting a new cigarette in his mouth. Cupping his hands around the tip and his lighter he slowly breathed the murderous smoke into his lungs, savouring the flavour and intoxication that only a cigarette can provide. Standing in the deserted road, the only sounds of distant cars and a dog barking, Thomas processed what he had just seen and debated with himself whether or not this would be worth reporting to his superiors. Shaking his head. He turned back towards his car hidden in the shadows. This news could wait. No one would be surprised that Berkant had punished his son in such a way. Many would be more surprised he hadn't done it sooner. What this meant for the dynamics of their relationship was what intrigued Thomas more.

Would Arif keep showing the same unfaltering loyalty that he has for so many years? Or would this be the straw that finally broke the camel's back? As smoke curled away from the end of his cigarette, flowing from between his lips and nostrils, Thomas considered his next move. Berkant was getting nervous, that much was clear. But he wasn't the type of man to be rash and make mistakes. He was focused, calculated and even now, as his empire began to collapse around him, he would still have planned several steps ahead on the chess board that was London, to make his successful exit.

His cigarette almost finished; Thomas looked down at the bloody, useless flesh that was once a strong muscle in Arif's mouth. Following Berkant might be his best option, but it could also lead to a false trail. Finding the blind man should really be his top priority, but finding him was proving harder than expected.

He removed the burnt-out cigarette from his mouth and dropped it to the floor, stepping on it as he walked back towards his car. His options were few and equally dangerous. Enemies and potential allies were being killed and mutilated on both sides and Thomas wanted to be alive when this was all over.

Starting the engine of his car, he decided to follow Berkant for now. Even though it might lead him nowhere, it meant that he was moving and moving, even if you're not sure it's in the right direction, is better than standing still. He set off, accelerating the car quickly to close the gap between himself and Berkant.

As the car light disappeared around the bend in the road, a watchful fox slipped silently from a nearby bush, sniffing around the floor. It followed the scent of blood and found what it was looking for. Its nose inspected the fleshy mess before scooping it up in its mouth and darting away to its hideaway to enjoy its evening meal.

*

Zoe walked out of the front door of the orphanage without speaking to Matthew. She felt it best to let him rest and she was sure that he would try to come with her if she told him she was leaving. She moved slowly along the pavement, her paranoia keeping her on full alert as she was sure she was being watched.

At the end of the street was a lone parked car. Walking at a quick pace, she made it to the car without being attacked. The car was not in the best condition: rusted along the edges; a cracked windscreen and missing one of its wing mirrors. Zoe tried the door and wasn't surprised to find that it was unlocked. Taking this car was surely doing the owner a favour she thought to herself as she sat behind the wheel. Leaning forward, she exposed the ignition wires and it only took her a moment to start the engine.

Out of her pocket she pulled out the smart phone she had 'borrowed' from Mrs Wilkinson, she planned to return it to her, at some point. A quick online search revealed there were half a dozen different bars in the greater London area with the name Admiral's Arms. Tired and frustrated, Zoe hit the steering wheel with her clenched fist just once. After one long deep breath, inhaled and then exhaled, she felt ready to begin her search.

Without looking back down the street, she pulled away quickly, heading towards the city in search of the Admiral's Arms pub. The roads were deserted, apart from an occasional fox or stray dog. She was alone. She glanced at the phone on the passenger seat showing the address of her first destination. Her knowledge of London's streets and criminal haunts had been honed and developed over the years she had worked in the police and undercover in the criminal underworld.

The city looked like something out of an apocalypse movie at this time of night: near empty streets, apart from the occasional drunken reveller or wandering tramp; abandoned cars with broken windows, stripped of anything of value; dark and deserted buildings with boarded up windows and coated in years of graffiti. She needed sleep, she needed more food but what she wanted more were answers. Why had the last words of her mentor been the name of a random pub? Who or what was waiting for her there that could be of any use to her? William was dead and so was Charles. She had left all the evidence and information she'd been collecting behind on the roof. For all she knew Berkant, or someone who worked for him, had already collected it. She had nothing.

She struck out hard against the roof of the car in frustration. Cursing her situation, she pulled the car over with a violent swerve. Zoe felt trapped. She rolled down the window, letting the cool night air rush over her. It didn't help. She felt hot, constricted and a wave of grief poured over her like a tidal wave of emotion. She slammed her head onto the steering wheel, then again and again harder each time. She didn't know how to feel. Tears began to pour down her face as she tried to punish herself for William's death, wanting to crack her skull open.

Zoe hadn't cried like this in years; her body shook as she gave in to her emotions and let the grief consume her. Nothing mattered to her anymore and she wanted all of this to end. Zoe had dealt with death so many times, but this was different. William had been like a father to her and had guided her throughout most of her career. He had always been there for her when she was undercover, being a familiar voice and trusted confidant during times of stress and loneliness. Now, with him gone, she felt more alone than she ever had in her whole life.

Her eyes shut tight; flashes of William appeared before her. These slowly faded and were replaced with Matthew, Charles and Berkant. The events of the last forty plus hours rushing through her mind. Zoe snapped her head up, suddenly feeling focused. All sadness and grief evaporated in an instant and was replaced with one feeling; revenge. She fired the car back into life and slammed her foot against the accelerator as she thrust the car into gear. She wanted Berkant. More than that, she wanted his head on a silver platter and she was now feeling more determined than ever to get it.

Chapter Seventeen

Matthew sat bolt upright as if a gun had gone off next to his head. His senses were on full alert. Slowing his breathing down, he slowly turned his head from side to side to listen for any sounds of an intruder in his room. He remembered where he was and that he should be alone, but he wasn't. The scratchy white sheet slipped to his waist, exposing his bare chest. Matthew carefully placed his hands on his legs over the sheet, ready to strike if he needed to.

Whoever was in the room with him was just as silent as him, he couldn't hear any movement, so either they were standing still and watching him, or they could move as quietly as a ghost. He sniffed the air, hoping for a scent to pick up on: aftershave, perfume, cigarettes or the lingering smell of their last meal. Nothing. He was at a disadvantage here: no weapons, in an unfamiliar room and with an unknown presence before him.

His options were limited at best. He could throw himself out of his bed to the floor and wait for the attack, but without knowing where this person was, he could be shot or stabbed before he'd gathered his surroundings. If he was quick enough, which he was sure he was, he could roll under the bed – hoping for some cover while his attacker gave away his position.

His fingertips brushed the cotton under them. It was time to move. He took a slow inhale of breath, he would move to his left, once on the floor he'd get under the bed, wait, then throw it up as best as he could towards whoever was in the room with him. As his fingers tightened around the sheets to throw them off him, the presence made itself known; four paws landed softly by his side, making him jump slightly. The cat started purring loudly as it brushed its head against his hand, seeking some attention.

"Jesus," he exclaimed, using all his self-control not to smack the cat away. Sighing, he caressed the cat's soft fur over its head gently, giving in to its demands. He didn't know how long he'd been asleep, but it had been enough. Ignoring the cat's meows of protest, he climbed out of the bed. After standing still for a moment, he reached out; one hand rested on the bed, the other searched around for his other surroundings, a wall, a table, something.

"Going so soon?"

Matthew stopped in his tracks; he had been hoping to avoid another talk with his old mistress.

"I felt I had overstayed my welcome."

"Well, I'm not going to lie, your presence would probably bring more trouble here than I need." Mrs Wilkinson stood in the doorway, arms folded.

"I'll be on my way then. Where are my clothes?" He ran his hand along the edge of the bed, feeling for the suit he was wearing when he arrived.

"Two steps forward, on the chair to your left." Her clear, concise instructions brought back memories from his childhood and he couldn't stop the smirk slipping across his lips. His hands found his clothes hanging over the back of a chair.

"Thank you for folding them."

"I ironed them as well. I'm afraid I didn't have time to wash them, there aren't many dry cleaners open at this hour." Although her voice was tinged with sarcasm, there was some warmth to it.

"You've done more than enough."

"I'll let you get dressed and then I assume you'll be leaving?"

"I will, yes. You won't see me again." Matthew carefully lifted his jacket off the chair and moved it to the bed. Turning back, he picked up his shirt and began to pull it on.

"Be careful, Matthew, whatever it is you end up doing. You'll be in my prayers."

*

Aaron looked out onto the dark street as he prepared to lock the doors of his pub. Something felt different tonight. There was a tension in the air that he was sure meant trouble for him. He closed the door firmly and locked the dead bolts.

Aaron moved quickly behind his bar. From underneath he pulled out his semi-automatic twelve-gauge combat shotgun, a memento from a previous life. His eyes slowly swept across his bar, looking over to the frosted windows for a sign of life outside. He slowly thumbed shells into his weapon; he hoped that he wouldn't need it tonight, but he had a strong feeling that he would.

A distant sound distracted him from his weapon; a car was approaching from the far end of the street. Nothing unusual Aaron thought, cars pass by all the time. Still, he was cautious. Aaron made his way around the bar and over towards the door, his shotgun held tightly in both hands. Headlights illuminated the entire pub as the vehicle came to a halt outside. The lights cut out, leaving the bar lit only by the few lamps Aaron hadn't yet turned off. A car door slammed and hurried footsteps approached before fists pounded on the door. Aaron moved slowly and carefully, his eyes sweeping across the windows as he held his weapon by his side with one hand. The pounding continued on the doors. One hand tightened its grip on his gun, while the other unlocked the door, slowly.

"We're closed," he called out over the noise of the drumming fists as he pulled the door open enough to get a look at the drunken reveller. The fists stopped attacking his door, allowing him to get a look at his uninvited guest. There was a manic glint in her eyes, overflowing with determination and urgency. She wasn't like the usual clientele of the Admiral's Arms; she was younger, stronger and sober. Aaron kept the shotgun out of sight as he looked into her fiery eyes. "Come back tomorrow when we're open if you want a drink."

"Is this your place?" she demanded looking over his shoulder into the dark pub. Aaron, in return, looked over her head, seeing the run-down car abandoned across the pavement.

"It might be. Who wants to know?"

"Did you know William Blaine?"

Aaron's hand tightened even more around his gun. He adjusted his hand slightly so as ready to move the weapon into a firing position if he so needed because William's name was usually followed by trouble.

"Who are you, girl?"

"A friend. I was. He told me to come here." She paused, looking into the weathered eyes before her and sizing him up, debating whether or not she was at the right place. "Well, he told me to come to The Admiral's Arms."

Sighing, Aaron rolled his eyes and opened the door enough for the girl to slip inside. She passed by him quickly, without a second glance at the car she had arrived in. Aaron didn't give the car a second look either as he quickly scanned the dark street before closing the door with a snap.

The door closed and locked, Aaron turned around to face his uninvited guest. She had moved to the bar, keeping at least an arm's length away from him; it wasn't hard to miss the large gun in his hand. He looked into her eyes and hers bore right back into his. There was a fire inside her that was burning hotter than hell itself. She was dangerous and she wasn't afraid of him.

"Who are you then?" he asked again, resting his weapon in both hands with the barrel pointed at the ground, relaxed but ready to be raised and fired in a heartbeat.

"I'm Zoe, Zoe Garland. I work for the police." Although tense, she kept her arms by her side. She was unarmed, having lost her weapon in the crash earlier. she was out gunned in her current situation, but confident in her speed over the old man if she had to get out of his line of fire.

"I've no time for any more of your lot," Aaron replied, never taking his eyes away from hers. "William, he's all right, but the rest of you bring nothin' but trouble. So tell me lass, why did he send you here to do his dirty work?"

"He's dead."

It took Aaron a moment to process those two words. His hands weakened around the gun for a moment as he looked at her. Although he and William weren't close, deep down he'd still considered him a friend.

"I'm sorry to hear that. I really am. But why has he sent you here? I won't be holding the wake here if that's what you're thinking?"

"I don't know why he told me to come here but he did. Has he told you something about a case? Did you two work together or something?" Zoe nodded towards the gun in his hands. He held it comfortably; he was clearly familiar with it.

"Actually, he arrested me. He used to come by now and again for a drink and ask me to spy on m'customers." The bitterness in his voice couldn't be hidden.

"Anything recently?" Although this was the right place, Zoe could feel her frustration growing. This man had no information that was useful to her. He shook his head, she could see his grip tightening around the gun.

"Just asking about some dodgy colleague who was having a meeting out back."

"A meeting about Berkant?"

She'd hit a nerve. For a moment, she was certain he was about to ready the weapon and aim it at her. There was a dangerous flash across his eyes at the mention of that name.

"Say that cunt's name in my pub again, lass and I'll drop you."

Finally, she might be getting somewhere. She eyed the weapon again, then looked back at him.

"We have a common enemy then."

"Don't make us friends."

"I don't need friends. I need Berkant dead and all his friends buried in a hole with him. A few days ago, I'd ask you to tell me what you know and what you've heard so I could build the case and have him arrested and put away by the book. But after the things I've been through and watching my friend and mentor die in front of me, I couldn't care less anymore. Prison is too good for Berkant. Hell, a bullet to the head is too good for that prick! So please, either help me find him and kill him, or give me that gun and let me find him myself."

They stared each other down, the ex-con and the ex-cop. Nothing more than strangers, but now suddenly united in their joint hatred of a man who had affected them both at some point in their lives. No words passed between them, but an understanding quickly formed.

Aaron opened his mouth, preparing to speak, but he was silenced. The bar was lit up by sweeping car lights that stopped outside, illuminating the both of them. They heard several car doors slam.

"I get the feeling you won't have to look very far." The gruff barman cocked the weapon, the first round thrust into the chamber. "Behind the bar. Keep out of sight," he ordered, taking control of the situation as a polite knock rapped against the frosted glass in the door. Zoe didn't argue. Silently, she ducked down and slipped behind the bar, grabbing a discarded corkscrew as she went. As she hid out of sight, the bar tool in her hand, she heard her new ally take a deep breath, his heavy footsteps the only sound after that as he moved back towards his door.

Aaron had the sense that trouble was on the other side of the door, so he made no effort to hide his gun. Undoing the dead bolts, he opened the door slowly, stepping into the doorway to block any attempt to step inside, his large bulky frame creating a barrier. Aaron was greeted with an equally large and just as strong man; Berkant. He looked into Aaron's eyes with a small smile on his lips. Aaron felt his blood boil as he looked back.

"The fuck you doin' here?" Aaron raised the gun, pointing it straight into Berkant's face. His two bodyguards were quick to the draw, guns raised, pointing over Berkant's shoulders and aiming right back at Aaron. Berkant hadn't flinched as the gun was aimed right between his eyes. From this close range the gun wouldn't just take his head off, it would be obliterated.

Aaron held his weapon tightly, looking at Berkant, then to the two guns either side of him held by his two bodyguards. Both men were tall, large and clearly very strong. Behind all three men, hanging back, was the fourth member of their team. Aaron recognised Berkant's son, Arif. He stood back away from the others, no weapon raised but still looking just as dangerous. By the light of a streetlamp, Aaron could see his chin and neck were stained with dry blood.

"Good evening, Aaron," said Berkant, speaking normally, as if shotguns were pointed at his face every day. "It's been a long time."

"Not long enough. Get away from my pub and take your cronies with you."

"I'm afraid I can't leave just yet. I have a few loose ends I need to tie up before I leave."

"Oh aye? Loose ends, eh? 'Fraid you and I have no business to discuss. Fifteen years I went away because of you, so why would I have anything you need? Fuck off."

*

Matthew made slow progress once he had left his childhood home. Although he knew where he was and could plot a route in his head, he had no idea where he should be going and his body was still sore and bruised from the crash earlier. He felt moving was better than just standing still so he kept walking with no clear direction in mind. Cursing to himself; he clenched his fists as he walked at a swift pace, feeling the need to hit something or someone. He turned left at the end of his current street and made a plan to head back towards the centre of the city. He may not find Zoe or the bar she was so desperate to find, but he might run into one of Berkant's men and take out his pent-up frustration on them.

As he continued in his new direction, he heard a car glide past him in the night, the first car he had heard in a while. He thought nothing of it until he heard the car suddenly stop and begin to reverse back towards him. This was it: he'd finally been found by Berkant or one of his people. Matthew stopped and prepared himself for the fight. His senses on alert, he listened closely as the car came to a halt in front of him. Only one car door opened. He was surprised but that would make this easier.

"Matthew Bartimaus?" came an unfamiliar voice. Matthew froze. Who was this stranger and how did they know his full name?

"Who are you?" he asked. He didn't feel like confirming anything about himself until he was sure who he was dealing with. He kept listening out for other footsteps or vehicles in case of a surprise ambush.

"I'm Special Agent Thomas Foy." Thomas instinctively reached into his jacket for his card but, remembering who he was dealing with, thought better against the pointless gesture.

"More police! I seem to be a magnet for you. Are you taking me in?" Matthew didn't have any plans to be arrested, but after the last couple of days he was starting to consider whether or not prison was worse than dealing with all these people.

"Not tonight no, Matthew. Luckily for you, I'm asking for your help."

"Lucky for you you're not trying to arrest me," Matthew replied with a casual shrug.

"Perhaps. But for now, you and I have a … common goal, shall we say? And I don't think you're doing much good wandering around the streets of London by yourself."

"Who are you?" Matthew asked. He couldn't decide whether he liked this person or not. He seemed to know more than Matthew liked, but he was keeping his cards as close to his chest as he could.

"I'm just someone trying to put away the bad guys, nothing more. If it means I have to work with other bad guys, I don't mind. Just as long as someone goes to prison."

"I have no intention of sending Berkant to prison."

"Neither do I." Thomas turned away from Matthew and walked back to his car, "Get in and I can take you where you need to go." He didn't wait for a reply. Closing his car door as he climbed in, he fired up the engine and looked at Matthew through the passenger window.

*

Outside the Admiral's Arms, Berkant calmly placed his palm on the end of the gun and gently pushed against it as he stepped forward into the bar. Aaron didn't pull the trigger, nor did he resist Berkant. Stepping backwards, he kept the gun raised, watching Berkant and his two men step inside, spreading out either side around their boss, their guns still aimed at him. The tension and silence that filled the room could only have been cut with a diamond. Nobody spoke. Zoe, hid behind the bar and hardly dared breathe lest she gave herself away.

Berkant made the first move. With speed like that of a Cobra striking, he snatched at Aaron's gun, pushing it out of his face and grabbing it with both hands. As the weapon was forced away from his target, Aaron fired a round. The gun went off like a cannon hitting a wall across the bar, shattering several glasses and bottles along the way.

Berkant hadn't flinched or loosened his grip as the gun discharged. Instead, his two hands tightened around the weapon even more as he fought against Aaron to get it out of his hands. Aaron quickly recovered from the shock of Berkant's attack and his hands gripped around both ends of the weapon. Berkant forced him back against the wall, both men growling like grizzly bears as they wrestled each other for the gun.

Although taken by surprise by the gun going off, Berkant's two guards recovered quickly. They had not fired their own guns, they knew better than to do that; Berkant could handle himself. They kept their eyes on their boss and his adversary, weapons raised ready to strike if needed.

Zoe slowly looked out over the bar, she had had to duck and cover a moment earlier when Aaron's gun had gone off as the exploding bar had sent shards of glass raining down over her. Aaron and Berkant were still fighting each other for control of the shotgun and Berkant's men were too focused on them to notice her.

She took her chance. She threw herself over the bar. While she was in the air, she launched a pint glass at the head of the nearest heavy. She hit her target. The glass burst against the bald head, blood mixing with the broken pieces of glass as he fell to the floor, clutching his wound and crying out in surprise and pain. The second turned to see the cause of his partner's cry.

Zoe was on him in a flash; she was running at him as soon as her feet had hit the floor. Charging at the second guard, while the other hit the deck, she leapt at him, raising her right knee and striking him in the chest. As her kneecap crashed into his body, she heard several ribs crack from the impact. Their bodies went straight into the wall behind him. As his head cracked against the faded picture hung on the wall, Zoe drove the corkscrew in her hand into his neck.

She was like a deranged animal, as the semi-conscious body slid down the wall to the floor, she continued to strike his neck and face with the makeshift weapon. Her hand became a blur as she thrust the silver tool in and out of his flesh. His blood poured and spurted out of his body as the strikes rained down on him, soaking his face, clothes and Zoe. She didn't relent, her grief for William and her anger at his death were fuelling her rage as she did everything she could to kill this man.

To Zoe's right, Berkant and Aaron were still fighting: neither would relinquish the weapon. Aaron pushed back against Berkant, forcing his back against the bar. Berkant retaliated with a hard headbutt to Aaron's face. The pain made Aaron cry out as his head was split open, blood slowly flowing down his forehead and his nose. He didn't loosen his grip though, he kicked down at Berkant's leg, forcing him below him as he fell to one knee. Berkant roared up into his face as he got himself back to his feet quickly to continue this fight.

Zoe was so overcome with blood lust that she had forgotten about the first heavy she had hit with the pint glass. She hadn't stopped stabbing the second with the corkscrew; there was nothing left of his face except a bloody pulp of torn flesh and muscle. Her head was yanked back with such force her neck could have been broken. Her first target had recovered and had started his attack.

His bloody hands grabbing her hair, he pulled her off his deceased partner and flung her into the door of the bar, sending her crashing out onto the street with such force that one of the door's hinges gave way, leaving the door barely hanging on by the other. Berkant's bodyguard crashed through the door after her, causing the remaining hinge to give way. The door crashed out onto the street, the glass shattering against the pavement. His face was covered in blood and full of a rage that few had ever survived.

He towered over Zoe like a murderous gorilla, wiping the blood out of his eye with the back of his hairy hand. Zoe was on all fours, coughing and choking after being thrown like a rag doll through the door. From inside the bar, she could hear Berkant and Aaron crashing around as stools and tables were knocked aside and more bottles and glasses were broken. She didn't have time to recover. A dark shadow fell over her; looking up she saw her attacker.

Zoe tried to stab his foot with the corkscrew, but to no avail. He was wearing steel capped boots. He kicked her hand away easily then sent a much harder kick into her stomach. She was lifted off the ground and onto her back from the force of the kick. Clutching her stomach, she cried out in pain and curled into a ball, holding herself tightly. Two giant hands grabbed her by her jacket, pulled her to her feet and then lifted her off the floor. He grabbed and held her face with one hand and slammed his head against her nose, breaking it instantly and causing blood to gush out of her nostrils. She couldn't speak. He struck her again, knocking out a tooth. He threw her down to the floor where she landed on her back.

Through her blurry eyes, she saw him walk back through the broken door into the bar, perhaps to help Berkant? She wiped her face, feeling the warm blood on the back of her hand. She spat the blood and the broken tooth out of her mouth. The sound of heavy footsteps caught her attention: the gorilla was returning. In his hand was his pistol. He had gone inside to get the gun he had dropped when the pint glass had hit him.

He pressed his large heavy foot against her chest and pushed her onto her back. Her hands grabbed at his boot weakly to try and force him off her, but she was pinned down. He looked down at her. She looked so small and helpless to him right now that he felt he could simply crush her like an insect under his boot. This was too easy for him. Looking away from her for a moment, he noticed the *mute*, Berkant's son. He hadn't moved since he had stepped out of the car. The gorilla gave Arif a contemptuous look and tossed the gun to him.

"Make yourself useful," he said, pressing his foot harder into Zoe's chest. Arif caught the gun easily in one hand. He looked from the bloody girl on the floor, back to the bloody bodyguard standing over her, crushing her with his boot. The beaten mess on the floor looked back up at him as he held the gun. She had taken a beating but there was still a fire in her eyes. She hadn't given up and she wouldn't stop fighting until she was dead.

Arif raised the gun, taking aim at her head. From this distance, he could easily hit her right between the eyes. She looked at him, her fierce eyes boring into his, daring him to pull the trigger. Arif changed targets, moving as fast as his father. He pointed his gun at the towering beast standing over the girl and fired. The bullet passed through the centre of his forehead killing him instantly. The heavy body fell backwards to the floor in a heap, freeing the shocked girl on the floor.

Arif turned the gun quickly towards the car where Berkant's loyal driver sat frozen in surprise. Arif fired another round, catching the driver in the head and killing him instantly, sending blood across the driver's side windows.

Arif tossed the gun aside, feeling a small sense of retribution at the death of the man who had helped his father cut out his tongue. His revenge accomplished; he turned his attention to the undercover cop on the floor. She had been a thorn in his side for too long and he finally had his chance to end her.

Zoe rolled over into her knees, coughing as she spat her blood onto the floor. Wiping her mouth, she looked up at Arif, wary of him and what he had just done. Was he helping her? Had something happened between him and his father?

Slowly getting to her feet, she didn't take her eyes off him. Her whole body was sore, but she didn't want to show any weakness in front of Arif. He just stood there, silently watching her as she stood up, staring back at him. From inside the bar, came the sounds of the two giant men fighting and crashing around the pub: their roars of rage mixed with the destructive sounds of furniture and glass bottles being destroyed as they attempted to kill each other.

Never taking his eyes off Zoe, Arif gestured with his hand, signalling for her to take her time and catch her breath. He took his jacket off and tossed it onto the bonnet of his father's car. Zoe was up, she shook her head to clear her senses, Arif nodded and prepared himself for what was to come.

Zoe raised her fists, gently bouncing on the balls of her feet, she moved closer, ready to fight. She attacked with her right, fist aiming for his jaw. Arif was quick to block and countered with a strike to her stomach; Zoe tensed as best as she could, gritting her teeth against the force of the blow. She grabbed his arm with both her hands and landed a strike with her forehead on his nose, breaking it. Arif struck her cheek with his elbow, and they broke apart.

Neither paused to recover, each threw punches and kicks, doing all they could to connect, but the other could always block or counter where needed. Arif was slowly gaining an advantage, Zoe was still hurt from her earlier encounter and it was starting to show. Arif trapped her hand under his arm and rained down several blows onto her head, swinging his fist over his own with every blow. Each hit had a devastating effect on Zoe: her eye and bottom lip were becoming swollen, large bruises were discolouring her face and more blood was flowing freely from her wounds.

Arif dropped her to the floor after the fifth blow, she collapsed onto her back, gasping for air and wiping the blood out of her only usable eye. He stepped towards her, ready to continue the onslaught.

Zoe kicked out hard into his knee, forcing it into an unnatural angle and almost breaking it. Arif's mouth opened as he screamed in pain from the surprise strike. Zoe saw for a brief moment that his tongue was gone. While he grabbed at his knee, staggering backwards, Zoe rolled herself backwards and up onto her feet. She took her chance, while Arif was still holding and looking down at his injured knee, she rushed forward and swung her right leg in a fast, hard, roundhouse kick.

Connecting with his head, Arif fell to the floor, landing on his knees and grabbing his head. Zoe struck out with her knee, aiming for his forehead. Arif was prepared and he blocked her knee, pushing her back. Zoe didn't slow down, she attempted again with her other knee. He blocked again. She punched at his head and got a glancing blow against his cheek. He pushed her back as she attempted to punch him again and quickly got to his feet. The two exchanged punches and kicks, blocking each other but more were landing on their target as each fighter became more injured and tired.

Zoe attempted to sweep Arif's legs, but with her swollen eye she fell short of his shin. He stepped back, avoiding her and took his chance, landing a strong kick straight into her chest and sending her sprawling over the bonnet of his father's car. They both paused, Zoe clutching her chest and Arif's hands returning to his knee which was beginning to swell after her earlier strike. Gasping for breath, Zoe tried to sit up and look at Arif, but she fell back as the pain in her chest was too great for her to support herself.

From inside the bar, the crashing sounds of Berkant and Aaron were still going strong. It sounded as if they were trying to kill each other with their bare hands. Arif looked towards the bar and shrugged, choosing to ignore what was going on inside. He took a step closer to Zoe as she lay across the car like some sort of brutally beaten model. He'd had enough of her now. She had proven a tougher opponent than he had expected, but he was done toying with her and wanted to end her life.

Limping slightly, he walked over to the car, opened the driver's door and leaned across to the glove box. Opening it, he found what he was looking for, his father's Ozekes fighting knife. The silver blade gleamed in the streetlights.

He gripped the worn wooden handle tightly as he slammed the door shut and looked towards the bonnet. Zoe was gone. He was instantly on high alert, looking around quickly, searching for where she had gone. She wasn't under the car or on the roof waiting to surprise him. Spinning around, Arif cursed himself for letting his concentration slip, thinking she was completely incapacitated. She couldn't have run into the bar, his father and Aaron were still fighting and her presence would have interrupted them. He looked over at the car down the street. Another black car was pulling away and rounding the corner at the end of the road very quickly. Had she made a run for it?

A hard punch connected with Arif's head, sending him rolling across the floor. His father's knife dropped out of his hand and spun across the ground, stopping next to a storm drain. He hit the edge of the pavement and stopped. The street was spinning around him and small lights flashed in front of his eyes. Even with all this, there was no mistaking who had struck him. Matthew had finally joined the party.

Matthew stood next to the car with his fists clenched by his sides, looking towards Arif on the floor, having followed the sound of his body hitting the concrete. Zoe stepped out from behind the car, clutching her body and wobbling slightly with each step. She placed a hand on the car for support.

"What kept you?" she asked Matthew, a look of shock mixed with gratitude spread across her face.

"My ride was late," he replied, his body still facing towards Arif. He listened intently to his every move, but the sounds from inside the building behind Arif distracted his concentration.

"How did you get here?" Zoe asked, puzzled. She knew he had no money or weapons.

"Looks like we have more friends in high places. He found me and picked me up. He'll probably be calling for back up now. Perhaps you could prepare for them while I deal with him?"

Zoe nodded, then realising that he couldn't see that gesture grunted, "Sure." She slipped around the back of the car. Looking in through the open rear door, she saw a discarded mobile phone. Taking it, she moved away from the carnage, knowing she needed to make contact with her own people sooner rather than later.

Matthew took a step closer to Arif who was slowly getting to his feet. His battered and bruised face full of hatred and rage.

"Good to see you, Arif," Matthew said, with only the smallest hint of sarcasm. Arif placed his hand on the bonnet of the car and tapped the metal with his finger to give Matthew his response in Morse code. Reaching out for the car next to him, Matthew's hand found the body and he tapped his reply, smirking as he did so.

Arif shot forward, ignoring the pain in his body he thrust his fist towards Matthew's face. Matthew listened to Arif's body coming towards him and blocked, striking him in the abdomen, hard. Arif keeled over, but quickly recovered, striking Matthew's face with the back of his hand with a force so hard that Matthew's head bounced off the car next to them and his glasses fell to the floor from his face. Arif crushed them under his boot as he rushed forward, grabbing Matthew's body. Spinning them both to gather momentum, he threw Matthew into the air and onto the road. Matthew grunted in pain as he landed on his shoulder and rolled, but he recovered quickly and got to his feet. He turned his head side to side quickly, trying to pick up where Arif was, but the noise from the bar was loud enough to hide Arif's silent steps.

Arif kicked him in the chest, making his broken rib scream in agony. He staggered backwards, gritting his teeth and prepared himself for the second blow. He caught Arif's leg and slammed his elbow hard onto his thigh, attempting to break it. Arif had expected this blow. He moved his leg enough in Matthew's grip to avoid a break and headbutted Matthew against his forehead. Matthew's head swung backwards, but he struck back against Arif's head just as hard, still holding tightly to his leg.

Arif opened his mouth in a garbled cry of rage and jumped up. Wrapping his other leg around Matthew's body, he threw his weight backwards, rolling them both to the floor. As Matthew's body fell over him, he kicked out, sending him flying over his body into the air before landing on his back on the pavement outside the bar.

Matthew lay there, his back screaming in pain. He was sure more bones were broken and several organs severely damaged. He rolled over onto his stomach slowly, catching his breath. His hand fell against a storm drain, the cold metal brushed against his fingers and so did something wooden. Berkant's knife. Matthew shook his head, clearing his senses. He could hear Arif's feet hitting the road as he ran towards him.

Matthew grabbed the knife and shot his hand forwards. The blade struck true, stabbing deep into Arif's shin. Arif's scream could probably have been heard on the other side of London. He grabbed his bleeding leg, falling onto his other knee in shock. Matthew didn't hesitate, his hand still tight around the knife, he pulled it out and stabbed it back into Arif's thigh. He pulled it out again and, as swiftly as the other two strikes, forced the knife into the side of Arif's body. He felt Arif grab at the knife, attempting to take it from him. Matthew got to his knees quickly, holding it tightly with his own two hands. The two men, the two brothers, pressed their heads together and each attempted to take control of the blade deep inside Arif's body.

A booming gunshot distracted them both. The shotgun inside the bar had been fired. The sound of a strong and heavy body hitting the floor followed. Arif and Matthew froze, each asking themselves the same question. Who had fired the gun? Heavy footsteps could be heard walking slowly out of the bar, along with the next round being loaded into the chamber.

"Either finish him off or let him go, Matthew." Berkant's voice sounded tired but still carried the same strength and control it always did. He walked down the two steps from the pub door, pointing the shotgun at the back of Matthew's head. Matthew slowly took his hands off the knife, Arif's tightened around it as he held the blade inside him, knowing that to pull it out might lead him to bleed out.

"It didn't have to be this way, Berkant," Matthew said slowly, turning his head slightly over his shoulder towards his former boss.

"You're right: it didn't. But things are never that simple when it comes to you are they?"

"They used to be." Matthew slowly got to his feet, his hands still raised in the air while Berkant took a step back, keeping his gun out of Matthew's reach. "I always did what was asked of me and I did it well. You tried to kill me. Why?"

"Too much blood on your hands. All the people you've killed for me, the lives you've ended to help our organisation get to where it is. It all comes back to you and therefore me. If I was to go home with you by my side, there would have been too many questions to answer and we'd have targets on our backs before we left London. With you gone, I could have gone home and started fresh without any concern for my life. You just bring too much trouble with you."

Matthew lowered his hands. He could hear Berkant's heavy, slow breathing. If this was it, so be it. But he wasn't going to die without putting up a fight. He knew Berkant was too clever to get too close to him, so he had to hope that he could move quicker than him. Berkant wouldn't wait much longer. Matthew threw his body to the ground as fast and hard as he could. As he hit the floor, he rolled away from Berkant towards Arif, who was still kneeling and holding the knife in his body.

As Matthew dropped, Berkant fired the round. The shotgun went off, narrowly missing Matthew and blowing out the windscreen of the car. Matthew reached out and found what he was looking for; Arif had loosened his grip on the knife's handle when his father had fired the round. Elbowing him in the face, Matthew grabbed the knife and threw it as hard as he could in the direction of the gunshot.

Berkant, who had followed Matthew with his eyes while he chambered another round, saw the flash of the blade as the knife spun through the air. Trying to block the speeding weapon with the shot gun, he exposed his neck enough for the knife to strike him. The knife penetrated his skin, diving deep into his neck and severing vital arteries. Berkant grabbed at his neck desperately. Dropping the shotgun, he pressed both strong hands to his wound to try and stop the flow of blood escaping from his neck.

As he fell to his knees, Matthew rose to his feet. He could hear Berkant's staggered and gargled breath as life slowly faded out of his body. Matthew walked slowly towards the dying man. The closest thing to a father in his life was slowly drifting painfully away before him. Matthew didn't have time to dwell on memories. He reached out and found the knife, now soaked in blood, and pulled it out with such aggressive force that Berkant's wound was ripped open even more, splashing blood over Matthew's face and suit.

He turned away without a word to the old man, knife in hand – ready to finish off Arif. Behind him Berkant's lifeless corpse keeled over in a bloody heap. His hand reached out and felt the car that had brought them here. He was sure Arif was kneeling next to it, further along from him. He moved slowly, preparing himself to end another life.

In the distance, the sounds of several car sirens were beginning. Zoe had made contact with her people. Something was wrong though. Matthew stopped. He couldn't hear anything but the increasing wails of the police and other emergency services. There were no slow breaths of a dying man, no drip-drip of blood hitting the floor.

Matthew gripped the knife tighter and reached out with his free hand. Arif had gone. He crouched on the floor and found a small pool of blood from Arif's wounds when Matthew had left him on the floor. Slowly moving his fingers around the pool of blood, he found what he was looking for; a trail. Arif must have pulled himself away while his father was dying. Matthew hit the car next to him in frustration and tossed the knife away across the road, cursing loudly in frustration.

"You okay?" Zoe asked, slowly walking from around the back of the car. She looked down at Matthew kneeling on the floor, head hung as if in defeat. "He won't get far. I'm sorry I didn't come back sooner."

"Don't be," Matthew replied, raising his head towards her voice and pulling himself to his feet. "He might not get very far. I got a few good hits in." The sirens were growing louder now: they would be here in a minute, maybe less. "Are you okay?"

"I'll live," she answered, shrugging. She moved to Matthew and wrapped one arm around him, pulling him first to his feet and then into a small hug. Matthew was taken aback by this gesture; he couldn't remember the last time he had been hugged. It felt very strange to him to feel affection, warmth and kindness from another person. He slowly lifted his own arms, they felt heavy, weighed down and resisted his movement. He returned the hug for a moment before releasing Zoe and stepping back.

Several marked and unmarked police cars shot around the corner at the far end of the road, followed by a swat van and a number of ambulances. Zoe stepped back to look around the car and waved them down as they sped towards her.

"This is going to be hard to explain. I can't promise I can protect you."

"I don't think you can do anything for me now," Matthew replied, counting the sounds of the various speeding police cars and other emergency services.

"Where will you go? Another London safe house?" The vehicles were skidding to a halt outside the bar now. Doors were flung open and bodies leapt out, shouting orders and questions to each other.

"No, there's nothing left for me here now." Matthew shook his head as he spoke. Berkant may be dead, but Arif had gotten away and they had a large family across Europe. "Will you be all right? I could give a witness statement?" he asked, smiling at her, his face awash in blue and red lights.

"Don't make jokes, it doesn't suit you." Hard as she tried not to, Zoe let out a small chuckle. "I better go and explain what's going on now. Get yourself out of here before someone decides to start asking questions."

"Maybe we'll see each other again? It's good to know I have a friend on the inside now." Matthew smiled in her direction. He turned to walk away from her and the small army that was swarming the street and the bar like a plague of locusts.

"We'll see," she added, smirking to herself as she watched him walk slowly and inconspicuously away from the crowd behind her. Sighing, she turned away from her new ally to go and report to whoever was in charge.

Milton Keynes UK
Ingram Content Group UK Ltd.
UKHW020234281123
433366UK00008B/192